In the

Fields

WILLOW ASTER

Copyright © 2013 by Willow Aster
Cover by Tosha Khoury
Interior Book Design by JT Formatting

www.willowaster.com

Printed in the United States of America

First Edition: September 2013
Library of Congress Cataloging-in-Publication Data

Aster, Willow
	In the Fields / Willow Aster. – 1st ed
	ISBN-10: 1492188034
	ISBN-13: 978-1492188032

	1.In the Fields—Fiction. 2.Fiction—Coming-of-Age
	3.Fiction—Contemporary Romance

WARNING: The details described in this book may not be suitable for readers below the age of 18 as descriptions of rape, alcoholism, child neglect, and abuse are depicted.

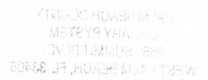

*Dedicated to anyone
who has ever felt like they
don't quite belong.
There's a place for us all.*

PROLOGUE

1977

THERE IS NOT one specific minute, hour, or even day that changed my life. It was one summer; one twisted summer when everything derailed into endless complication.

It was the summer I said goodbye to my childhood.

THE MEMORIES ARE suffocating me. I should have never come back.

I walk into the kitchen, a place so familiar and yet, I'm a stranger here. My hands shake as I pour my umpteenth cup of tea. I lean against the counter and stare out the window. It looks the same as it did all those years ago. I see the place it happened. I feel the sweltering heat of the day. I hear the cries and curses that were spoken.

My breath is ragged as I abandon the tea and walk into my old bedroom. Pale lavender, with a few stuffed animals sitting on top of the chest of drawers—nothing has changed. When we left, Nellie kept everything together for us, never giving up hope that we would be back. I'm not sure if I left everything because I thought she might like to have my things, or if I simply never wanted to see them again. Maybe a little bit of both.

I make my way into my parents' bedroom. I will always think of it as their room, even though they haven't slept here together in years. A picture of Gracie and me sits on the nightstand, turned toward the bed. The tears fall then, and as much as I try to fight them, they're unrelenting.

In my dad's closet, I pick up one of his shirts and try to smell it, hoping to feel connected to him somehow. I don't smell anything but cotton. I hang it up again, feeling disappointed with myself and the shirt.

The screen door slams and I hurriedly swipe the tears away. Leaving the bedroom and hopefully some of the ghosts along with it, I square my shoulders and take a deep breath.

Gracie stands at the sink, her ringlets bouncing with each movement. Her face is shining with sweat, but she doesn't seem to mind the heat. She's eating a peach and with every bite, the juice drips down her chin. I hand her a towel and she grins up at me. Her face falters when she sees my splotchy face, but I put my hand over hers with a smile and she relaxes.

"You all right, Mama?"

"I will be, baby girl."

She lays her head on my stomach for a minute and pats it, and then leans back over the sink.

"This is the best peach I've ever eaten," she says with her mouth full.

"Mr. Talbot's peaches—I've had a few of them in my day," I say.

"I filled up a basket and put it on the back porch. Do you think we can make a pie?"

"I don't see why not. We don't have to be at the funeral home for a few hours yet. We'll be overrun with pies shortly from all the little old ladies in town, but I happen to have all of Miss Sue's recipes right here." I tap my right temple. "All other pies are just a waste of time."

Gracie beams.

Anything to distract myself from the memories of this place is a welcome relief. As we get all the ingredients assembled, Gracie chatters nonstop, not minding if I answer or not. I've been distracted since we got here, but she's been too excited to notice. She has heard stories about Tulma for as long as she can remember. I felt I had to keep it alive for her somehow since I knew I'd never be back, but here I am. Inside this God-forsaken house.

Before I know it, she's putting the pie in the oven. My heart turns over with love for her. I hope and pray that everyone will be kind to her. A fierce protectiveness overtakes me at the thought of anyone mistreating her. If someone so much as looks at her cross-eyed tonight, we'll leave. Another middle-of-the-night getaway. She doesn't even know to be anxious, and I seem to be enough for both of us.

Gracie goes back outside and stretches out on the hammock my dad put between the two oak trees closest to the house. If it had been there when I was a child, I would have spent a lot of time reading there. I finally move away from the window and hope the past will finally be put to rest.

NEW BEGINNINGS

TULMA, TENNESSEE
MAY, 1971

DO YOU EVER wish to be invisible, but when you are, feel desperate to be noticed?

This morning I woke up at 6 o'clock, took a quick bath, unrolled the pink foam curlers my mom insists I wear every night, made scrambled eggs, ate them, put the left-overs in the refrigerator for my parents to eat when they got up, let Josh the dog out, picked up my dad's beer bottles from last night, ironed my mom's shirt for work, dusted off her Miss Tennessee picture, and was on the bus for school all before 7 o'clock.

This is my daily routine. There are a few variations, but it mostly stays the same. To mix it up sometimes, I make waffles instead of eggs or iron my mother's shirt first, but I find that any change throws me off schedule.

I hate routines. I wish I could sleep in and that when I went into the kitchen, my mom would be standing at the stove, saying, "I've got your breakfast all ready, sweetie."

I'd say, "Oh, thanks, Mama, how did you know I was hungry for pancakes?" She'd tuck a loose strand of hair behind my ear and kiss my cheek while I ate my delicious breakfast. My dad would saunter in, smelling like after-shave and say, "How are my girls this morning?"

I'm going to be fifteen in a month. I hope to get my wish for a normal family then.

TODAY MISS GREENER has a baseball cap with a pink feather peeking out over her ear. Her grey hair is going every direction, tamed only by the cap. Most days, she doesn't care about her mop-top. She's proud of her hat collection and can't be bothered by whether they ever match her outfit or not.

As she opens the door of the bus for me, I feel the gust of wind on my face and it cools me off for a second. May is usually the nicest time of year, not too hot yet, but we're having record temperatures this spring. Yesterday, it hit 100 degrees and the humidity was so thick you could bounce it like a ball.

"Caroline, how are you this refreshing morning?" Miss Greener is perpetually sunny.

"I'm good, Miss Greener. I thought of you this morn-ing. The peony bush out back looks almost as pretty as yours."

"Oh my, I'll have to take a look at that on Saturday. Are you still up for me bringing over my azaleas?"

"I can't wait." I take my place on the right side of the bus and take my book out while we stop every other minute on the way to school.

I'm fully engrossed in my Beverly Cleary book by the time Clara Mae gets on and plops down beside me. She immediately starts telling me about a crazy dream she had and once I tear myself away from my book, I'm fully engrossed in her story, laughing at the way she goes on about it. This makes her sit up taller and talk even faster.

I can't figure it out. Outside my home, in the real world, people like me. I could do jumping jacks all day long in front of my parents and they wouldn't even blink, but at school and even around town, where I'm horribly shy and would rather just be left alone, people reach out to me. Maybe my shyness disguised as standoffishness makes kids at school try harder. I guess I can just pretend to be mysterious, when really I'm about as bold as a bowl of noodles.

The black girls love my long hair. It falls in soft waves with a halo of frizziness around my scalp. I don't care for it very much, but they think it's beautiful and soft. Jackie does six tiny, perfect cornrows on my head before she gets in trouble from the teacher. My hair gets greasy from all the hands, but it doesn't bother me a bit. When they play with my hair, it makes me feel like I'm one of them, and I like that. I like to take out Jackie and Beck's braids and arrange their hair in pretty, cottony curls.

My mama used to tell me that if I let all those little black girls play with my hair all the time, I'd turn into one. *Don't let them touch you too much,* she'd say, *or it'll wear off on you!*

It backfired on her, because I never minded that thought one bit.

Black folks intrigue me. If I was black, then I could

be done with the pink foam rollers. I could sing like Sister Bessie. I heard her at a funeral once and the next Sunday I asked if we could go visit the church where Sister Bessie sings.

"That would not be appropriate, Caroline," my mother sniffed.

To me, not appropriate is not wearing a slip under a white skirt, but I didn't say this.

My family is not racist. Really.

"We don't have anything against black people," my parents say.

I rolled my eyes at my mom for saying that once and got my mouth popped.

"I ain't got nothin' agin niggers," my grandpaw says. "They's good people, I got lots of nigger friends."

The n-word is his favorite word. This has always *really* bugged me about him.

"They need to be with their kind; we need to be with our kind."

Well, that settles it then.

THE ONLY TIME my mom seems proud of me is when we're out in public. When we're at the store, someone will inevitably stop her to say hello. She's the teller at Tulma First Bank on Pope and Third Street, so everyone feels like they know her.

"Such a pretty little thing," they say, sometimes reaching out to touch my hair or pat my cheek.

My deep down shyness rears up and I try not to

stiffen. My skin gives me away, turning a mottled red on my neck and cheeks. My mother practically falls over with the big head every time I'm paid a compliment.

She smiles her pageant smile and says, "Thank you," and then, "What do you say, Caroline Josephine?"

Sometimes I'm even swept up in her beauty when she gives me that smile. If it would only pop out at home—I might be more inclined to believe in it. She will never let me forget she was Miss Tennessee. Or that her waist was only 22 inches when she got married. Or that every man in the county wanted to date her. I do think she's beautiful, but I'd like to think it on my own without her ever lovin' constant reminders. And just for once, I'd like for something besides beauty to matter to her, especially *my* beauty.

When I'm feeling a mite bit rebellious, I think dumb thoughts like:

I wish my teeth would all fall out. Then what would Mama say...

Maybe when she's telling me to quit eating because I'll get chubby one day, I'll just stare at her and shove all the food in my mouth. At every meal. Until I do get chubby and then she'll be so mortified.

If I didn't wash my hair for two weeks, she wouldn't puff up with pride every time someone stopped us on the street to compliment me. It would sure save time at the grocery store.

I'm afraid my mama doesn't bring out the best in me. And I must be a real wimp because I just bite my tongue and do whatever she says. *Yes, ma'am. No, ma'am. Whatever you say, Mama.*

Because that's what good girls do.

TULMA HAS A population of 6,579. We did have 6,583 until Mr. Jefferson, Jocelyn Sanders, Berlin Smith, and baby Edna passed away. It's a river town with one bridge leading the way in and out. Tulma Elementary, Tulma Middle School, and Tulma High are all connected with each other, sitting in a row on Main Street. It's the most impressive structure we've got in town, which is kinda sad when you think about it.

Today in gym, we're learning to waltz. I love to dance but feel nervous at the thought of having to pick a boy partner. There's only one boy I want to dance with. Ever. My hands start to sweat.

I look over and catch his eye. Isaiah. Isaiah Washington. He walks over.

"Hi, Caroline. Do you have a partner yet?"

"No, do you?" I try to act nonchalant.

"I do now," he takes my hand, "if it's okay with you."

I smile my answer.

As all the other boys in class cut up with their partners, rolling their eyes at how juvenile it is to dance with a girl of all things, Isaiah and I dance the waltz like we were born doing this very thing.

Isaiah has mesmerizing eyes, flecks of gold in green. His hair has soft, short curls. His skin is smooth and clear and the color of milk chocolate. He is the most beautiful person I have ever seen.

He smiles at me. "What are you thinking right now, Caroline Josephine Carson?"

"I'm thinking...I hope we don't get a lot of homework

tonight."

His eyes crinkle. He knows I'm lying.

My heart returns to normal as I walk back to my class. The dance ended way too soon.

ISAIAH AND I had a class together last year. He's a year ahead of me, but we've shared some of the same classes. We became friends while working on a project together in Miss Spain's history class. While we were supposed to talk, study, and basically breathe everything pyramid-related, we were getting to know each other. Isaiah was a straight A student, possibly the smartest kid in school. I admired that. Any awkwardness flew out with the chickens when he cracked a silly joke about elephants in the refrigerator. He was smart *and* funny. I was in love.

Once our project was completed, I didn't get to talk to him much, but I'd catch him watching me. Whenever our eyes met, he'd give me that smile of his that seemed like I was the only girl in the world. I thought I might be imagining it, but a month later, he passed a note to me in gym that said:

Caroline, your smile is better than my mama's chocolate pie, which is one of my favorite things.

I like you.

If you don't like me the same way, just ignore this... I'll understand.

If you do, can I call you tonight?

I sent a note back with my phone number. He smiled when he read it and tucked it into his jeans' pocket. As soon as I walked in the door that afternoon, the phone was ringing. I ran to answer it and we talked for an hour.

And the next day and the next. Nothing was different at school. We didn't talk, didn't sit by each other, didn't do anything to draw attention to ourselves, but in the afternoons, I began walking home from school and so did he. He had always taken his bike to school, but we realized that after everyone else in the group got to their houses, we had fifteen minutes to walk together, just the two of us.

Isaiah was romantic from the very beginning. He knew I liked wildflowers, so he picked them for me as we walked. He wrote poems for me like this one, which I still have in a little box he gave me for Valentine's Day...

Someday...
I will hold your hand
Dance in the sand
With our favorite band.
Someday...
I will steal a kiss
Little miss,
It will be bliss.
Someday...
I will shout that you're mine,
Caroline...
Till the end of time.
Someday.

Since that first day he called, he has been my favorite person and I've been his.

I still feel empty every day when I turn to go to my house and leave Isaiah for the day. Sometimes I see his mother standing in the doorway of their tiny ramshackle house. He never invites me in, but he waves until I'm out of sight.

"Bye, Miss Caroline," his mother calls.

She always has a smile for me, but never asks if I want to stay awhile. I always wish she would, but know better than to ask. Today Sadie is wearing a handkerchief around her head and has a bowl in her hand, stirring, as Isaiah goes in the house. Maybe if I rush home, I can talk to him a little longer before my parents get there.

WE LIVE ON the outskirts of town, just a mile or so past Isaiah's house, but the scenery changes dramatically as soon as I turn the corner. Fields of fruit grow on one side of the road and a pasture for the Talbots' horses stretches out on the other side. Our house is a little rambler on the far corner of the Talbot's field. On the edge of town lie beautiful green mountains and we are nestled in the first valley.

Mama says we would be well off if Daddy wouldn't drink away our money. Daddy says we'd be well off if she'd stuck to pageants and to just shut up. It never goes too far because Mama does bring home the money. She has had her job for fifteen years and even though she's constantly remembering the good ole days when she didn't have to do anything but look pretty, I think she actually likes her job. She would never admit it, but I assume she does since she's there every waking minute. Even Saturdays.

When Daddy is having a good bout, he works const-ruction in Tulma and the neighboring towns. Once he made it a year without taking a drink, but eventually he gave in and went back to the bottle. This time has been three months of solid drinking, and I'm beginning to think the daddy I used to know is gone.

When I was little, Daddy would tell me stories, not just little nursery rhymes, but long, detailed stories that he would add to each night. Clovis the Bunny was one of my favorites and if I was sick, or had a bad dream, or just couldn't sleep, Daddy would come in and tell me the adventures Clovis had been in that day. Nothing could make me laugh like the thought of Clovis hanging from our curtains or Clovis scaring the postman by talking like an old lady.

I can see my house just a football field ahead. I try to remember all the nice things about my daddy in the time it takes to get to the door. If I think nice things about him, it will stick. He will remember to be strong and will come home sober and happy.

When I finally reach the door, I'm sweating like my Aunt Josephine, who always has wet marks under her armpits. Josh is so happy to see me; he does a little dance around my feet. This is the one time of day that I'm happy to be home. Just me and my dog.

I step in the shower and wash quickly with cold water and get out just in time to hear the phone ringing. Isaiah knows the exact time to call. I run to the phone and we talk for an hour and a half today. I stretch it out until I hear my mom's car turning in the driveway.

I've been preparing supper as I talk to Isaiah. The cornbread is ready to come out of the oven, the black-eyed peas are simmering on the stove, and the pork chops are all ready.

"I'll see you tomorrow," I whisper to Isaiah.

"Sweet dreams, Caroline," he whispers because I'm whispering.

"Sweet dreams back."

This is our hanging-up ritual. I know I won't get a chance to talk to him again for the night. I hang up quickly before my mom can catch me on the phone with him. We're very careful to not get caught. She would never approve of me loving a black boy.

FRIENDS & ENEMIES

DADDY DIDN'T COME home last night and Mama is spittin' mad. She's already up when I come out of the bedroom, rubbing the sleep out of my eyes. There are no pancakes on the table, in case you were wondering.

Mama is pacing the floor, muttering to herself, while Josh tries to keep up with her fast strides. I can't hear what she's saying, but there are a few four-letter words flying around that she has always instructed me to never dream of saying, on account of it not being ladylike and all.

I get done with the chores a good ten minutes earlier than usual. I don't want to stick around any longer than necessary. I shock Miss Greener—she's used to me running down the road while she holds the bus for me.

Clara Mae invites me to come over to her house the next day and I tell her I have to check with my mother. Lord knows, I don't need to rile her up any more than she already is.

I barely see Isaiah today. In gym, we take a break from the waltz and are divided into teams for dodge ball. I was hoping to have a little chat with Isaiah, but instead I'm running for my life to avoid the ball. He's on my team, so we're in close proximity, but neither of us speaks to the other. It's hard to not stare at him, but I try to save all my looks for our walk home.

MY GRANDMA, NELLIE, surprises me by picking me up from school. I wish I could let Isaiah know that I'm not walking home with him, but you don't make Nellie wait around. She's in an extra hustle-bustle mood.

"Your mama said you need some new clothes," she says when I get in the car. She drives a black '57 Chevrolet Bel-Air with a white hardtop. My grandpa washes it every Saturday. Nellie says Paw loves it more than he loves her, and I'd say it's not too far from the truth. They might be neck and neck.

We drive to the fabric store and she lets me pick out material for three dresses, six blouses, and three skirts. She absolutely will not let me pick out material for pants. If I'm gonna do such a heathen thing like wear pants, I'm gonna have to get them on my own dime, she says. She gripes about the fashions all the way home from the store.

"That girl in there was wearin' her pants so tight, I could see her religion!" she huffs.

My grandma is an exceptional seamstress. Even though I would like to wear pants sometimes, she makes such beautiful dresses that I can't feel bad about it. Clara Mae says she'd give anything to wear a dress like my white poplin one with the blue glass buttons. Now that I'll finally have something else to wear, I can give it to her.

When we get to her house, I help carry in the fabric

and go to the back bedroom to get measured. I've grown two and a half inches since the last time we did this. I'm taller than anyone in my class, but didn't realize I had grown so much in the last few months. Isaiah must be growing right along with me, because he's still taller than me by a couple inches.

I blush as Nellie says, "Girl, we need to get you a new bra yesterday!" I've noticed that things are progressing quite rapidly there, but haven't known exactly what to do about it. I don't tell Nellie about wrapping a small table-cloth around my chest until Mama takes me to get a new bra. She would ask why I don't just tell my mother mine is way too small now, but I can't explain how that would humiliate me to no end.

Thankfully, in third grade, Jody told me everything about "my visiting aunt Dottie," so I knew what to expect when that came a while ago. Jody failed second and third grade and was extremely proud to know something that none of us knew. I didn't believe her at first, but she was telling it straight. I never told Mama when I got it and she has never asked.

I sit by Nellie and cut the material while she threads the machine. She has her own handmade patterns that she pins onto the material. She lets me sew all the easy seams while she takes a turn at cutting. We've done this many times, since as far back as I can remember. I think I could probably do it myself, but it's more fun with her.

My Nellie is tall and very skinny. She hunches over the machine like a spindly match. When I hug her, I can feel her bones jutting out, but she's still nice to hug. Her white hair sits atop her head, invoking thoughts of an imposing schoolmarm. She has always insisted I call her

Nellie. When I think about it, I'm not really certain why she doesn't like Grandma and think I will ask her why.

"Nellie, why have you never wanted me to call you Grandma?"

She stops cutting and has a pin in her mouth when she answers, "Child, do I look old enough to be a grandma?"

"Well, yes," I say. My, aren't we brave today.

Her eyes narrow and for a minute I am very afraid. You just never know what will set off Nellie. Another minute creeps by and then she throws her head back and lets out a loud guffaw. Nellie can laugh like nobody's business.

Relieved, I laugh too.

Grandpaw wanders back to our room and asks, "What's all the commotion back here?" When he says here, it sounds like heah.

"Hi, Grandpaw, how are ya?" I get up to hug his thick middle.

He hugs me tight, patting my head and says, "Hey, Little Caroline, how you?"

And then, "Have I told you about the nigger who went into the five and dime?"

Honestly, it has not even been one minute. Here we go.

"*Yes*, Grandpaw, you have…" I roll my eyes as he repeats the punch line for probably the millionth time. I've given up trying to get him to stop talking like this. He doesn't need me to laugh because he's already laughing so hard. Nellie is laughing right alongside him.

SIX HOURS LATER and I have half of a new wardrobe. We whipped up the skirts, four of the blouses and got a good start on the dresses. I must admit that my new clothes are exquisite. I thank Nellie as we're driving home.

"Oh, glad to do it, Honey. Lord knows you deserve a little something pretty."

When we pull up to the house, the lights are off. Mama's car is not in the driveway. Daddy's truck isn't either.

"Where do you suppose everyone is?" Nellie asks. "It's late."

"Oh, they'll probably be home before too long. Mama sometimes works late during the week." I don't mention Daddy's lack of attendance last night.

"Well, do you want to stay with us tonight? I don't like leaving you out here all by yourself," she says as she stifles a yawn.

"No, I'll be fine. I'm just going to bed."

"Well, if you're sure…" she pauses, then seems satisfied with my answer.

"Goodnight, Grandma," I whisper that last part and she swats my backside as I get out of the car.

I hear Mama come in around midnight. I've dozed off and on, but can't help but worry about her. I'm relieved when I finally hear the door latch and her heels clacking softly in the living room. She has been working so hard lately. Last week, she came in late three nights and was dragging around the rest of the week. Before I drift off to sleep, I think that her boss, Mr. Anderson, is so cruel to take a mother away from her daughter like he has all these years.

I FIRST NOTICED Leroy and Les a month ago. I was downtown with Miss Greener, picking out seeds to plant in our gardens. She has taken me flower shopping the last two springs, after we realized our mutual passion for flowers. I was softly touching the wisteria blooms and out of the corner of my eye, I caught the commotion by the cashier.

Two guys that looked a little older than me were laughing and weaving in and out through the plants. The taller one, Leroy, had grabbed a shovel and was chasing the shorter guy, Les, around the store. I was laughing until Mr. Clayton, the owner, came around the counter and grabbed the guy holding the shovel.

"Boy, give me that right now and get outta here," Mr. Clayton was not quite as tall as Les and Leroy seemed to know it.

He put the shovel up to Mr. Clayton's neck and said, "Ask nice."

"I don't have to ask nicely, it's my shovel," Mr. Clayton growled.

Leroy dug the shovel into Mr. Clayton's neck just enough to make his face turn all red. The other boy stood, laughing, egging on Leroy.

"Please put down the shovel," Mr. Clayton said.

Leroy, taking his slow, sweet time, gradually let the shovel inch down.

When the shovel was leaning against the counter, Mr. Clayton said, "Now, I said to get out of here, boy."

They turned on him so fast, it was a blur. Leroy

smashed Mr. Clayton in the nose and knocked him down. Les took over then, his fists flying, as blood poured out on the floor. Leroy grabbed the shovel again and I don't know what he would have done next if someone in the back hadn't called the police.

Kenny, a good-sized farmer grabbed Leroy before he used the shovel on anyone. That gave Ben and Samuel the nerve to pull Les off of Mr. Clayton. Several people had tried to step in, but just got hurt in the process. Sheriff Sanders threw a handcuffed Leroy and Les in the back of the squad car and Mr. Clayton was taken in an ambulance to the hospital two towns over, since he was in such bad shape.

Miss Greener and I hightailed it out of there, grateful to get away. My parents came home talking about it; word had gotten out around town that Mr. Clayton had been beaten up by two black boys. It sparked a whole week of conversations about how bad this area is getting, how black people are just taking over and what are we going to do if they can just pick up a shovel and beat someone up in the local flower market?

Isaiah and I talked about it on the phone that night.

"Leroy and Les are angry. About everything and everyone."

"Why do you think it got worse when Mr. Clayton called Leroy "boy"?

"It's a matter of respect. They shouldn't have done all that they did, but he shouldn't have called him "boy" either."

I didn't understand what was so wrong about that, but vowed since it bothered Isaiah so much that I would never do it either.

IT HAS BEEN more than a little unsettling since Leroy and Les have gotten out of jail. They only spent two weeks in there and it doesn't seem to have fazed them. This past week it seems as if I see them everywhere. The first time I saw them, I was waiting for Nellie outside the Piggly Wiggly. I was lost in thought, as usual, daydreaming.

"What are you doing out here all by yourself?" Leroy asked, as they circled me. He reached out and touched my collar, "You're lookin' mighty fancy."

I stood still and did not breathe, willing my face to not turn red. Up close, Leroy and Les look older than I thought, maybe sixteen or even seventeen.

"The cat got your tongue? You think you're all high and mighty? You too good for us?" Les sneered his ugly old gold tooth in my face.

"No, I don't think I'm too good," I whispered.

"Oh, she speaks!" Leroy said. "Ain't you some-thing…" He had his hand on my sleeve when Nellie came out.

She marched over to us and said, "Come on, Caroline, let's get home."

"Caroline, her name's Caroline, did you hear that, Les?" Leroy mocked. He looked me over again and came near me one more time. It wasn't intentional, but just as he came closer to me, I took a nervous step and his shoe caught on mine. He went flying. He was stunned for only a moment and then he jumped up and brushed the dirt off his pants.

"I didn't mean to do that!" I cried.

He kept his distance, but then spit, and the spittle came just short of landing on my right shoe.

Then I wished I *had* done it on purpose.

Nellie dragged my arm all the way to the car. "Oh, Caroline, I'm afraid you've started something now. You stay away from them boys."

"Yes, ma'am." I couldn't hide the tremble in my voice.

When I get around to telling Isaiah about this encounter, he sounds scared. "I don't trust them. I know you take care of your—" he pauses an uncomfortable length, "just—will you tell your parents about this, Caroline? Don't try to handle them on your own. I wish you weren't on their radar now. They're dangerous." He groans and I wish I could see him instead of just hearing him on the phone right now. It would make me feel a lot better.

I nod and when he says my name to see if I'm still there, I say yes out loud and hope that he will change the subject. There's no way I'm telling my parents about this.

I DECIDE TO give Clara Mae the excuse that I can't come to her house because I didn't get to ask Mama's permission. We plan for me to come over next week. I really just want to go home because I miss Isaiah and want to actually *see* him when we talk today.

At the end of the day, when we have finally said good-bye to the rest of the group, Isaiah says, "I don't have to go right home today, Mama had to go see her sister this afternoon. So I can walk you home, if you'd like."

"Really? I'd love it if you could."

This hasn't happened before. I'm so glad I didn't go home with Clara Mae.

We talk and talk and I'm telling him about my daddy not coming home again and Mama also staying out late all the time. He tells me if I ever get scared to call his house and let it ring three times and he'll find a way to call me back.

"I wish you lived even closer to my house, so I could be right there if you ever need me." Isaiah looks over at me and holds out a flower for me. I take it and smile. "Close enough that you could just flash a light and I'd come runnin'."

He takes my hand now that we're away from town. It never fails to make my stomach drop down to my big toes.

"I still will, you know." He stops and faces me. "If you're ever home by yourself and scared, call me and I'll be here in two seconds flat. My bike has superpowers. And I have it set to come straight to you."

I laugh and we start walking again.

"Caroline?"

I look at him and we stop again, lost in each other.

"I'm gonna make you laugh every day for as long as you let me," he vows.

My cheeks get hot and he chuckles. He puts his hand near my face like he's going to touch it and then snaps it back like it's been burned. I laugh harder and I'm sure my cheeks are smoking steamstacks by now.

We're in the fields by my house, taking our time, when Leroy and Les ride by on their bikes. I've never seen them out here and don't want them to know where I live.

"Isaiah, let's just walk past my house," I whisper.

They pull up right in front of us, blocking our way. "What's going on here? Where do you think you're going?"

Isaiah says, "Leave us alone, Leroy."

"You don't live out here," Leroy says. "Aw, I get it, you want a little one on one." He snickers and turns to Les. "He likes the white bitch." He does a singsong voice, "Prissy white bitch." He loses the laugh and snarls. "I think we've interrupted something here. Y'all headed to your lovenest?"

"She's my friend," Isaiah says.

"Yeah, she's your friend," Leroy laughs. "You think this girl is your friend? I bet she's not your friend at school. Do you think she's his friend at school, Les? Cause I bet she don't even know he's alive at school." He shakes his head. "But this don't look like no 'friendship'... friends don't hold hands and talk all lovey-dovey." Leroy cracks up at himself again. "I have some issues to settle with her though. I need you to let me have her for a little while. She tripped me the other day. You better know, Isaiah, that I don't take to that."

"I don't even know why you're talking to her," Les says. "She's trash."

"She's pretty trash, though." Leroy laughs and turns to Isaiah. "You need to get on out of here, boy, and let me handle this one." He eyes me up and down.

"Her dad is expecting her home in a few minutes," Isaiah says, taking my arm and walking around them.

It works. We quickly walk past and they take off on their bikes. Leroy yells, "I know where to find you, Miss Caroline." Their laughs grate on my skin.

I rush home and lock all the doors. Isaiah calls me

when he gets home, but we don't talk long, the encounter has left us shaken.

❀ 3 ❀

TRUTH & CONSEQUENCES

I'M REALLY BEGINNING to wonder if Daddy is coming back when another two weeks have gone by without any word from him. Two teachers have held me after class to see if I'm all right. I'm distracted and can't stop wondering where he is and if he's okay.

Isaiah asks his uncles if they had heard anything about Daddy. They work construction on the other side of town. They thought he'd taken work in Memphis.

I am determined to find out what in the world is going on when my mom comes home tonight. My dad cannot possibly have left town without telling me. He's left me to fend for myself a lot, but he'd never leave town this long without giving me warning. He knows my mother has it out for me.

I'm thinking about all of it as I sit in class trying to dissect a frog. I didn't think I would like this at all, but it truly is fascinating to see any kind of creature's insides. The knife is a struggle, though—it seems too big for this little frog. As I'm trying to open the stomach and figure out where my dad really is, the knife slips. Blood goes shooting everywhere.

I'm hurriedly sent to the nurses' office and Cindy tries to stop the bleeding, but it just keeps gushing. She begins calling my parents; first their work numbers, then the house, then my grandparents. No one answers anywhere and I can tell she doesn't know what to do next.

"Is there *anyone* else we can call?"

Miss Greener answers on the first ring and is there within twelve minutes. She says she'll take me to the doctor to get stitches. We rush to the car with Miss Greener practically lifting me off the ground. She buckles me in and then proceeds to drive like I'm on the verge of dying.

"Whoa, Miss Greener, it's only my hand!"

The blood has filled a towel, though, and I don't know if it's her driving or the cut, but I'm feeling greener than a toad. Guess that's what I get for dissecting its kin.

Just when I think the ride will never ever end, we reach the clinic.

The doctor sees me right away and gives me nine stitches between the thumb and first finger of my left hand. Dissecting casualties.

On the way home, Miss Greener looks over at me. "Caroline, are you all right, honey?"

I nod, not trusting my voice to speak. I'm afraid if I start crying, I won't be able to stop.

"It's okay to cry, you know. You've been through a lot today. I know your finger must really be hurtin' and you haven't even made a peep."

I look out the window and focus on swallowing down the huge lump that has taken over my throat.

She puts her hand on my shoulder and leaves it there for the rest of the drive.

When we reach my house, there's a grey car in the driveway. I've never seen it before. Maybe Daddy's back and he bought a new car. This makes sense. He's been talking about needing a car and there's nothing nice to buy around here. He probably *did* go to Memphis just to get a good deal. I'm so ready to see him. So much has happened since he has been gone. I run in and he's not in the living room. I hear a sound in the back bedroom, so I run back there.

It isn't Daddy.

I stumble as I try to quickly back out of the room. Miss Greener is in the living room now and I run straight to her. Suddenly, I'm desperate to get her out of my house. I wipe my face and try to smile at her. The words start pouring out of me. Frantically.

"Thank you, Miss Greener. I'll be fine now. I'm just going to rest for a while. Thank you so much. You were really so kind to take such good care of me today. I really appreciate it. I'm just gonna...I'll just go lay down now."

I take her hand and walk her to the door, just as my mom and Mr. Anderson come out of the bedroom. My mom is talking to me, but I can't hear her. I just want Miss Greener to go home.

My mother is still buttoning her shirt when she sees our company. "Why, hello. Caroline, why are you home? Miss Greener, what brings you to my home in the middle of the day?"

Neither of us answers and my mom is thankfully silent for a moment. "Well, this is..." she trails off, smoothing her hair.

Miss Greener is flustered and red, but she calmly says, "Caroline got a pretty bad cut today. She had to have stitches. Nine. Of. Them."

"Why didn't you call me? Caroline, why didn't you let me know?" My mom is at my side, holding up my hand, not noticing me wince.

"The school tried every number they have for you, as well as your husband's numbers." Miss Greener glances at Mr. Anderson as she says this. "Cindy also tried Mr. Carson's parents but wasn't able to reach anyone. We had to act quickly."

"Yes, well, thank you. We'll take it from here. Thank you, Miss Greener." My mom dismisses her.

"Caroline, are you all right? Do you need anything else from me?" Miss Greener asks.

I want nothing more than to say, "Take me with you." But I don't.

"Thank you, Miss Greener," I whisper.

"Anytime, dear. Just let me know if I can do anything else," she whispers back as she hugs me goodbye.

When she leaves, the room is quiet. The tension is so thick you could get up in it and crawl around. I want to scream and kick and cry and say mean things to my mother. Instead, I sit and wait for her to speak.

When she does speak, it's to Mr. Anderson. "You should leave, now, Grant," she says.

Grant?

I guess when she's been doing what I just saw them doing, she can call him Grant.

Yes, you can leave now, Grant, I mimic in my head. *My dad will be home soon.*

"Are you sure? Is she all right?" He nods at me.

At this, I jump up, take his arm, and drag him out the door. "*She* is fine! Now leave!"

27

Mama grabs me. "Caroline, stop this instant." Her voice is as sharp as that stupid knife. "That is no way to speak to Mr. Anderson. You apologize right now!"

"I will not. You—get out of my house!" I run to my room and slam the door.

A few minutes later, I hear the car start and he peels out of the driveway. My mother walks back into the house, pauses by my door, and keeps walking to her room.

I sit on the floor by my window, the fields coming in and out of focus. I try to ignore the hate that's churning.

IT'S DARK WHEN I come out of my room again. The bathroom is calling; otherwise, I would have stayed in my room forever. My mom is sitting in the dark, drinking the alcohol she berates my dad for drinking. When I walk by, she lifts her head. Her words have a slight slur that I've rarely heard from her. I'm used to this from my father.

"When you're my age, you'll understand this, Caroline. Your father...he has never appreciated me. Ever. Do you hear me, Caroline?"

She takes another swig and looks at me. "You're a pretty girl. Used to getting plenty of attention. You just wait. One day, people won't notice you anymore. You just wait." She laughs bitterly.

I go over to the coffeepot and begin making strong coffee. She continues to talk, and I pour a cup of coffee when it's ready. Her head begins to get heavy. I walk over and take the bottle out of her hand, giving her the coffee. She takes a sip and reaches up to smooth back a wavy strand of hair that has gotten loose.

She really is beautiful, I think. If her insides didn't make me cringe so much, maybe I could appreciate her pale, creamy skin and her Elizabeth Taylor eyes.

"I deserve better than this dump. Do you know that President Kennedy came through one time and noticed me? He did. He flirted with me and made your daddy so jealous. Have I told you that before?"

I nod. I've heard it many, many times.

"I was gonna get out of here. Your daddy had big dreams." She laughs, tears running down her face. "Look at where those big dreams got him. He's a drunk, Caroline. Nothing but a filthy drunk."

My heart feels like a hard rock. It beats, but it's dead. I can't listen to her. I've played out this same story with her one too many times.

I'm not sure if she notices when I leave the room and go to bed. I stay awake all night, unable to even close my eyes. When the sun comes up, I close them and sleep the long sleep of someone who has known grief and recognizes it for what it is.

I OVERSLEEP THE next morning too, and since my hand is screaming at me anyway, I stay home. After Mama leaves for work, I go out to the living room. There's a row of bottles by the couch. It seems my mother has taken over where my dad left off with the drinking, and by the looks of things, she's able to keep up with him in that department. I make some promises to myself to stay away from alcohol, since it seems to turn the people I love into idiots.

Then, I'm ashamed of thinking that of my parents.

In the afternoon, I go sit by the pond past the Talbot house. My journal gets the brunt of all my wrath. I write until the lead in my pencil breaks and then I just sit and stare at the water. I hear a rustle in the tree behind me and Isaiah walks through the clearing.

"I thought I might find you here," he says with a grin.

"How did you know?" I can't help but smile back. It feels strange—my face has been almost taut with not smiling for so long.

"I just listened...a little bird told me where you were."

He pulls a wildflower out from his pocket and puts it behind my ear. Squished and all, it's beautiful.

"I've been worried about you. Is your hand okay? I tried calling last night and when I didn't see you at school again today, I knew I had to come find you."

"It's feeling a little better."

He waits for me to say more, his eyes pulling me in.

"I...I think my dad isn't coming back, Isaiah. My mom and Mr. Anderson..."

Isaiah puts his arm around my shoulder, and I begin to cry. He sits there and lets me cry, holding me for a long time. I realize once I stop that he doesn't seem surprised.

"Did you know about my mom?" I pull away.

"It's a small town, Caroline, you know how people like to talk around here. I didn't want to think it was true, but I've heard some things."

"It's true. I saw them. It was awful, Isaiah. The day I cut my hand, I saw them. I'm so mad; I can't even look at her—I think I hate her." It all comes rushing out.

Isaiah has never heard me talk like this, but he

doesn't seem bothered by my words, just that I'm going through the feelings. "I don't believe that you hate her."

"I do."

"I've never seen anyone love their mother so much. Even when—" he stops.

"Even when what?"

"Well, even when most people wouldn't."

"Yeah, well, I'm starting to wonder why I ever did." The tears well up again, but I'm done crying. I get up and pull Isaiah up with me.

"Let's go get our bikes or something." Now that I'm cried out, I'm ready to move.

"I have to get home and help Mama with supper," Isaiah says. "She didn't want me to stay out long. I told her I needed to check on you since you weren't at school again today."

"And she let you come?"

"Yep. She just made me promise to hurry back. So I better go." He touches my face as he says it.

Isaiah has never touched my face like this. My heart beats fast. Everything else goes still. He leans over and kisses me. Right on the lips. It's over so quickly; I barely blink. But it's still really nice.

I didn't know it was possible, but Isaiah blushes. He waves and runs off before I have a chance to say anything.

Later, I'm still standing in the same spot, wondering if it felt good to him too. And...I wish I could have at least puckered up a little bit.

4

GLIMPSE OF ISAIAH

I FEEL LIGHT as I jog home from Caroline's, like I could run for miles and not even be winded. I can't believe I kissed her. I have to hold back from laughing when I think about my nerve. I think I shocked us both.

I've been drawn to Caroline from the first time I talked to her in class. I could tell she was an old soul like me. I'm a little older than her and have always had a lot of responsibility since I've never had a dad around. Every black boy I know without a father has either grown up fast or gotten into trouble. Even though Caroline doesn't know what any of that's like, she has also had to grow up before her time.

I wish she had parents who were there for her. She deserves that. She needs someone to love her and take care of her, and I'd like that person to be me. I know we would come against it—there would be hell to pay for us to really be together—but I can't let her go. I love her too much.

I had hoped it wasn't true about Caroline's mother. For a long time now, everyone in town has whispered of an affair going on between Mrs. Carson and Mr. Anderson. You just can't keep something like that a secret in a small town. I wonder if she wanted to get caught.

Caroline...thinking of her makes my heart ache. She's so beautiful. So good. When she told me about her life at home the first time, and every time since, I wished I could take her out of there and bring her to my mama. Sadie Washington, my mama, is the finest woman I know. She knows how to truly love and cherish someone. But Caroline has never spoken a bad word about her parents until today, and even then, I know she didn't really mean all that. She just needed to let it out to someone. She seems like the parent most of the time.

Opening the front door, I call out, "Mama, I'm home."

"Hey there, Love. Supper's 'bout ready. How was Miss Caroline? Did you find her?"

I pause and try to tone down any excitement in my voice. "Yes, ma'am, I did. She's had a really rough couple of days."

"Bless her heart, that child has more rough times ahead of her, I'm afraid."

I stand in the doorway and Mama turns and smiles at me before going back to slicing tomatoes.

"Mama, did you know about her mom and Mr. Anderson?"

She stops in mid-slice. "Does Caroline know? Oh, child. I do wish she didn't have to know all that." She shakes her head and arranges the tomatoes on a plate. "That girl has a sadness about her that breaks my heart."

Caroline has a ready smile for everyone, but her sadness is always right there, just beneath the surface. The first time I made her laugh, I felt like I could leap tall buildings in a single bound. Me and Superman, together. It became my goal right then to make Caroline Carson happy. I want that more than anything.

"What's gonna happen to her parents?" I ask, knowing she probably doesn't know, but wishing she had any good twist to put on the situation.

"Well, you just never know. Just never do know, son."

"Do you ever wish you were married, Mama?"

I lean over on her shoulder then, as she stirs the cornbread batter.

"Me? Oh, Lawd. I have enough to handle with the likes of you." She laughs and turns around, placing her hands on my cheeks.

"Look at you. You're way up there now, gettin' so tall! You, my man, you're going to meet a wonderful woman one day and that will be that. You're going to be a good husband and a good father. I can see that in you now. You have the right stuff in you."

I've already met her—I think it, but I don't dare say it. I smile at Mama, wishing I could tell her how one day I will marry Caroline, but I know she wouldn't really believe me. I want her to take me seriously, but the thought of her son marrying a white girl is just not imaginable.

I kissed her today. And I can't wait to kiss her again. Those thoughts wind through my head as I set the table; everything else blurs. When Mama finishes up with supper, we sit down and eat. While we're laughing and talking about the little, everyday things, I wish Caroline could be as lucky as me.

AFTER THE TABLE is cleared, I finish my homework while Mama sits at the sewing machine. She's considered the best seamstress in town. She used to only see black folks, but when Miss Ellen moved further south, Mama got the white folks' business. It helped her business more than double when white customers began knocking on her door.

She hems Mr. Gentry's pants and watches the clock. I hope he's not the one picking them up. Mr. Gentry is the owner of the funeral parlor in town and while he would never even speak to Mama if they ran into each other on the street, in private, he seems to take every chance to make her uncomfortable. She's finishing the pants as the doorbell rings, and I answer the door.

Mr. Gentry steps inside, nodding at me and then looking at Mama.

"Are those pants ready yet, Sadie?" He walks over by her and manages to make even that question seem dirty.

"They are, Mr. Gentry." She holds the pants up for him to take.

"How many times do I have to tell you? You can call me Fred," he says softly, holding onto her hand underneath the pants.

She pulls her hand away, and I step closer to her.

"Thank you, Mr. Gentry, that will be 35 cents," I speak up. I want this piece of trash out of my house. Now. He doesn't acknowledge me, just rakes his eyes over Mama.

"Are you raisin' your prices on me, Sadie? You don't need to get uppity on me now, even if you are the only seamstress in town. I send you a lot of customers, you know. Not many people want to come to a colored lady's house. Even if she is the prettiest colored in town." He snickers.

I inch closer to Mr. Gentry and glare him down.

Mama speaks softly, "And we appreciate all your business, Mr. Gentry. Remember I told you the other day that it would be 35 cents?"

"I'm just giving you a hard time, Sadie. No need to get your tail tied in a knot, boy." His eyes gleam as he laughs at me.

I want to punch his face so bad, but I take deep breaths instead.

Mama walks to the door, holding out the receipt for the pants. Mr. Gentry pulls out his money and is still laughing as he leaves.

"Dammit, Mama, I wish you didn't have to work for people like him!" I practically chew a hole in my jaw, as I watch Mr. Gentry walk to his car.

"You watch your mouth, Isaiah Cornelius Washington!" she yells at me. "Don't you be lettin' him bring you down to his level! If God wanted you to use that kind of language, your mouth would come equipped with soap!" she cries.

"Yes, ma'am. Sorry, Mama."

Mama doesn't tolerate language.

"He's harmless, Isaiah," she says, after she's cooled off, but I can tell she's troubled by the visit.

She pulls out a book from our tall bookshelf and says, "Read to me for a while, son."

Her smile calms me down, and I take the thick book from her hands. We may not have much, but we're proud of our book collection. I've already read all the classics several times over. If there's one thing Mama has instilled in me, it's to be hungry for knowledge. Otherwise, she says I'll never go anywhere in this life. And she desperately wants me to go *somewhere*, hopefully far, far away from Tulma. As long as I take her with me when I go.

Tulma isn't a bad town; it's a nice place. If you're white, it's a *wonderful* place. It may be small, but it has a charm all its own. The views by the river are beautiful and the weather is hot, but not nearly as hot as further south.

Mama has grown up here and it's home, but she wants more for me. She wants me to go to college and not be held back by the small-minded people here. When she imagines leaving her family and her church, though, I can tell she gets sick at the thought. We'll just cross that bridge when we come to it, I guess. Mama nestles beside me as I begin to read.

BIRTHDAY WISHES

TODAY'S MY BIRTHDAY and the last day of school. I haven't been back since everything happened, not quite a week, so I can't say that I'm happy to be going on my birthday. Nothing like feeling conspicuous when there's nothing you could desire any less.

And yet, I'm not ready for school to be over. No school means endless days of being alone. I think I might go mad with all the time I'll have on my hands.

Last year on my birthday, my dad and I ate dinner together while my mother was out late for a work party. My dad got more and more drunk as the night went on. We still had a nice time together; for the most part, he handles his liquor pretty well. Except the times he doesn't. But on my birthday, he seemed to try extra hard to be pleasant. He gave me a necklace that I've worn ever since. It's a gold chain with a small, gold "C" on it. I never take it off.

My mother came in dressed up from her party, and she came over and patted my cheek. She pulled a cupcake from behind her back and gave it to me. I still remember exactly how it looked: pale pink frosting with a white daisy in the center. The frosting was delicious. I ate it slowly, so I could savor each bite.

WHEN I GET on the bus, Miss Greener is so happy to see me. She pulls me close as I step up the stairs of the bus. Her grey fedora threatens to fall off as I clumsily hug her.

"Caroline, how are you doing, sweetheart? I've been extremely concerned about you. How's your hand?"

"It's much better."

"I've been wanting to come check on you, but thought I better just wait until you came back." She looks at me, saying a lot with her eyes. "Will you let me know if there's anything I can do?"

"Yes, I will. Thank you." I take my seat and get my new book out to read.

"Oh, and Caroline—happy birthday." Miss Greener beams at me and passes back a package of all kinds of flower seeds. The packets are tied together with a bright yellow bow.

"Thank you, Miss Greener! I can't wait to try these... thank you." I lean back in my seat, looking over each packet.

THERE'S A CARD from Isaiah in my locker. I save it until I have a quiet moment in study hall. The tears come with the very first sentence. I lay my head on the desk and read the rest with the card on my lap.

Dear Caroline,

When you were born, the angels stopped what they were doing and said, "I want to be just like her."

God said, "There is only one Caroline. You will just have to be satisfied with watching over her."

So that is exactly what they do. They watch over you night and day. Keeping guard over you as you sleep, smiling at the funny things you say, in awe of your beauty and wishing to be your friend.

And then there's me, always here, standing just on the edge of wherever you are, but so happy for every time our worlds collide. When everything else blurs and it's just you and me. You make me believe anything is possible.

Happy Birthday, Caroline.

I love you,

Isaiah

Besides being the sweetest words I've ever read, he *loves* me. Hearing him say that makes it feel like everything might be okay.

CLARA MAE AND her brother Thomas catch up with me as I'm getting ready to walk home.

"What are you doin' the rest of the day, Caroline?" Clara Mae asks.

"I really don't have any specific plans," I tell her.

"Why don't you come over to our house for a while? You can still beat your mom home, if you want," Thomas says.

All the girls in town swoon over Thomas. I can see why they do. Every year in the Tulma High yearbook, he wins the student poll for Most Handsome and Most Popular. Guys like him too, since he's a good football player.

I like him because he's nice. He's seventeen but has never seemed bugged by having me around. He's crazy about Clara Mae, which endears him to me more. I've always been a little envious of their relationship. It would be nice to have an older brother.

Clara Mae hooks one arm through Thomas's and another through mine. "Come on, we're not taking no for an answer."

I look over my shoulder and see Isaiah waiting around to see if I'm coming. In a single glance, I try to silently apologize. I want to tell him how much his card means to me, but it also sounds so good to have a place to go instead of home.

"What, you'd rather hang around school instead of coming to our house?" Thomas laughs. "I know we're not very exciting, but it's gotta be better than this!"

I look past Thomas and say loud enough for Isaiah to hear, "Sure, I'll come over, but I have to be home by 5:30." That will still give me time to talk to him before my mom gets home.

The hurt in Isaiah's eyes is unmistakable. I immediately want to take it back, but before I can say anything else, they've turned me around and we're marching to their house. I feel awful about hurting him, but they're doing everything they can to make me laugh. Our arms still looped together, Thomas stops suddenly, making us all jerk to a stop. Just when we come to a full stop, he takes off, practically running, with us trying to keep up. He does the same thing over and over again until we get home, and by the time we're there, I'm laughing so hard I can't breathe.

We walk into their sunny kitchen and Mrs. Owens, who asks me to please call her Miss Suzanne every time I come over, is just pulling cookies out of the oven. It really is that perfect.

We go outside with our cookies and eat them under the big willow tree in their backyard, and I wonder why I've put off this visit for so long. I always enjoy myself when I'm here. A few minutes into our conversation, I'm reminded.

"Do you have a big party planned, Caroline?" Thomas asks. "Your mother seems like she would throw big parties. I still remember the church carnival she put together last year. Do you remember that magician she hired? Where did she even find him?"

"I think he was from Memphis," I answer, wishing I could change the subject already.

"Your mother seems really cool. When I went in the bank last week, she invited Clara Mae and me over to your house sometime for supper. I thought that was nice."

"Yeah, that would be nice. You should come." *Maybe she'll even show up for you.*

Clara Mae pipes up, "She is *so* beautiful. Has she ever shown you her dress when she won Miss Tennessee? My dad still talks about how pretty she was the night she won. I think it makes my mother jealous, though." Clara Mae laughs. "Daddy says she was the prettiest girl this side of Texas, besides Mama."

"Well, now Caroline is." Thomas grins at me, his

eyes bright.

"So what are y'all doin' this summer?" Desperate to change the subject.

"We're supposed to go on vacation in a month, but other than that, I think we should swim. A lot." Clara Mae sticks her toes in the water. "The pool is ready. Next time you come over, we'll go swimming."

"That sounds great. You know I love to swim, but I'm still not very good."

"Oh, I bet you are." Thomas is looking at me in a different way today. I feel extra fidgety under his steady gaze.

"Do you have any new dolls, Clara Mae?" I wish Thomas would go inside.

"I do! Come inside, I'll show you." Clara Mae has a huge collection of porcelain dolls.

Thomas groans, "Aw, come on! Let's go down to the river. That's way more fun than those silly dolls! Don't they scare you just a little with their eyes, all blink-blink and real-looking?"

"Come on, Caroline, my brother is trying to hog you as usual." Clara Mae takes my hand and we run inside to her room.

The dolls are beautiful. I've never really played with dolls and feel that fifteen is surely too old to start, but I still appreciate Clara Mae's collection. She has every kind imaginable. At first I'm afraid to touch them, but Clara Mae pushes one into my hands. I set it carefully beside me and watch as she takes one and plays with the doll's hair. She's really good, keeping me completely mesmerized with her twists and turns of the curls into an elaborate hairdo. Before I know it, Mrs. Owens is knocking on the door, saying, "Caroline, are you ready? It's almost 5:30."

I'M SO GLAD I went—it took my mind off of things. I just hope Isaiah isn't too upset with me. After I wave goodbye to Mrs. Owens and Clara Mae, I look down and on the doorstep is a small box. It's wrapped in pretty lavender paper. I carefully tear the wrapping off and open the box. Inside, there's a small wooden jewelry box. The wood is dark walnut and perfectly smooth. I rub it over and over, loving the soft finish. Inside the jewelry box, a tiny "I + C" is etched into the wood. It's the most beautiful thing I've ever been given. This must be what Isaiah has been making. He has hinted several times that he was making me something, but I didn't imagine it would be so special.

I run inside and wait for him to call. And wait and wait.

It's after 6 o'clock and still no call. Still no word from my mother, either.

Nellie calls at 6:30 and says, "Grandpaw and I will be over in a jiffy with your present, dear. You're not in the middle of dinner yet, are ye?"

"No, come on over, we haven't eaten yet."

"All righty, we'll be over shortly." Nellie always hangs up on me. I don't think she means to, just once she has said what she wants to say, she's done.

True to their word, they're over in a jiffy. By this time, my stomach is rumbling, but I haven't started supper. In the back of my mind, I think my mom will probably be home any minute with a plan for supper. Grandpaw & Nellie come in the door with big hugs and kisses.

"How does it feel to be fifteen?" Grandpaw asks.

"Well, about the same as fourteen so far," I say with a grin.

"You look an inch taller already. You better slow down or you're gonna pass Nellie up."

He pokes my ribs and makes me laugh.

"I wish I'd stop, I'm already the tallest girl in my class. And taller than most of the boys too."

Except Isaiah.

"Oh, don't you be ashamed of that," Nellie speaks up. "You look like one of them models."

"A damn fine model!" Grandpaw whistles.

"Edward! You hush your mouth." Nellie swats Grandpaw's backside.

"Well, she *is* a damn fine beauty. Anyone can see that."

"You just mind your mouth, mister." She glares at him and then turns to me, smiling. She's hilarious the way she can turn it on and off like that. "Pretty is as pretty does, Caroline. You're sweet and that's what matters."

"Thank you, Nellie." I blush for about the fiftieth time that day. I also wonder why my mama doesn't seem to agree with Nellie's theory on beauty.

"Now where is that mother of yours?" Nellie asks.

I notice she doesn't even mention my daddy. I wonder if they've talked to him. They'd be who he'd call over Mama right now, probably.

"I haven't heard from her yet. I'm not sure," I answer.

"Well, it's gettin' to be late. Have you had your supper yet?"

"No, ma'am."

"Well, where is that girl?" Grandpaw asks. "Why don't we take our birthday girl out to eat and leave a note for Jenny to meet us."

"That's a right fine idea, Edward. Turns out you *are* good for somethin'." Nellie gets her purse. "Does that sound good to you, honey?"

"Yes, ma'am, it does. I'm hungry. Where should we go?"

"Well, there are only two choices that are open this late around here. How 'bout Dixie's?"

"I love Dixie's!"

"Let's get a move on then."

DIXIE'S IS A restaurant in an old Victorian house, just this side of the river. The owner, Dixie, is a warm, buxom woman who laughs loud and often. Her laugh reverberates so in the uncarpeted house that Grandpaw says he's only going to think of sad things to say. I love Dixie—I've loved coming here since I was a little girl. She makes the best mashed potatoes.

"Why, hello, Caroline! My, you've grown up since the last time I saw you!" Dixie shouts.

"Hello, Miss Dixie." I smile shyly.

"Do you want your regular?" she asks.

"Yes, ma'am."

It's no time before Dixie brings out her delicious roast beef, mashed potatoes and sweet carrots. For dessert, we have warm bread pudding with rum sauce. I eat until

I'm stuffed and realize I've managed to be happy this whole day, even without my mama and daddy.

MAMA NEVER SHOWS up at the restaurant and isn't home either. Nellie is bewildered by her and says she's worried about that girl.

"I think we should call the police, Edward. She wouldn't miss Caroline's birthday like this. Something is *wrong*."

"No, Nellie. I'm sure she just got caught up in work or something…" He doesn't look me in the eyes.

"You know, she did mention that she had to work late," I say before I can think. My gut twinges a bit with the fib.

"She did?" Nellie asks. "Well, I'm glad to hear that, although I can't believe she would do that on your birthday. I'm sorry, honey."

"Oh, it's all right. I had a nice time with you." I kiss their cheeks. "It was a really nice birthday. Thank you."

"Our pleasure, dear. Would you like us to come in for a while?"

"No, ma'am, it's okay. I'm good. I'll just read for a while and go to bed. I'm sure Mama will be home soon."

"Ok, dove. We love ya."

"I love you, too."

They watch as I go inside and when I look out the window, I wave. They drive away, tooting the horn once as they go.

I have a hard time sleeping. Mama doesn't come

home. I never talk to Isaiah. I miss my daddy. I'm fifteen years old.

TO-DO LISTS

FIRST DAY OF Summer Vacation To-Do List:

1. Take my time getting up.
2. Read a while.
3. Leave my bed unmade all day long.
4. Take Josh for a walk.
5. Write in my journal.
6. Go to the library.

I've done the first five things all before 10 o'clock. At precisely 10 o'clock, I'm also showered and on my way to the library. It's a 15-minute walk and I'm sweating by the time I get there. The humidity has kicked in full swing. How did Scarlett O'Hara manage to never sweat? I s'pose she never walked even this far in the heat. She probably never had need of a library either, come to think of it.

I go to the self-help area and look at all the parenting books. I see a book called *Making Divorce Easier for Your Children*. I take it and *Learning to Cope after Divorce* over to a table and read them both for a long time. I have an encyclopedia covering the books, so if anyone walks by, they won't see what I'm reading. It's close to imposs-ible to keep secrets when you know everyone in town, but I'm going to try anyway.

Learning to Cope After Divorce says it's important to get out and resume living a full life. Don't just wallow in self-misery, but get out and see people. Experience life, it says. In *Making Divorce Easier for Your Children*, it encourages parents to each give one-on-one time with their children. Make sure you let your child know it's not their fault that you can't live together, it says.

I'm deeply immersed in the books when Miss Greener walks up to my table.

"Boo!" she whispers in my ear.

I jump out of my seat like a scalded dog.

"Oh, sorry, Caroline! Didn't mean to scare you that bad." She laughs.

"Hi." I smile at her, while furiously scrambling to hide the books.

Miss Greener has a way of looking untidy even when I know she has just brushed her hair. For once, she's not wearing a hat. She's wearing a dress and the tops of her knee-highs are showing. This is fancy for her.

"Would you like to go grab a shake?" she whispers.

I nod, excitedly. "Let me just go put my book away."

I quickly put all the books in place and we walk across the street to the diner. Harriet's is the other restau-rant in town—a down-home, old-fashioned diner complete with black and white-tiled floors.

I realize I'm starving when I sit down.

Miss Greener, in her all-knowing way, says, "I'm kinda hungry for a burger, how 'bout you, Caroline? My treat…"

We order burgers and fries and chocolate shakes. It tastes wonderful. We talk to all the regulars and enjoy the small talk for a while.

"George misses you, you know."

"I miss him, too." I wipe my mouth with a napkin and take another sip of my shake. "Is he still chewing that bone I brought over a couple weeks ago?"

"Oh mercy, he finished that one at least a week ago now! You know that dog, he can't leave the bone alone until it's gone." Her shoulders shake as she laughs. "He is something *else*."

George is a huge mass of hair and thinks he's human. I used to walk him for Miss Greener when she worked another bus route, but now that she's on my route, I only see him if I go visit them. I take Josh with me every now and then to say hello to his buddy.

"You'll have to come see us soon. Bring Josh…"

"Yeah, I'll do that. I've missed George. I'm sure Josh misses him too."

When I've finished my food, Miss Greener leans over and says, "Caroline, I know you're going through a rough time right now."

I hate the flush that rises when a touchy subject comes up or when close attention is paid to me.

"I've heard about your daddy being gone, and well, I know about your mama too…'specially after the other day and all. I'm worried about you. I just want you to know I'm here for you. If you need to talk—do you have anything you'd like to talk about?"

I sit there, quiet and embarrassed…that she knows so much and that it's so obvious that I'm such a mess. *Please don't cry. Please don't cry. Please don't cry*, I chant inside until I feel the knot go away.

"I'm hoping this is just a phase my parents are going through. Maybe they can work things out."

"Maybe so, maybe so. These things can take time, though."

If I didn't love her so much, I would be offended at this talk, but I know she's just worried about me.

"It's ok." I find that I cannot say anything else.

She looks at me, waiting for more.

"It's gonna get better," I whisper.

"I'm sure you're right, honey. Will you just promise me that you'll call or come to me if you ever need anything? Anything at all. Will you promise me that?" She takes my hand and her eyes are full of tears.

I'm so touched by her concern that I want to tell her everything. I want to tell her that my mother never came home last night...that we haven't spoken in a week...that she didn't remember my birthday. But I just say, "Thank you, Miss Greener. I will. I promise."

There's a commotion by the door and Les and Leroy burst into the restaurant. They saunter over to the bar, taking notice of all the customers in the place. Leroy spots me and walks over to our table. Les sits down and picks up a menu, watching our every move.

"It's Miss Caroline," Leroy says. "You're looking mighty fine this mornin'." He mouths, *White bitch*.

I just look at him and then at Miss Greener.

"You ignorin' me, girl?" He leans down into my face. "I'm talkin' to you."

"Hi, Leroy," I manage. He makes me so nervous that I begin to shake.

"That's more like it." He runs his fingers down my

hair and then gives a curl a sharp tug.

Tears prick my eyes, and I knock his hand away. Miss Greener stands up.

"Hey! You leave her alone, do you hear me?"

"Whatcha gon' do 'bout it?" He puts his face as close to Miss Greener's as he can without touching.

"You keep your hands to yourself. Be nice," she says, not backing down.

"Oh, I'm gonna be nice, all right. I'm being nice." He holds his hands up and backs away, laughing.

We leave, not saying anything until we get outside. "Try to stay away from them, Caroline. Leroy, especially, is pure trouble."

"I know. My Nellie says the same thing. They both make me nervous."

"Well, you just be careful. I'm sure they're just talk, but Leroy seems to have it in for you, so be cautious. Just watch out for yourself. I know you walk everywhere and summer is upon us, so you'll be out a lot. Maybe you can call Clara Mae and the two of you can go places together." She grins at this thought and that seems to settle it in her mind. "Clara Mae and Thomas would be happy to hang out with you this summer."

"I'm sure we'll hang out some."

"Good. Well, I have a doctor's appointment in a half hour. Can I give you a ride home?"

"That would be great."

I try to catch a glimpse of my mama as we drive past the bank, but I don't see her. It's hard to get a good look in the window.

"Why don't you come over tomorrow and see us? Maybe help me plant some things? I'm needin' your help somethin' fierce."

"Sure. What time would you like me to come?"

"How about 10?"

"I'll be there."

FIRST DAY OF Summer Vacation Afternoon To-Do List:

1. Read.
2. Clean the bathroom.
3. Clean the kitchen.
4. Go ahead and make the bed.
5. Take Josh for another walk.
6. Weed the garden.
7. Try not to panic that my mother is still not home and hasn't called.

Isaiah calls when I get back from my walk with Josh.

"Hey. What are you doing today?" he asks.

"Oh, you know. Just staying busy."

He chuckles. Isaiah knows I'm already stir crazy. I was stir crazy in this house before summer vacation ever began.

"I miss you," I tell him.

"I miss you too—"

"Isaiah!" I interrupt. "The box! The card. So beautiful. I will keep them both forever," I vow.

"I'm glad you liked it." He sounds pleased.

"I *love* it," I say and then get all flustered with the word *love*.

He laughs again. "I'm glad about that too, then," he says.

THE NEXT MORNING, I sleep late. I didn't go to sleep until the sun was shining this morning. I have to stop doing that. I tiptoe to my mother's room; her bed is still made. My stomach is clenched and the panic rises in my chest. Is she coming back?

I take Josh out for a while and when I get back to the house, I've settled down a bit. It isn't like I wasn't alone a lot to begin with. She's just staying out a little longer than usual. I need to stay calm. She'll be back.

I go in her room and look in her closet. Only a few items are missing. She'll have to at least come home for more clothes. This is a small consolation.

Feeling like the house is closing in on me, I walk over to Miss Greener's house. At the last minute, I decide to leave Josh at home. He seems worn out from our earlier walks. She lives close to the school. It's just her and George. George really does take over the whole house, standing neck and neck with the kitchen counters. His large ears stand to attention, the only distinct feature on his face, since his eyes are completely covered by hair. He's quite the character. When he jumps up on me, he lays both paws on my shoulders. He's very charming and seems particularly happy to see me today, almost knocking me down to lick me.

As usual, Miss Greener is bright and cheerful. Before I know it, I'm feeling somewhat cheerful myself. Working in the garden will do that to you. Especially with these two. Miss Greener hums "In the Garden" in at least five keys too high, and George starts to howl along when she hits that long drawn-out note going into the chorus. I laugh till I cry.

When we go in for lunch, Miss Greener hands me a tall glass of sweet tea and I gulp it down. She makes tall, loaded sandwiches for the three of us, George included, and we inhale them, in between chattering.

Miss Greener and I became close when I started seeing her every day on the school bus. We realized our mutual love for flowers early on, and she began inviting me over to pick out what I wanted her to divide for my garden.

When I come over, I'm at home. Not enough to rummage through the fridge on my own, but enough to laugh and talk freely. I feel peaceful at her house.

As I help clean up, I ask if she needs any more help with her garden.

"If you're able to come back tomorrow, I have a few more things I'd like you to do," she says.

I'm thrilled that I have another reason to come back so soon.

"Same time?"

"Same time, honey. That sounds good. Here let me give you a little bit for what you did today."

She begins getting money out of her wallet.

"Oh, no, I'm not taking that! I'm glad to help. You know that." I hand the money back as fast as I can.

"You take this. I would have had to hire someone to do all the work you did today. You worked hard. Think of it as a little summer job." She grins and puts the money in my pocket.

"It was too fun to be a summer job." I grin back.

"Well, good, that means you'll hurry back." She puts her arm around my shoulder. "Now come on, I'll drive you home."

"Oh, don't worry, I'll walk. It won't take me long."

"Are you sure? I don't mind driving you."

"I'm sure. I need to go do a few things in town anyway."

"I'd be happy to take you somewhere if you'd like, Caroline. Where would you like to go?"

"Well, I was just going to stop by the bank."

"Oh, I see...why don't I take you there? I don't mind waiting to take you home either."

"I'm fine to go on my own," I insist.

"I know you are. Let me take you, though. We'll just pop over there."

We get in her old car and she drives the couple of blocks to the bank. She shuts the car off when we get there and I think she is coming in, but she stays inside.

"I'll wait here for you." She nods and gives me a reassuring smile. "Take your time."

I try to remember the last time I came to my mother's work. She used to bring me here when I was little and show me off to her friends. They would all talk in sing-song voices to me.

Jeanette is the first person I see when I walk in the door. It's clear that she's shocked to see me.

"Why, hello, Caroline! How are you? It's so good to see you." She gives me a big hug. "What are you doing here? I would have thought you'd be with your mother."

"Oh? Yeah? I...didn't get to go." I laugh awkwardly

and try to stall to figure out what else I can learn. This isn't what I expected at all.

"Well, maybe next time. I hear that festival in Memphis is hard to beat. Do you like the blues, Caroline?" She looks at me so earnestly that if I were not so bewildered I would giggle.

"Um, yes, ma'am, I do." Memphis. I let out a deep breath. She's with Daddy.

"Me too. I'd sure love to go sometime."

"Well, maybe you can someday." I back up, hoping to make a quick escape. "It was good to see you, Jeanette."

"Oh, you leavin'? Was there somethin' I can help you with?" She's by my side in an instant. "We want to take care of Jenny's girl. It's not every day that we see you in here. This is a treat." She's patting my arm and leading me back to Betty, one of the tellers. "Betty, can you believe this is Caroline? Look how tall! I tell you what—you've grown a foot since the last time I saw you, girl!"

Save me now.

Miss Greener walks in right on time.

"Caroline, just checking on you. Did you find what you needed?" she asks, winking at me.

"I did, thank you. It's so good to see you, Jeanette and Betty." I walk out with Miss Greener. I think Jeanette is still talking as I leave, but I just keep walking.

"Did you see your mother?" She asks when we get in the car.

"No."

I don't tell her she's gone. I know better than to tell anyone she has left me alone. Miss Greener would want me to come stay with her while Mama is away and even though it drives me crazy, I'd rather be home.

"Well, hopefully you can make your peace with her when she gets home tonight."

"Yes, I'd like that."

I cannot express what a relief it is to know my parents are together. Everything will be all right now. I don't even mind that she didn't tell me she was going. I hope they can really work things out and that we can be a happy family when they come home.

I finally do sleep. A deep sleep. It's long overdue.

❀ 7 ❀

HARRIET'S

THIS MORNING I woke up at 8 o'clock, took a quick bath, let my curls air dry, ate a piece of toast, let Josh out, dusted off my mom's Miss Tennessee picture and sat down wondering what I should do next. I'm clearly back-slidden. My life has been greatly simplified since my parents left. Despite the obvious fact that I'm alone, I've made some decisions about a few things that are for the better.

First of all, I will never wear pink foam curlers again. This is a small thing, I know, but it brings me great joy to lie my head flat on my pillow at night, with no bumpy ridges getting in the way. My hair loves this new freedom and even though it *is* on the frizzy side, I think the curls actually look better. I don't know if this is really true since I'm the only one usually looking at me, but that's the up-side of being by myself.

The second thing I've decided is I will only iron when an article is in dire need of it. If I hang the dress up as soon as I get it out of the washer, the wrinkles aren't too bad. My mother would be mor-ti-*fied* if she knew I was leaving the house in slightly wrinkled clothes, but...well, she's not here, is she?

I've left the dishes in the sink for the first time in my life. One day I even ate chocolate chip cookies for breakfast. And lunch. Okay, dinner too. But for dessert, I was sick of them and had some ice cream instead.

These are the small consolations. This is dealing with a bad situation in a positive way. I've learned to do that from years of experience and from the latest batch of self-help books I just got from the library.

AS I'M WALKING home from Miss Greener's a week later, I pass Harriet's and see a *Help Wanted* sign. I've been to her house three times and she has paid me every time, but the last time I was there I finished all the odd jobs she had for me. What she said about a little summer job got me to thinking that's exactly what I have to do, get a real one.

The food is beginning to dwindle. The shelves are getting bare and I've used almost all of the money Miss Greener has given me. I've always loved tuna, but if I never see another can, I will be just fine.

I still haven't told a soul that my parents are both gone. I don't know how it's escaping everyone, but no one seems to realize that I'm on my own. Either they don't truly realize both parents are gone, or they assume I'm with my grandparents. I come and go as I please and no one has said a word. Even Miss Greener, for all her intuition or nosiness, whichever it is, hasn't noticed. And my grandparents, as much as I love them, I'm used to them being distracted a lot of the time.

The whole situation makes me determined to be more observant when I'm an adult. So far, every adult I know seems to be in his or her own little world.

I haven't even told Isaiah, and there would be no way for him to know. Since school ended, I haven't been able to talk to him as much. He's helping his uncles at their construction job and tries to call in the afternoon, but he isn't always back home in time to do it.

I've spent a lot of time walking with Josh. He's loving all the extra attention. I stop by the library almost every day. I carry a big bag with a few books and snacks. Around noon, I'll usually pull out half of a peanut butter and jelly sandwich and eat it down by the water.

I walk into Harriet's and see Miss Sue at the counter. She's pouring coffee for Mr. Davidson, Tulma's mayor. It's not uncommon to see the mayor on a weekly basis at Harriet's. The word around town is that Harriet's is his favorite place to eat. Dixie's is also his favorite place to eat. Mr. Davidson is known for being a fair man.

Miss Sue is the great, great granddaughter of Harriet. She has run the place for at least twenty years and is what everyone in town calls an "old maid," except no one really knows exactly how old she is. I think maybe she isn't all that old. When she laughs, she looks like a little girl. And she actually laughs quite often.

A pie from Miss Sue will make your taste buds get up and dance. She makes the best pies in the South. I can't prove this for a fact, since I've never been anywhere else, but it's just something I know is true.

"Hey there, Miss Caroline. How are you on this fine day?"

"I'm good, Miss Sue. Hi, Mr. Davidson."

"Hello there, Caroline. You're looking more like your mother every day."

"Thank you."

"Would you like to sit at the counter, Caroline?" Miss Sue has a menu ready for me.

"Actually, I was wondering if I might talk to you for a minute...when you're not busy."

"Why sure, Caroline, I'll be right with you." Miss Sue finishes with Mr. Davidson and walks around the counter and leads me to a booth.

"Now. What can I help you with?" She smiles into my eyes. Her eyes crinkle in the corners when she smiles and her cheeks burst out on each side.

"I, uh...I saw that you would like some help and I'm...I wonder if maybe I could help you...you know, work here..." I'm overcome with nervousness. I think I really need this job.

"Oh, sweetie, that is so nice of you. But I was kinda thinkin' of someone a little...well, older. You know, someone who can be here past summer vacation..."

"I thought you might say that, but—" I lean in and say softly, "I really need this job, Miss Sue. I really do. And I can wash dishes. I can cook. I can clean better than most adults. I'm always on time. I can stay late. Whatever you need, really. Even after school starts back up, I could still come in...before and after. I will work *really* hard." I run out of breath talking so fast.

Her face is hard to read as she looks at me. I'm afraid she's going to say no, when she finally speaks.

"Well, for you maybe I'd rethink this. I believe you would be a good little worker. And I started myself when I was...really young. This job won't pay much, but I sure could use your help. I lost my best help last week and I can't seem to catch up."

"Oh, thank you, Miss Sue! You won't regret it!"

"How old are you, anyway?" she asks, grinning. "And how do your parents feel about you working here?"

I must confess I do contemplate fudging my age a little bit, for several reasons, but figure she would find out the truth eventually. I've known her my whole life, so if she really thought about it, she could probably figure it out herself.

"I'm fifteen," I say with pride. "And my parents are fine with it."

"Well, I'll be. Seems like the last time I asked, you were eleven. I thought you were maybe thirteen now. Fifteen is just fine." She studies me for a minute. "And you could pass for even older. You sure are tall. Are you sure you want to work here? It's hard work. Wouldn't you rather be out, enjoying your summer vacation?"

"I really do want this job, Miss Sue. I mean it. Besides, my parents both work all day...they would actually like me to be busy with something." I don't know where that came from, but it seems to settle it in her mind.

"Well, I tell you what, let's give it a try, why don't we. I'll give you cash once a week. You'll start out washing dishes. We'll see how that goes. It's busy around here, are you sure you can keep up?"

I nod. "I'm sure."

She pats me on the shoulder and says, "When can you start?"

"Well, I should go home and let my dog out. But then I can come back if you'd like."

Miss Sue lets out a loud laugh that nearly shakes the windows and says, "Well, all right then, it's a deal!"

I race home and take Josh for a quick walk, trying to hurry him up. He seems particularly slow today, stopping to sniff every flower, every bush, and every post.

ONCE I'VE DROPPED off Josh and have almost reached the diner again, I cross Third Street, just before Main. Out of habit, I look down to Pope Street and stop dead in my tracks. In front of the bank, my mom is getting out of Mr. Anderson's car. She tosses her head back and it's too far to hear her, but I know because I know her like I know myself: she's laughing. She's happy. She's with Mr. Anderson.

I run to Main Street, past Harriet's, past the school, and finally reach the river. I'm crying and my nose has started dripping. I can't breathe and I fall on the dirt by the water. As the tears fall, I realize how much hope I've put into my mama and daddy coming back together. I'm so confused...why aren't they coming home?

"Caroline...Caroline?"

I look up to see Thomas standing over me. He leans down until he's squatting in front of me at eye level.

"What's the matter?"

"Oh, Thomas..." I hate crying in front of anyone, but I can't stop. He leans over and hugs me while I let my tears fall on his white cotton shirt.

He's quiet as I cry and when I come to my senses, I jump up. "Sorry, I got your shirt all wet."

"Don't worry about that. I'm worried about you. What's going on? You can tell me."

"I'm sorry, Thomas. I have to go." I turn around and run as fast as I can.

I hear him calling my name as I run, but I don't look back. I run back to the diner, sneak in the back door, and go in the bathroom. I rinse my face. *You have to calm down. This doesn't mean anything. You have to stay calm. Everything is going to be all right. You have work to do.*

I try to smooth down my hair. My hair is in crazy ringlets from all the humidity. I blow my nose and tuck my shirt into my skirt. I still look a mess, but I go out the bathroom door and straight to the kitchen. There's a pile of dishes and I begin washing them.

There's a black lady standing by the large stove. She has a kerchief over her hair and is humming as she works. I notice the pile of orders sitting beside her. As she expertly turns over burgers, she's also toasting bread, making pancakes, an omelet and a tuna melt. She barely looks my way, but says her name is Ruby and that it's nice to have my help. I thank her and get to work. I have the kitchen looking spotless when Miss Sue walks in, wiping her hands on her apron.

"Caroline! I didn't even know you were back! Look at this kitchen! Good heavenly days, child, you weren't kiddin'! The place looks great. Look at her go, Ruby."

"You ain't kiddin'. The child hadn't stopped since she got here," Ruby comments.

I just keep working, busying myself with the mop. Betty Jo, the waitress, brings dirty dishes back every few minutes. She whistles at the clean floor. I barely hear them; I just focus on cleaning. I don't realize how quickly time flies. I'm mopping the floor for the umpteenth time and jump when Miss Sue puts her hand on my shoulder.

"Honey, it's eight o'clock, you need to be getting home."

"Oh, I didn't realize it was so late."

"Yeah, I'm sorry about that, I didn't mean to have you stay this long. We just had such a busy stretch there."

"It's okay."

"Tomorrow I'll just have you work 7-2. How does that sound? You can eat your breakfast and lunch here. In fact, any time you're working here, Ruby will fix you something to eat, so don't worry 'bout packin' lunches." She gives me her huge grin. "And tomorrow, I'll make sure you take breaks. Don't want to wear you out before you even get started."

"Thank you."

I wash my hands, say goodnight and start the walk home. The sun is fading, but it's still shining. All the shops are closed and the bank has been closed for hours. I still look at the bank parking lot when I pass Third Street, looking for my mom or Mr. Anderson's car. I don't see either and try not to hope for her to be home when I get there.

Josh dances his jig when I walk in the door, and I go outside with him for a few minutes. My bones are aching; my back is tired. My hands still look like prunes from all the dishwashing.

I look in the telephone book and find Mr. Anderson's number. I pick up the phone and dial his number. He picks up on the fourth ring.

"Hello?"

I open my mouth, but nothing comes out. I put the phone down and sit in a dark living room, waiting...

wishing...hoping.

IT'S THE MIDDLE of the night when I wake. It feels a little cooler in here than before I fell asleep. I think Mama might have come home. Please tell me I'm not dreaming.

I sit up and look around the room. I see her shoes and her purse. Oh, thank you, God. She has come home. I go to her room and crack the door. She's in the bed, sleeping. I stand over her, looking at her long hair laid out on the pillow. She looks beautiful lying there. I forget that I hate her and only remember how much I love her and how glad I am that she's finally home.

I WAKE UP extra early the next morning, before the sun rises. I was afraid to go back to sleep last night...afraid I would wake up and she would be gone again. When I go into the kitchen, I'm surprised to see my mother sitting at the table, in a pretty new dress. She absently fingers a few twenty-dollar bills.

She looks up when I enter the room, and her eyes are tired with circles around them. "Caroline—" she says.

I sit down beside her and don't say anything.

"I had to go away for a bit. I needed to talk to your father and figure things out with Grant."

I try not to move. I want her to tell me everything.

"Your daddy's not coming back, Caroline. I know you probably think that it's my fault, but I've tried. I've really tried…"

I'm holding my breath, willing myself not to cry. He was supposed to come home with her. We were supposed to be a family again. The tears begin running down my cheeks.

"He can't stop drinking. I can't make him stop. And Grant, well, he appreciates me, Caroline. I haven't had anyone take care of me for a long time." She's crying now.

What have I been doing all this time? I want to yell.

She goes on. "I've been a good wife and a good mother. I've sacrificed a lot for this family. I could have had a real career if I'd left a long time ago. Do you know that? But I stayed here, with your father, in this God-for-saken town. It's draining me dry, it really is." She's picking up steam now. "You know I love you, Caroline, but you're old enough—you're able to look out for yourself and I need some time. I just need time on my own...for a little while."

I can barely speak, but I need to know. "Where are you going?"

She has a far off look in her eyes. I wonder for the first time if my mom has completely lost her mind. But then she looks at me. She wipes her tears, smiles and puts her hand on my cheek.

"Oh, I won't be gone long. Don't worry. Don't cry, honey. You're going to be fine here. I'll check on you often. Just keep doin' how you have been—you've been taking good care of everything. I'll be back before you know it. I really just came back to talk to you about all this. I felt bad that I left without explaining anything, but you were ignoring me there before I left."

"Please don't go, Mama. I'm sorry I ignored you. I

was just mad at you about Mr. Anderson. Please stay home. It's so hard to be a—"

"Shhh, shhh, that's enough of that whinin'. I promise you I will be back before you know I'm gone. I just need to…take care of myself for once and get my strength back."

That's when I notice her suitcase by the door. She's leaving me today. I'm so stunned, I hold onto her arm, and beg. "Please, Mama, please don't go. I can't stand it in this house by myself. Please—please don't leave me here."

"Hush, child. What is all this carryin' on? When you're at school, we hardly see each other anyway. I work all day. It's just a few hours in the evening that we'd even be together. I should have just stayed gone."

"No! No, I'm so glad you came back. And I will work harder. I know it was hard when Daddy was drinking, but now he's gone and it can just be the two of us." I hate the desperate tone in my voice, but I can't stop.

"Listen, Caroline Josephine. That is *enough*. I need you to quit this hissy fit and listen to me. I have to go. You are going to stay here, watch the house, take care of that dumb dog and not say a word to anyone about it. I'm not ready for the whole town to know about me and Grant. And he's not quite ready for you yet. It's enough that Miss Greener knows, but she won't tell anyone. She knows better. If your dad finds out about Grant, now, that's another story—we wouldn't get a dime. Do you understand? So look at me…" She lifts my chin and looks into my eyes. "You're going to suck it up, be the strong girl I raised you to be, and when I get back we're going to be just fine. Do you hear me?"

I can't move. She's still gripping my chin. "I said,

'Do you *hear* me?'"

I blink and that's enough for her. I can't believe this is happening. She seems completely sober, so I can't blame alcohol this time.

She stands, picks up her suitcase, and walks out the door.

I run to the door, embarrassed at myself, but desperate to keep her. "Mama!" I yell, sobbing. "Everyone knows. Everyone already knows about Mr. Anderson. Please, Mama!"

She doesn't even turn around, but gets in her car and leaves me standing there. Alone. Again.

I sit on the front step and pound on the concrete. The love I felt for her last night is gone. I pummel the ground until my fists are sore. Finally, I stand up and walk in the house, get in the shower and let the water wash over me and my bloody hands.

I wish I could have been good enough for my mother to love me.

If I had known what would end up bringing her back though, I would have wished her to be gone for keeps.

ALL IN A DAY'S WORK

AFTER ALL THE drama of the morning, I'm still at work with ten minutes to spare. The shower took care of some of my splotches, but I still look puffy in the eyes. I walk to Harriet's and pray that I can stay dry-eyed as I work.

I s'pose I wouldn't have to work since Mama left the money on the table. I counted it before I left and there's a hundred dollars still sitting on the dining room table.

I really want to go to Harriet's, though. I'm craving company—to hear people talking to each other, to be useful to someone else, for really anything other than sitting in my house, wishing the day away. I think, deep down, I also want to prove to my mother that I really am just fine without her. She wanted me to take care of myself. I will show her that I can do just that.

I'm standing outside the diner, when I see Isaiah and three of his uncles drive by in a big blue truck. Isaiah is in the back of the truck and he yells, "Caroline!" He grins and waves until the truck turns and he's out of sight. It does my heart good to see him.

I go in the diner and am surprised by how many people are already there. It seems practically the whole town comes here for breakfast. I rush to the back and get started washing dishes. I let myself get lost in the work and try not to replay the conversation with my mother over and over again.

Miss Sue calls me out to the eating area a few hours later and asks me to clean out there for a while. Everyone is friendly and asks about my parents. It's the southern way, but I've never been more uncomfortable with it.

"Caroline, how are you doing? I haven't seen you in a while. How's your mama? Your daddy?"

They barely wait for an answer, just asking the routine questions you ask someone when you see them.

I try to duck the answers, while still smiling and being cordial back. My mother has taught me well, after all.

When things slow down a little, I mop the floor of the dining room until it's clean as a whistle, as Nellie says. Les and Leroy come in then and walk right up to me.

"Hey, chickadee. What have we here? You workin' at Harriet's now? How 'bout that?" Leroy grins.

He takes my mop and does a little dance with it. I try in vain to grab it back.

"What? Whatcha wanna do that for?" He holds it out for me and when I reach for it, he pulls it back. Les thinks this is hysterical and that makes Leroy want to keep pestering me.

Miss Sue is busying herself behind the counter. I can tell she's nervous about them being in the diner, but she tries to act like she's not watching.

"Caroline, I need your help in the kitchen," she calls.

"Oh, that's convenient," Leroy says. "What time you get done here? Maybe we can walk you home." He snickers. "Or is Isaiah already takin' care of that?" He shakes his head as he says this and leans into my ear. "Maybe I can beat Isaiah here and have you to myself? Would you like that?" He sticks his tongue in my ear. I leap back, wiping my ear and unable to keep the disgusted look off my face.

Miss Sue didn't see the last part because she went in the back to get Ruby. When Ruby comes out of the kitchen, the boys say, "Hey, Ruby."

"Hey, yourself. Leave Miss Caroline alone, Leroy, you hear? Now sit down, you here to eat or not?"

"Yeah, make us some of them pancakes of yours," Les says.

Leroy smiles cockily at Ruby and says to me, "I'll deal with you later."

Ruby backs into the kitchen, saying, "Come on, Miss Caroline. Help me back here." I can see in her eyes that they make her nervous, too.

"Oh, come on, let Caroline serve us..." Leroy pipes up.

I go back in the kitchen with Ruby and pick up the dishcloth. She starts the pancakes.

"Them boys...they need to be smacked upside the head. They's been on they own for as long as I can remember, though. Never did find their way." She shakes her head. "I don't agree with how they acting 'round here, but I sho do think the blame goes to they folks. I guess I can't talk, I don't have no children myself." She smiles at me then.

I smile back. Her eyes are kind.

LES AND LEROY are long gone when I go out of the kitchen. The lunch crowd comes and I go back and forth from the kitchen to the diner. It's 2 o'clock before I know it, but I don't want to leave. I haven't had lunch yet, so I ask Miss Sue if I can have Ruby make me something for lunch.

"Why, of course, honey. I can't believe you didn't eat! Tomorrow, you make sure you eat, now. Ruby will make up whatever you want. You don't have to check with me a'tall."

Ruby is happy to make me some pancakes. I can't stop moaning as I eat them. So divine. I go on about them and Ruby is so pleased, she makes me more.

"Child, how long it been since you ate?" she asks after I've been eating a while.

"I guess I have a hearty appetite, Miss Ruby." I lie. I didn't realize how hungry I really was until I began eating.

"Oh, I's just plain ol' Ruby," she says with a grin.

"I'm just plain Caroline too," I tell her.

"Girl, there ain't nothin' plain 'bout you." I grin at her and start to say something back, but she keeps going. "You know, I seen you before. Before yesterday, I mean. I seen you walkin' with that Washington boy."

I blush at the mention of Isaiah. "Yes, sometimes he walks with our group."

"He's a good boy, that Isaiah...come from a good family. I don't know his mama, but I hear he take good care of her..." Ruby shakes her head. "I'd give anything for a boy like that...or a girl." She looks at me and winks.

"You's a good girl too. I bet yo parents is right proud."

I don't say anything; I just keep eating. These really are the best pancakes I've ever had.

Ruby goes on. "I think this girl is all dried up, though. Don't think I'm gon' be havin' any babies 'round here at this late date!" She cackles, showing her white teeth. They are perfectly even and look as bright as Ivory soap.

"You have really nice teeth," I blurt out.

It thrills her. "You think so? Mama always did say it was my best feature." She grins extra big.

"Well, your eyes are real nice, too," I say with all my heart, grinning back. I think I've found a friend. My heart wells up a little bit at the warmth I feel from her.

"Why, thank you, child! From a looker like you, I take that as a s*upreme* compliment. I'm sure I don't need to tell you how pretty you is. You's gon' have the boys dropping like flies, if they ain't already!"

I laugh and shake my head. "Thank you for the pancakes, Ruby." I rub my belly. "I think I may be done."

"Well, you sho did do some damage, sho nuff. I hadn't never seen no child eat like you just did. If I didn't know better, I'd think you hadn't eaten in a month!"

I give her a wobbly grin. If she only knew.

I stall and manage to stay at the diner past 4. Before I go, I call Nellie and Miss Greener to tell them about my new job at Harriet's. I know they'll wonder about me if they don't see me as often. They're both pleased that I have something to keep me busy for the summer.

Nellie and Grandpaw don't usually eat out during the week, but Nellie says they'll stop in now that they have kin running the place. Miss Greener goes to Harriet's several times a week, so she says she'll see me in a day or two.

As I head out, I hope that Josh hasn't lost his bladder, but he's pretty good about holding it. I decide to take a few more minutes and walk past Isaiah's house. It's only a few minutes out of the way. Before I get there, I pull out my tablet and write him a note in our not-so-secret code—pig latin.

Isaiah,
It is afesay otay allcay ymay ousehay. Ymay arentspay are onegay.
I issmay ouyay.
Ovelay,
Emay

Translated, that is:

Isaiah,
It is safe to call my house. My parents are gone.
I miss you.
Love,
Me

I feel better already as I tuck the note in the spoke of his bicycle. Isaiah is very particular about his bicycle. I've never known anyone to take better care of his things. He'll notice it right away.

When I get home, Josh licks my face all over and then is ready to go out. I don't know what I'd do without this sweet dog. I'm pretty sure he keeps me from losing it.

I stay full from all the pancakes for quite a while, but eventually start to get hungry. I'm scrounging through the cupboards trying to find something to eat when the phone rings.

I run to the phone and it's my mother.

"Hi, Caroline," she says.

I don't say anything to her.

"Caroline, are you there?"

I still don't answer.

"I can hear you breathing, Caroline, I know you're there. Well, anyway, just listen, I guess. This is a number where you can reach me." She rattles off a number. I don't bother to write it down. She repeats the number. "I'll be back soon. Make sure you don't let it slip to anyone that I'm not staying there or we'll be out on the street. Do you hear me?" She sighs. "Okay, Caroline, I'll let you go. I love you. All right?"

I hear the dial tone. I'm numb. And dry-eyed.

I go to the phone book and look up Grant Anderson's number. It's the number my mother just gave me.

I go back to looking in the cupboards and realize there's nothing. Well, at least I'll get a good breakfast in the morning.

I'M FALLING ASLEEP when I hear the phone again. Thinking it might be my mother again, I'm tempted to ignore it. She has never taken well to being ignored.

I run to catch it in time and I'm so glad I did. It's Isaiah.

"Caroline?"

"Isaiah!"

"Are you okay?"

I'm quiet for a long minute.

"Caroline?"

"I am. I will be."

"What's going on over there?"

"Will you promise not to tell a single soul, Isaiah? You can't tell your mother! Do you?"

"Of course, you're making me nervous, though. What is it?"

"My dad isn't coming back. My mom left. I'm not sure when she's coming back. She made me vow not to tell anyone because she's afraid my dad will find out she's having an affair with Mr. Anderson. I'm sure he already knows."

"What do you mean, she left? Where did she go? So you're there alone?"

"I have been for weeks."

"What? Caroline, why didn't you tell me?" Isaiah sounds shocked and a little angry.

"I haven't talked to you in a while!" I say defensively.

"I know and I'm sorry. I've been working hard, trying to help my mom. I've really missed you. I don't think we've ever gone this long without talking, do you?"

"No, we haven't." I can't help but sound a little sullen. "I thought maybe now that school is over you were forgetting about me."

"Are you kidding me?"

"No."

"I think about you all the time. My uncle has started teasing me about my daydreaming. He asked me the other day if I had a girl."

"What did you say?"

"I said yes."

"Really?"

"Is it okay for me to say that?"

"Well, yes...but did you tell him who?"

"No, but I wish I could."

"Well, I'm just glad that you weren't calling me because you don't like me anymore or something…"

"I don't regret a single moment with you, Caroline."

We're both smiling. And silent. My face is hot and I'm glad he isn't here to see my red mess.

"I can't believe they've left you there alone. They could get in serious trouble for that."

"Really? Well, I don't want them to get in trouble, I just want them to come home, so we can get back to normal."

"It sounds like things might not get back to normal, Caroline." His voice is soft and now I wish he could be here with me. I would feel better if he were here.

Neither of us knows what to say. For a few minutes, we're both quiet.

Finally Isaiah says, "Tomorrow I'll ask my uncles if I can get done early. I can come hang out with you for a while. We can go by Talbot's Pond or down by the river. Maybe take lunch."

"That sounds great, but I got a job too! I have lots to tell you!"

I tell him about working at Harriet's, about Miss Greener helping me with work, about Ruby, and about Les and Leroy coming into the diner. We talk for a couple of hours. His mother has been in bed, so we're both free to talk. He's whispering and I find myself whispering too.

Before we hang up, we plan to meet by the river at 2:30. He'll call the diner if he can't make it by then. I'm going to bring lunch with me and we'll go swimming. He thinks it'll be fine since he will still be working most of the day.

"Caroline?" Isaiah whispers.

"What?" I'm so sleepy.

"I promise I'll take care of you one day. And I'll do my best to take care of you now, too."

I can't think of anything to say. I'm afraid to wish for that. Finally, I tell him, "I can take care of myself, Isaiah, you don't need to worry about me."

"I know. But you shouldn't have to take care of yourself," he says. "And I want more than anything to do it for you."

"It means a lot that you want to," I whisper. "Really, it does."

"That's what love is about, Caroline. And I love you more than anything."

THE NEXT DAY, I fly through my work. Eating regular meals again gives me renewed energy. Ruby has eggs, bacon, and toast waiting for me when I get to work. Mid-morning, she motions me over to her and gives me the first piece of her apple pie. I eat a hamburger for lunch and am working up my nerve to ask her if I could take some food home with me.

She looks at me with narrowed eyes, still grinning, but says, "Where do you put all this food, girl?"

"I'm a growing girl, you know." I laugh.

"You've got that right." She laughs and then leans over to whisper, "Miss Sue can't pay you what you worth, so I will just feed you 'til you can't eat no mo'."

She gives me the rest of the chicken pot pie and half of a rhubarb pie to take home. At the last minute, she puts in a pan of warm biscuits and a jar of honey. "Just bring that pan back in the mornin', darlin', I won't need it tonight."

I sneak two forks in the bag and take off to meet Isaiah. I run down Main Street, past Third, and this time I don't even look to see if my mother is there.

AT THE END of Main Street, the bridge leads out of town. On either side of the bridge, the water laps against the mud and rocks. I go through the trees, down the steep ravine and when the space between the trees opens up, the view is spectacular. It's the only reason I can think of to live in Tulma. We don't have a huge expanse of the Tennessee River; it looks more like a lake here, but it's a really beautiful lake. In some places, it trickles down to just a small stream that you can skip across.

Isaiah is already waiting. We know the path to take where no one will see us. We wind back through the trees and follow the river a while. I follow him and watch his white shirt-tails blowing in the breeze. He has his jeans rolled up around his calves. We've only been here once before, last summer, when we planned another day together. These sacred days are few and far between, and there's excitement in the air to know we have a few hours to spend with one another.

When we find a secluded spot, Isaiah spreads a blanket out on the dirt and I pull out the food. I can't believe I'm even hungry after all I've eaten today, but I think maybe I'm making up for lost time. I dig into the food with relish and Isaiah does too. We don't say anything—just watch the water, feel the breeze and eat until we've finished every bite. When we've licked the honey off our fingers, we run to the water to rinse them.

"Want to get in and swim?" Isaiah asks.

"Sure, let's do it!" I jump in, dress and all, and decide the next thing on my To-Do List is buying myself some jeans, maybe even shorts, with my money from the diner. What Nellie doesn't know won't hurt her. She's already in the dark on a lot of things—jeans aren't gonna make that much of a difference.

❀ 9 ❀

THE ALMOST PERFECT DAY

I JUST WANT to pause this day. If it could never end, I would be so blissfully happy. I've put out of my mind all the grief of yesterday. My tears are done. I will cry no more for my parents...not today, anyway.

There's a quiet breeze by the water. I can't remember a more pleasant summer day. The sun is shining down on us and feels so good as we swim. The heat is surprisingly mild, in the low 90s.

I wish I had packed a swimsuit, but I forgot it on my way out the door. I probably wouldn't have had the nerve to wear it in front of Isaiah anyway. I tie the dress together in the middle and it works fine.

I did buy myself a bra after that embarrassing day with Nellie and have never been more glad to have it than now. I went to Woolworth's and bought one with my saved money, however, I think I already need a new one. I may have already grown a few inches taller, too. I wasn't kidding when I told Ruby I was a growing girl.

Isaiah and I swim for about an hour. We dunk each other for a while, laugh, float on our backs, and talk like we haven't seen each other in ages. I can tell him anything.

"Caroline?"

We're lying on the shore now, drying off. I'm staring up at the clouds, trying to memorize how I feel right now. I want to bottle up this day in my memory and bring it out whenever I need to remember something happy. Something good.

"Can I ask you something?" he whispers.

"Yes."

"Do you think we'll get married one day?"

"Are you asking me to?" I turn to face him and grin. "That's not much of a proposal." He looks so serious, I stop teasing and answer him truthfully, "I don't know. I wish we could...do you think we will?"

"I know I will always want to. It just isn't done, you know, not around here anyway. Maybe we could move somewhere else?"

"Where do you think we could go?"

"Mmm, I don't know, maybe California?"

"Do you ever wish you were white?"

"No. Do *you* ever wish I was white?" He leans up on his elbow and looks over at me.

"No, never, but I've wished I was black many times."

"You have? Why?"

"Well, for lots of reasons...I wish I could sing like a black person..."

"Well, not all black people can sing, you know..."

"You don't think?"

"I don't think, I *know*!" Isaiah laughs. "You should hear my Uncle Clyde. He can't carry a tune to save his life!"

"Hmm, well, every black person I've ever heard sings really good."

85

"What else?"

"Well, my curls and big lips would fit in better."

"You do have the best lips," he grins, "and your hair is perfect. If you had hair like mine, the curls wouldn't be quite so... soft. And it would take a lot longer for you to do your hair."

"Yours always looks nice. And soft, too."

"You think so?

I nod.

"What else?" he asks.

"I like brown skin."

"That's a good reason. What else?"

"We could be together. And everyone could know…" This is the main reason I wish I was black.

He stares at me for a moment, studying my eyes and then my lips. My heart skips as I look back at his. I put my hand on his cheek and want to cry with how much I love him. He takes my hand and kisses it. Then he leans back on the blanket, still holding my hand. "Caroline?"

"What?"

"There's not one single thing about you that I would change."

"Really?"

"Really."

This makes me smile.

"I do wish I could tell the world that you're my girl, though."

"Me too."

It's hard to leave our enchanted spot, but we reluctantly go. Isaiah needs to be home for supper. He wants more than anything to take me to his house, so I don't have to be home alone, but I'm blissful enough from his attention today. I have a bounce in my step as I walk toward town.

After Isaiah and I part ways, I decide to stop in Harriet's and give the biscuit pan back to Ruby. I go in through the back, and she's whistling as she cooks.

"Hey, girl! I didn't expect to see you back in here tonight!"

"I know. I was around, so I thought I'd bring your pan back. Thank you, we really enjoyed the biscuits." I don't want her to know who helped me eat them, but I also don't want her to think I ate them all myself.

"Oh, you're welcome. You had your supper yet?"

"No, ma'am. What are you making there?"

"Well, I's tryin' a new recipe. It's slow out there tonight. Everyone out enjoyin' this weather. I need to see if we want to add this here to the menu." She points to the big pot on the stove. "I tried a different way of cookin' my dumplins. See there...they's lookin' good, ain't they?"

"They sure do." My mouth waters, just looking at them.

"And then I shred the chicken. Cook all afternoon, so it be as tender as a mother's love."

I think Ruby would be a perfect mother.

"I'd be glad to sample it for you." I grin so wide at her, my cheeks hurt.

"Here, sit yo'self down and I make you up a plate. You want some carrots along with it?"

"Yes, ma'am, that sounds delicious!"

"You is my new favorite person to cook for." Ruby beams. "Is they anything you don't like to eat?"

When Ruby says favorite, it sounds like favor-*ite*, the emphasis on the 'i'. Grandpaw says it the same way.

"Liver and onions." I wrinkle my nose.

"Well, naw, that don't even count. I don't know any child under the age of...fifty...who can wrap they stomach 'round that!"

I laugh and she joins in. When she laughs, her eyes disappear, her shoulders bounce up and down, and often, she wipes tears from her eyes. I find myself always trying to make her laugh.

I sit down and eat the chicken and dumplings and they are delicious. Even the carrots are tastier than any I've eaten. I groan and moan and eat everything she puts in front of me.

"This definitely has to go on the menu!"

Ruby looks very pleased. "Well, let's see if Miss Sue think so."

We walk out the swinging door into the diner and Miss Sue is talking to some customers. There are only a few filled tables tonight. As soon as there's a lull, Ruby motions for Miss Sue to come sample her dumplings. Miss Sue's eyes just about roll back to all whites when she tastes them.

ON MY WAY home, I see three little black girls with braids bouncing as they jump rope. I admire their skill for a while and the songs they jump to, one after the other. I can't help but think about my conversation with Isaiah. If I could be part of his world, his everyday world, I think I would be the happiest girl alive. I'm tired of hiding it.

Distracted, I walk past Thomas without even knowing it. "Caroline!" he calls.

I stop and turn around and Thomas is standing across the street in front of the school field waving. He's still dressed in his baseball uniform. The guys from the team play throughout the summer, usually after supper when the day has cooled.

I wave back and he crosses the street to meet me.

"Hey, how are you doing?" he asks, studying my face.

I'm embarrassed that I left our last conversation crying. I haven't seen him since then and he looks so worried.

"I came to your house yesterday, looking for you. I was worried about you after the other day. Is everything all right?"

"Sorry to worry you. I got a job!" I smile brightly, trying to change the subject.

"Really? Where? Why do *you* need a job?" He wrinkles his nose. "It's summer break. You need to be hanging out with me—Clara Mae, too—before we leave. You know we're leaving for our trip soon. If you're working all the time, the summer will be gone."

"Well, I can hang out sometime in the afternoon. And evenings, too…"

"Good, how about coming over right now?" With this, he takes my hand and starts walking toward his house.

I stumble a bit to catch up with him and he doesn't let go. While we walk, I'm a bit confused about why he's still holding my hand but too nervous to let go. I'm still a little shy around him. He must still be feeling sorry for me, not knowing why I was so upset a few days ago.

"Well, I guess I could come over for a while." I laugh. I don't think I have much choice in the matter.

We walk past the oak trees, past the white Victorian on the corner, and past Mrs. Stanley's rosebushes. My heart stops cold as I see Leroy and Les ride by us on their bikes. I begin to walk faster, hoping they won't see me.

Leroy turns his bike around and drives past us another time, looking me in the eyes…letting me know he *has* seen me. I can't explain it, but I feel a sick, cold dread in the pit of my stomach and want to be sick. His eyes pierce into mine and I glance away quickly, unable to look at him any more.

Thomas doesn't seem to notice Leroy. He's still holding my hand. In fact, he laces his fingers in mine, and I think my heart is going to beat right out of my chest. What's going on here?

Leroy rides off with Les, and I breathe a little easier. But I'm still sweating over the encounter. I look up at Thomas and he's gazing at me with a look I don't recognize. Not from him, anyway.

We get to the edge of his driveway and he stops. He turns me to face him, lightly holding onto my arm.

"Caroline, can we talk for a minute before we go inside?"

"Sure, Thomas. What's up?" I look at him, and for a moment I'm afraid that he knows everything. He looks nervous.

"Well, it's just—we've known each other for a long time. Forever, really. And I know that you're a lot younger than me and everything—even though you seem so much older than Clara Mae…" He looks at me as if expecting me to say something, but I really have no clue where he's going with this.

He stutters along. "I know since you're close to Clara

Mae it could seem weird, but I think she'd be totally fine with it. You're her favorite person in the world. I just—well, I just really, really like you and...I want to know if you like me. I think you do, but we've never talked about it...and I want to know if you would like to...go steady..." He stops then and takes a deep breath.

I'm stunned. I don't know the first thing to say. I take a step back, open my mouth to speak and nothing comes out. What I wouldn't give for a mother right about now. Somehow I think she would know the right thing to say in a time like this.

I try again, opening my mouth to form a word, but shut it again.

Thomas moves his hand down my arm, holding my hand again and says, "Caroline? Did you hear what I said?"

I nod my head.

He smiles, the light reaching his eyes. It's plain to see why every girl in town is smitten with him. Even Miss Greener flirts with Thomas Owens when she sees him.

"Do you have anything you'd like to say?"

I take a deep breath and say, "Wow, Thomas, you've shocked me with this one."

Brilliant, I know, but it's all I can come up with.

"Really? I thought you always knew how I felt about you."

"No!" I laugh, feeling a bit hysterical. "Not really! I can't say I *ever* really thought this!"

His smile fades just a little, and he shakes my hands with his. "You do like me, though, don't you?"

"I like you so much, Thomas. I've just never thought of you...like *that*," I admit.

He lets go of my hands then and when I look in his eyes, I'm horrified to see the shadow that has crossed over his features.

I grab his hands back, wanting to make him happy again. "Thomas, please don't be upset with me! Please. I never meant to hurt you. I just never knew. I never knew you...I guess I'm just...you know, younger than you think..." I stop because I realize that I'm not too young to know how I feel about him, and I would never want to say something that I didn't feel.

"I love both you and Clara Mae. You are so important to me. Please! Let's stay how we are," I plead with him, now shaking his hands in mine.

He gives me an awkward smile and says, "I'll always be your friend, Caroline. And," he leans down and whispers in my ear, "I'll wait for you to feel the same. Maybe in a couple years you'll be ready for me." With that, he gives me a full smile and kisses my cheek.

We go in the house, and Mrs. Owens is in the kitchen. I think she lives in there.

"Caroline! So good to see you, honey! How's your summer goin'?"

"Pretty well. I've been staying busy. I'm working at Harriet's now."

"Oh my! Well, that's great! Just don't work so hard that you can't still come see us."

"No way. I can always make time to come over here."

To me, Mrs. Owens is the personification of a beautiful lady. Her hair is blonde, her eyes are a deep green and when she laughs, her whole face lights up. She loves her children and this may be what I find the most beautiful. Her feelings for them are evident in the way she looks at them and talks to them. She makes me feel special too, each time I'm here.

"Why don't you plan on coming over as often as you can before we leave for our trip?" She suggests as she spoons large spoonfuls of cookie dough on a tray.

"That sounds really nice."

"Clara Mae!" Mrs. Owens calls. "Caroline is here!"

Clara Mae comes bounding out of her room and hurries over to hug my neck. She immediately launches into what she'd like to do now that I'm here. I look over at Thomas and he's watching us from his stool at the counter. He looks dejected, and I feel bad that I made him sad.

I stay in Clara Mae's room most of the night. We listen to our favorite records and dance around singing in her hairspray bottles. We collapse on her bed in giggles when she does a particularly clumsy dance move.

"Why don't you just spend the night, Caroline? I know it would be fine with my mom."

"Oh, I wish I could, but I should get going to let Josh out." I really do wish I could stay. "It's been so much fun."

"Aw, let your parents do it for once. Come on, stay!"

"I can't. You know, I actually better get going now. It's getting dark out."

"Shoot. I shouldn't have said anything." She pouts.

"I'll come back soon, I promise. How about day after tomorrow?" I ask.

"Okay." She gives in. "Come on, I'll ask Thomas to walk you home."

"No! I mean—it's no trouble! I can get home by myself."

"He won't mind." And before I can say another word, she's yelling, "Thomas! *Thooooomas*!"

He comes out of his room, freshly showered and in his sweatpants and jersey.

"Can you walk Caroline home? She needs to get home to let Josh out."

"It's really not a big deal, Thomas. I can walk home myself," I insist.

"Don't be silly. Of course, I'm walking you home."

I tell Mr. and Mrs. Owens good night and we start the walk home.

It isn't a far walk, but it feels like forever because neither of us says a word the entire walk home. When we finally reach my door, I turn to tell Thomas thank you for walking me home and the next thing I know, he's kissing me. What in the world?

This is a kiss altogether different from Isaiah's kiss. I can tell Thomas has done this before. I really don't know what to do. Why I don't just push him away, I don't know, but I have it ingrained in me not to hurt anyone's feelings. Guilt washes over me, but I just let him go on and kiss me. When he tries to get a bit more serious about it, I push him back.

"Sorry, Caroline," he says. He turns and runs down the road.

10

COMPLICATIONS

WELL, THIS SURE puts a kink in things. All night, I lie awake thinking about Thomas professing his feelings, the kiss, and Isaiah. Then I go back to the kiss...

Clara Mae and I have talked about kissing quite a bit. We're big fans of romantic movies and have studied kissing extensively. When we found out that tongues are actually involved—again from Jody, the fount of all worldly knowledge—we didn't watch our favorite movies for a while. Then, when we did, we tried to determine if we could see it happening there on the screen. It almost ruined the whole thing for us.

So when Thomas tried it on me, I was curious about it, but appalled. I can't believe he likes me and that he kissed me. I mean, *really* kissed me!

I would hate for Isaiah to ever find out. He would be so upset. I would die if I knew he had kissed someone else. And even though I know my feelings haven't changed for Isaiah, I can't help but feel that I caused this to happen with Thomas. I must have done something to make him think I liked him. And I must have made him think he could kiss me. And then for me to not stop him right away!

I toss and turn all night. I don't think I can live with this guilt.

———————————— ❀ ————————————

WHEN I REACH Harriet's, I'm weary before I've even begun to work. I know my eyes have dark circles under them and try as I may, I can't keep my shoulders from slumping as I walk into the kitchen.

"Mercy, girl, what is wrong with *you*?" Ruby, I have learned, is not one to mince words.

"Oh, just a few things," I say.

"Lay it on me," she says. "Or do you just need some of Ruby's good ole breakfast?"

"Let's start with the breakfast." I sigh. I have fifteen minutes until the rush. Ruby has a plate of scrambled eggs, toast and bacon made up for me in no time. I eat and gradually feel a tiny bit better.

"Do you ever wish you could just go back to being a child? I mean a really little child—where everything is just easy?" I chew my eggs and look at Ruby, who has stopped cooking to look at me with a strange expression.

"Honey, you *is* a child. What you got to be all worried about? Now, when *I* was yo age, I worked hard, but that was just what we do. Now, times is a'changin'. You come in here and you work, and I can tell this is not a new thing for you neither. You work just as hard as I ever did. What I don't know, is why is you carryin' so much weight on those shoulders? Yo mama and daddy work hard. Why you here at Harriet's, honey? And lookin' so tired all the time."

"It's a long story, Ruby."

"Well, if you ever is up to telling me, I will be right happy to listen."

Just then, Miss Sue comes in with several orders and we get to work.

IN THE AFTERNOON, Harriet's is full. A bus of elderly folks comes through town and we serve right through the afternoon. Miss Sue asks me to help Betty Jo carry all the food out in between washing dishes and cleaning tables. I'm cleaning a table when I see Thomas walk in and sit at the counter. I blush when I see him, and it seems to amuse him.

"Hi, Caroline." He grins.

"Hi, Thomas."

I busy myself wiping the table across from him until it sparkles.

"You look pretty today."

"Thank you."

I go clean the table furthest from him and when I come back by the counter, he's still watching me.

"I came by to invite you to our house tomorrow night. It's my birthday and I'd like it if you came." Thomas looks a little unsure as he says this.

"Okay," I say softly. Then I lean over and whisper in his ear, "But no more kissing, Thomas. Okay?"

And before he can answer, I go in the back to tackle the dishes.

When I'm done washing, I go back out and Thomas is gone. A few customers ask for coffee, and I don't have time to think about him as it gets busier.

I enjoy talking to all the different people that come through. In my short time at Harriet's, I've already met a lot of folks that I've only seen around town but never talked to until now. Already they're calling me by name and asking how my day is going as I walk by their table.

I work late, until six. This time, Miss Sue doesn't apologize. She seems to realize I enjoy the work and that she won't hear complaints from my parents. She's appreciative of how hard I work, and I'm glad I have something to keep me busy. When I open the door to leave, the hot air rushes to my face and I realize I've missed a whole day of being outside. But I don't mind...it feels nice to be appreciated.

I take a chance and walk past Isaiah's house. He's outside, playing basketball with a couple other boys. I stand watching them play until Isaiah notices me. He hands the ball off to someone else and runs up to me.

"Hey! How's it goin'?" His grin stretches across his entire face.

"It's good. I'm just on my way home from Harriet's. I worked late today. It was busy all day long."

"Wait one sec. Let me tell my mom where I'm going and I'll walk you home."

"Okay! How 'bout I wait over there?" I point across the street. "I can sit on the other side of that fence until you come."

He nods. "I'll be right over." He runs in the house while I walk across the street and around the corner. I sit down and lean my back against the fence. It has been a while since I sat down. My feet ache.

A few minutes pass and I hear Isaiah tell the guys he has to go. Their protests carry down the road. For a moment, I debate telling him what has been happening with Thomas, but the next thing I know he's in front of me and I just want to enjoy his company.

"Ready?" He pulls my hands until I'm standing. I look up into his face that I know so well and know for me there will never be another. I forget everyone and everything when I'm with Isaiah.

Once we're in the clearing past his house, he takes my hand again and we walk the last stretch hand in hand. My heart pounds as he laces his fingers through mine. Everything else fades as we walk. I want to stretch out our time for as long as possible. Talking about our day, I tell him how much fun I'm having at Harriet's and how much I like Ruby. He tells me what he's liking and disliking about going out with his uncles every day.

We don't hear Leroy until he's in front of us. We stop because he has pulled his bike around so we can't go any further. I let go of Isaiah's hand and wait for everything to fall apart.

"So, it's just like I thought," Leroy says. "You's playin' it both ways, ain't ya."

I know then that I should have told Isaiah about Thomas before Leroy ruins everything.

Leroy looks angry and I'm terrified. I have no idea what he'll do next. He gets off his bike and circles us. He's the same height as Isaiah and gets in his face. "You think you're something—carryin' on with this high and mighty trash. Let me tell you somethin', it ain't gon' work."

He leans over into my face then. "Why you wanna

waste time on these boys? I show you the real thing." He grabs my chin hard when he says this.

"Leave her alone, man," Isaiah puts his hand on Leroy's arm. "Leave her alone."

"Shut up, I ain't talkin' to you." He yanks my hair back until I'm looking at him. He's pulling my hair so hard, I'm disgusted with myself that the tears are rolling down my cheeks, giving away my fear.

Isaiah hits Leroy in the gut, hard enough to make Leroy drop his grip on my hair. I quickly move back. Isaiah then barrels into Leroy, knocking him on the ground while they pummel each other. Isaiah gets a few hits in, but Leroy is an experienced fighter and he gains ground fast. Blood is flying, splattering on the dirt and grass and my shoe. I feel helpless, watching Isaiah getting hurt. When Leroy gets the upper hand, I see a stick on the side of the road and grab it. I hit Leroy over the back with a hard thwack. He yelps and rolls off of Isaiah. Isaiah jumps up, grabbing my hand, and we run to my house.

"This ain't over. I'm not finished with you!" Leroy yells.

We get in the door and look out the window. Leroy slowly gets on his bike and rides away.

"He's not going to let this go, you know," I tell Isaiah.

"I know."

He winces and then I take in how hurt he really is. His face looks awful. He has a black eye and there's blood around his mouth and nose.

"Let's get you cleaned up."

We go into the kitchen and he washes his hands. I get the first aid kit and gingerly wipe his face.

"You need to go stay with your grandparents, Caroline."

I stop wiping his cheek and think about this. If I go stay with them, I won't be able to see Isaiah. Our long phone conversations will be over. The thought of that sounds worse than anything imaginable.

"I'll try to come home from Harriet's earlier. We just don't need to be seen together for a while."

"I don't like you out here all alone, Caroline. It's not a good idea. We've made him mad and now that he knows we're together, he's just gonna get worse. The best thing would be for you to go to Nellie's and stay there until your parents come home. He knows where you *live*, Caroline." He grips the counter as I wipe around the cuts on his eyebrow.

"My mom made me *swear* that I wouldn't let anyone know she's gone. I can't leave, Isaiah. She would kill me, *especially* if I went to my grandparents!"

"She's not here! And you're not safe! He's not gonna leave you alone. I know you want to think the best about everybody, but he's trouble." His voice gets more panick-ed with every word.

"I know he's trouble; it's obvious that he's trouble! But I can't go to my grandparents. My mom could come back anytime and when she does, I need to have every-thing how she left it."

"Caroline—" He shakes his head. "I admire you for so many things. But, you keep making excuses for your parents. It's painful to see them hurt you over and over. Please, for me, do this. Let someone help you. Go to your Nellie's house. We can think of something to tell your mother when that time comes."

101

His pitying tone is the last straw. This is the first time I've ever been angry with him, and I don't like it. "I'll worry about that when the time comes. I can take care of myself, I've been doing *just fine* my whole life."

His eyes flash and he looks hurt. "I know you have." He stands up and looks me square in the face. "If you won't let me help you, maybe you'll let Thomas."

"What are you talking about, how did-?" I stop before I say too much. I don't want to tell him about Thomas when we're upset with each other.

"It's a small town, Caroline. Word gets around fast when the most popular kid in Tulma likes the prettiest girl in town. I think you're probably the last to know how Thomas Owens feels about you."

"He's just a friend, Isaiah. I don't like him like that. I told him that. I like *you*." All my anger is gone in a rush. Now I'm just mortified that he knows about Thomas.

"I bet you didn't tell him *that*." His face is red and now he looks mad. Then he shakes his head. "I'm sorry, Caroline. I know you like me. I like you too. I *love* you. And that's why…" He pauses and looks away. "I think we have to stop this now. It's only going to get us in trouble. You're meant to be with someone like Thomas anyway."

"What are you saying? I told you—I don't want to be with Thomas!"

"That may be true now, but you're wasting your time with me. It's never going to work for us, Caroline. We both know that deep down. We're just kids, anyway…if we can't even hang out in public now, what makes us think it will work later?"

He takes my hand and kisses it. "Think about what I said about going to your grandparents. You need to do that. Please be safe." He walks to the door and turns around. "I won't be calling you anymore."

I follow him and reach out for his arm. "Isaiah, please don't go! We need to talk about this. Now you're leaving too." I begin to cry, and he reaches over and holds me.

"Don't cry. I never want to make you cry. I am...I'm trying to stop a bad situation from getting worse. Leroy—this town—it's never going to happen. You know it too. It's best that we try to stop feeling this way now instead of dragging out the inevitable."

"I'm never going to stop feeling this way. I thought you were never going to stop either."

"I haven't. We're just too...different."

"We are very much the same," I say firmly.

"I have to go."

"You said you wanted to marry me someday, Isaiah," the words rush out. "What about all the things you said to me? Just a few days ago, all the promises you made..."

"I meant it...all of it. And I wish I could be the one to take care of you. More than anything. But you deserve way more than I'll ever be able to give you. Someone, maybe not Thomas, but someone like him, is going to give you the life you deserve."

"Quit bringing Thomas into this. I don't like Thomas. This has nothing to do with him."

"You know what I'm trying to say. You know I don't want this any more than you do. But what happened today just proves that we can't do this. We're asking for trouble if we try to be together. I can't risk putting you in danger, not to mention all the humiliation that comes from being with a nigger."

My face crumples when he says that. "Isaiah, don't

say—"

He holds his hand up to stop me. "It's the truth, Caroline. It's time we both face it." He puts his hands around his head and closes his eyes for a second. "Do everything you can to avoid Leroy."

With this, he turns around and walks out the door and out of my world.

11

ISAIAH

THE RESOLVE I have with Caroline crumbles the moment I close her door. I want to hit everything in sight. The road blurs in front of me. I'm so sick of doing the right thing. I'll never understand the way this world works. Why can't I love whoever I want to love and it not affect anyone but us? It doesn't matter. I'll never know the answers.

She's better off without me. She doesn't deserve any of this. I've just been a distraction from the one she'll end up with—Thomas Owens. He's the kind of guy everyone expects Caroline to be with, and she'll thank me one day... when they're happily married. Maybe now that I'm out of the way, she'll be able to see Thomas in a different light.

I can't imagine not talking to her anymore.

The hurt on her face is going to haunt me forever. I never imagined I'd be the one to hurt her like that. I was so stupid to believe all the promises I made to her at the river the other day. It was one of the happiest days I can remember. I wanted to hope that things could be different for us.

Every step toward home is painful. Leroy managed to

hurt me in places I didn't know could hurt. I'd give anything if I could have hurt him worse, made it so he could never get to Caroline. He'll be watching me, just waiting for a chance to make me pay for today. The thought is already squeezing my chest, but I'm more afraid for Caroline than myself. I have to find a way to keep her safe.

My nose and eyes are running. I wipe my nose on my sleeve and blood covers the shirt. Mama will be furious with me for fighting Leroy. Everyone knows Leroy doesn't fight fair. This won't end well.

I push the front door open as quietly as possible and look in the living room mirror. It's bad. I back up to sneak into the bathroom and Mama calls out, "Isaiah, I'm in the kitchen. Supper's ready, you're just in time. Come on, wash your hands."

I decide to get it over with and walk on back to the kitchen. When Mama sees me, she cries out and rushes to me.

"Baby, what happened to you? Who did this?"

"Leroy."

"Why would you be fighting with Leroy? You know to stay out of that boy's way! What happened?"

"I have a few things to tell you."

"Well, let's get you cleaned up and you can tell me everything over supper. Do you feel up to eating?"

"I can always eat." I attempt a smile, but my face crumples up instead. My whole body aches.

"Oh, baby. Come on, let's get you fixed up."

Mama lovingly tends to my wounds and when she feels they're properly taken care of, we go to the kitchen and she fills a plate for me. I sit down carefully, trying not to groan out loud. I've finally manned up and stopped crying, but there's still a huge lump in my throat.

"Okay, start at the beginning, son. Are you ready to talk?"

I feel a little sick to my stomach when I think about all I have to tell her.

"You know Caroline is my friend."

"Yes."

"Well, she's my best friend. She's my girlfriend... *was* my girlfriend..."

Her face falls. "Oh, Isaiah..."

"I know it wasn't a good idea. But for years, Mama... for years, we've liked each other. We've talked on the phone every day. I walk with her every day. I love her, Mama."

Mama just looks at me with tears in her eyes. She hasn't said a word, but waits for me to finish.

I go on, "From the time I first saw her, I loved her. I know I'm young—" My voice gets wobbly and I swallow before continuing. "I know I'm young, but I know how I feel about her. I won't ever feel that way about anyone else. Ever."

"I know it feels that way now, Isaiah—" she starts.

"No, Mama. It's not going to change. Believe me."

"How did you manage all this without me knowing about it? I've seen the two of you walking, but I didn't see the harm in that. I haven't even seen you on the phone that much." She shakes her head. "A few years is a long time. Do her parents know about this?"

"No. They aren't around very much. I talk to her on the phone when I'm supposed to be doing my homework. Her parents aren't home then. Or I talk to her after you go to bed." I look at her guiltily, and she pats my hand.

"I wish I'd known how you felt sooner, Isaiah. But you know I would've tried to put a stop to it."

"Yes, ma'am."

"It's just not acceptable here. But really, it's not just here. Anyone who chooses that life has a long, hard road ahead of them. You know that. I realize it's not fair. It should be a fine thing for you to be with a nice girl like Caroline. Except for the fact that she's white and you're not...you know we don't mix like that around here, son. Do you remember what happened with Uncle Billy?"

"Well, I know he had to leave, but I don't remember why."

She takes a while to answer. Her voice stays calm, but she clutches a dishrag until her knuckles turn white.

"He got caught up with Mr. Davidson's daughter. Remember? He nearly got shot when they chased him out of town. They put a burning cross on our lawn twice, knocked out the windows with rocks...it isn't over around here, Isaiah. You know full well that those kinds of things still happen. But this is our home, like it or not, and we have to keep the peace. Our family is here. This is the only home we know."

"I know it. And that's why I ended it with Caroline today."

She can't hide her relief when I say this. "Oh, thank the good Lord. Son, can you just imagine what the white folks in town would do if they found out you like Caroline Carson, the very cream of the crop? They would not take that lying down, you can be sure of that." She pats my hand and gives me a concerned look. "So where does Leroy fit in?"

"Leroy has been noticing Caroline for a while and keeps showing up wherever she is. He keeps going out of his way to harass her. He has seen us together before and...well, he saw us today...holding hands..."

Mama groans. "Isaiah! Oh my, son. This is my fault. I'm to blame for not putting a stop for this. I'm so sorry. I should have never let you be friends with her. I thought it was harmless. I should have known...I know you think the world of her, but it would destroy you both, Isaiah." She leans over and grips my face. "Listen...I know it's going to be hard, but you're gonna have to stay away from her, you hear me? If you don't want to get run out of town, you're gonna have to just leave her alone. For her sake too."

"I know, Mama." I lay my head on the table. "I told her today that it was over."

"Well, you did the right thing, love. I'm sorry—I'm so sorry. I know it feels awful now...and it will for a long while. But it will get better, you'll see. You're young and you will find someone one day."

I shake my head but don't bother arguing with her.

"I know you don't want to hear any of this right now, but you have all the time in the world. It's not even time to be looking for all that yet!"

She wraps her arms around me and hugs me close.

"She doesn't have anybody!" I wail. "I'm the only one who really cares about her."

"Now, now...that's just not true. I'm sure she has a lot of people looking out for her."

I shake my head again, frustrated, but I don't say any more. I want so badly to tell my mother everything. If she knew Caroline was on her own, she would make sure she was taken care of, but I know Caroline will never forgive me if I tell her secret.

We talk a while longer, but it doesn't make either of us feel any better.

"I wish deep down in my bones that I could make everything all right, son. I wish the world were fair…that you could have all the privileges of anyone else, but it's just not our reality. I hope one day…" She wipes her eyes with her napkin. "All I can do is my best to keep you safe, love you, and encourage you to better yourself so you can get out of here one day. As sad as it makes me, I cannot let you get caught up in Caroline Carson's world. It would be the undoing of all of us."

I nod and we sit there quietly for a while. Mama gets up and brings back medicine. When I take that, she runs a bath for me. When I'm done in there, I go straight to my room and shut the door. I'm all talked out.

I lay on the bed and close my eyes. All I can see is Caroline crying by her door.

I can't do this.

But I have to try to stay away.

It's best for everyone.

Now that Mama knows everything, I know she'll be keeping a close eye on me. It's over.

It's torment. I can't get Caroline out of my mind. But now the image of Caroline is marred by Thomas Owens. I pretty much just handed her over to him. She's been the only one in my world who completely sees past my skin. In a town like Tulma, a love like that is miraculous. And I just gave that away.

12

EMPTY

ANY JOY I had, left, when Isaiah walked out the door. I feel like I'm sleepwalking. At night, I roam the rooms in my house. It's a small house, so it doesn't take long. I pace back and forth. I go through every drawer in my parents' room; something I would have previously never dreamed of doing. I touch their clothing, fold it, and put it back in the drawers.

In my snooping, I find letters my mom and dad wrote to each other. I read each one, trying to feel some of the love they professed to feel. It doesn't feel real—I can't imagine my parents saying these things to each other. I wonder if they meant any of it. If only I could read without the experience of my lifetime with them.

I'm so angry with Isaiah, I can't think straight. This whole time—our whole friendship—I've never once doubted his love for me. It's painful to know he can end things this way. I guess he never felt the way I thought he did. But when I think about all the hours we talked about everything that was important to us, I have to believe he does care.

111

I relive the day by the water. All the things he said—I thought I would cherish them forever, but now they feel like boils on my skin, oozing with the knowledge that he can walk away from me.

I have a brief memory of my daddy. I try to force thoughts of him away; it's just too hard, but the memories push themselves to the surface.

On my sixth birthday, my dad gave me a stuffed dog. We named him Scruffy. He had pitiful eyes that looked sorrowful and sweet all at once. My dad would make him talk to me and give me fits of laughter. Sometimes he would make him misbehave and I would cry and stomp my foot to make my dad stop. I slept with Scruffy every night and carried him around the house until I went to school. Truth be told, I still sleep with him every night.

I fell off my bike one afternoon and my dad was home. He saw me from the window and came running outside. I had a bad scrape on my knee, and he carried me in the house. He walked straight to the bedroom and picked up Scruffy, and they doctored my knee together. I was laughing by the time the bandage was in place.

This is one of the last times I can ever remember life being simple. I would give anything if Daddy and Scruffy could make everything better with a Band-Aid and a few jokes.

It's apparent something is wrong with me—that everyone I love keeps leaving me. I don't know why I never imagined Isaiah doing the same.

I don't sleep that night. I cry and pace and agonize. In the morning, I put on a clean yellow dress. It has tiny lavender flower-shaped buttons. It's a pretty dress—one that Nellie and I made the last time we sewed together. I always enjoy wearing it. Fingering through my curls and trying to smooth down the frizz, I tie a lavender ribbon around my hair. I open my mother's bathroom drawer and rummage through the odds and ends she left. A little mascara on my eyelashes makes my eyes deepen into a darker blue-gray shade. I put on her soft pink lip-gloss and examine the results. I still only see the sad eyes, but I may as well continue playing a part. That's what everyone always expects of me. I will do it for this one day, at least.

I think of my mother as I look in her mirror and I hate the parts of me that look like her. I don't hate her though. I don't love her either. I feel nothing. My daddy, too. Nothing.

I've thought all night about what Isaiah said about me making excuses for my parents and realize that's one thing he was completely right about. I've made every excuse in the book for my daddy, but really he left me just like my mother did. Neither of them is any better than the other.

I walk slowly to Harriet's, not really sure of how I even get there. It's a tunnel vision without the vision. I'm floundering and I don't know how to pull myself out of it. I do get through my day at Harriet's. I don't know what I would do if I didn't have this job, but it has been a long, hard day to see people and try to put on a happy face. I've been told many times to smile. I'm trying to not bring everyone down with my sadness, but I just can't turn on the fake.

Nellie stops by and says I'm looking sadder'n a cow in heat. She forces me to say yes to dinner that night. When I get done at Harriet's, I head home to let Josh out before going to Nellie's house. Maybe I will even take Josh with me. He seems to know I'm needing him right now. He never left my side during the night.

I turn on my street and pick a peach from one of the trees. Mr. Talbot has the best peaches. I never see him, so I feel fine about helping myself to one. He wouldn't mind anyway, he has always told us to pick whatever fruit we want. He has more than enough. I take a bite and the juice runs down my chin. It's so tasty that I pick another one for later.

When I turn toward my house, my heart stops cold. Leroy and Les are in front of my house, waiting. I look around and don't see another person in sight. Immediately, I turn around and start running toward town. The peaches go flying. The rattle of their bikes is just behind me. I stumble and scrape my knee on the gravel. The pause is enough for them to almost catch up to me. I jump up and run as hard as I can.

Leroy reaches me first and shoves me into the trees. I try to get loose, but he has a firm grip on me.

"I've been wanting to do this for a long time." He laughs.

IT'S STRANGE THE things you remember. When I think back on this day, I'll think of how the air smells, all heavy and humid. The peach trees swaying in the breeze, their scent combining with sweat and dirt. The white shoes on my feet, muddied in the dirt. My yellow dress...the blue, blue sky... a bird I keep trying to hear over my cries.

I didn't know anyone could be so cruel. I fight with everything I have, but Leroy is stronger than me. He punches me in the stomach, taking my breath. He pulls chunks of my hair out as I hit and kick and bite. I try so hard to get away and it only makes him fight harder. It feels like I'm in a dream where I want to run quickly and I'm in slow motion, not actually moving at all. Nothing I do works.

He knocks me down on the grass and I still try to crawl away. He has a knife. He cuts my leg and when I stop crawling, he puts the knife on my throat. It's the knife he had at the flower shop that day. I recognize it and I go still. He wants to kill me. The hate in his eyes; I just know.

"You don't need to fight me, you know you want me," he says.

The tears spill over and I can't see anything for a minute. I blink and kick him again. When I do, the knife digs into my skin. I yell and he leans on me, his face in mine.

"Look, you filthy bitch, you can stop yellin'. Ain't no one out here. Les is keepin' watch. You may as well just save your breath." He laughs again and puts the knife on my cheek. "Come on, don't make me mess up that pretty face."

He rips off my yellow dress with his other hand, the buttons popping with little pings on my arm. He grips me so hard, my breath comes out in squeaks. He pulls down his pants. I squeeze my eyes shut and beg God to please not let this happen.

The knife gets loose and since my arms are pinned, I bite until I make him bleed. He yelps and this just makes him mad. He beats me until every inch of me is bruised. I'm numb and almost out of fight. Somehow I get out from under him and try to get up and run, but I only make it a few feet. When he tries to knock me down, I kick him in the groin and he doubles over, groaning.

I turn around and try to make my way through the peach trees. If I can just make it to the Talbot house, I can find someone to help me. I'm almost to the pond. The house is just on the other side of the pond. He's running behind me, his breath coming out in shallow bursts. I think they're both chasing me. My legs feel like lead, but I keep pushing myself. I won't stop running. I won't stop running. I won't...

I round a tree and see the water. Please let someone be at the house. Please, please, please. Out of breath. They're getting closer. I feel the heat from his body. Too close. And then Les takes hold of me and I'm on the ground. He kicks me until I'm wheezing for air.

Leroy takes over then and he's on top of me, crushing my ribs, ripping my underwear as he pulls it down, hurting me...

I give up. My eyes are swollen; one is all the way shut and the other is a tiny slit, but I stare at the sky, not really seeing it. I listen for that bird. Maybe if I really concentrate, I can hear it.

Leroy keeps screaming at me to shut up, but I think he must be talking to someone else. It cannot be me making that noise.

"I'm gonna teach you a lesson," he says over and over. "And then I'm gonna slit your throat and watch you bleed."

The bird sings a pretty melody, almost making it sound like a magical day in the forest. Like Snow White might come out at any moment. I struggle to hear that song. My eyes close all the way now.

When Leroy is done, he climbs off of me and gives me one final kick in the stomach. Les comes back for his turn, but I'm barely coherent. I taste blood and try not to swallow it. I swim in and out of consciousness until the weight of Les is gone. Metallic meets my neck. I wish God would just take me now. I don't know how much time passes before I hear them laughing as they leave me in the dirt.

And then blessed darkness.

✿ 13 ✿

FIELD OF WHITE

I'M IN A field of white daisies. Everywhere I look there is white. The sky is white, the ground is white, the flowers are white…I see the angels Isaiah wrote about in my birthday card. They're lifting me up; holding me. Dressed in white. The only color is their eyes and their long black hair. Their skin is luminous. All light. Beautiful. I'm happy to know they're real.

Floating. In the air. Being held. Warm. I'm in a nice place that I never want to leave.

I hear them talking. I don't really want to listen, but they're trying to tell me something. I squeeze my eyes shut and breathe in all the white. They're persistent. I'll try hard to listen later.

Caroline! Again and again. It sounds like a song on their lips. *Caroline! Caroline!*

I shake my head. No, I'm resting now. I sleep a deep sleep surrounded by white daisies, a white sky and angels made of light with black hair.

"CAROLINE! CAN YOU hear me, honey? Caroline! Help me pick her up, son. Can you lift her? Careful…oh my soul, this child is hurt…"

"I've got her, Mama. I've got her."

"Okay, I'll help you hold her steady. Let's walk real slow. We have to get this baby to the hospital."

"Let's take her home first. Please. Maybe I can find her mother before we take her to the hospital."

"I don't think we have time, son."

"Please, I gave her my word."

"I'm sorry, honey, we can wait."

I WAKE UP gasping for air. I've dreamed this exact dream every night for the last three and a half weeks. Each time I wake up, I remember another detail. The tone of his voice…the fear in the air…they thought I was dying…

I'm getting out of the hospital today. My mother has come back. I'm pretty sure Nellie and Grandpaw hunted her down. For the first two weeks, a variety of people held my hand: Nellie, Grandpaw, Miss Greener, and Ruby, even Miss Sue.

Ruby has come to see about me every day, and she calls every night before I fall asleep, without fail. I don't know how I would have survived without her. The only one who has been here the most, besides Ruby, is Sadie. She was the first face I saw when I woke from the coma. She held my hair back when I threw up in the bucket by the bed. She washed my face with a warm washcloth and held my hand while I cried.

I've seen Isaiah twice since everything happened, not because he hasn't tried to see me. I just haven't been able to see *him*. The day after I woke up, he came in with Sadie. He leaned over my bed and whispered, "I'm so sorry, Caroline, so sorry..."

I couldn't stop crying and the nurse made him leave. I couldn't look at him. It hurt too much. I knew he was the one who found me and I should thank him, but knowing that he knew...it was just too much.

The second time I saw him through the door. Sadie walked in and he was standing by her, but stepped back as she came inside. Sadie brought a note from him that day, but I still haven't read it.

My headaches are getting better. The first week and a half, I didn't want to live, my head pounded so hard. Gradually, the pain has eased and it has been much more bearable. All of my stitches have been removed. I had twelve stitches on my neck and fourteen on my leg. My ribs should be feeling better and better the next few weeks. I have three broken ribs and there really isn't much you can do for that. The concussion...for the first few days, I was woken every hour and checked non-stop to make sure I hadn't slipped into a coma.

The police have questioned me thoroughly since I woke up and I've told them all I can remember. They're searching for Leroy and Les but still haven't been able to find them. Sometimes I dream that Leroy is here in this room, and I wake up in a cold sweat, crying. I think they took off as soon as they left me to die. For the first few days, the police were hanging around to see if I would live or die. Once I regained consciousness, they pounced on me to get my statement.

I'm feeling much better physically, but my head hasn't wrapped around the idea of what really happened to me. I don't know if I can be normal again. Everything I've ever known has shifted. I can't imagine ever being the same. I dread leaving these secure walls and going back out in the real world.

My mother says we have to leave Tulma. The whole town knows what happened to me. Word spread quickly that *the girl from Harriet's...you know, Jenny Carson's girl, Caroline...she was raped by two black boys.* My mother says no one will be able to forget and we have to go somewhere to start over.

I can't think about leaving. I'm not ready to go. This place is all I've ever known. But she insists we go...the sooner, the better. I believe she also had a falling out with Grant and that helped matters along, but maybe she really is trying to do the right thing by me. I'm having a hard time being in the same room with her. I can't imagine starting over someplace we've never been...together.

She came back a little over a week ago. I had been in here for two weeks by then and was starting to believe she was never coming. Nellie and Grandpaw weren't talking about it, but I could tell they were stewing about her. They had no clue she had been gone in the first place. I think they were pretty aggravated with me for not letting them know. For my part, I've been too lethargic with all the medicine they're giving me to be too concerned about any of it.

But when I actually saw her—she came in crying and hasn't stopped. I think she might really be sorry for leaving me. I don't know...but she has been very sweet and attentive. Well, she's being as attentive as she can be. She seems rather excited about leaving. Maybe once I can stop being so angry with her, this will be the right thing for us.

My dad still hasn't come. I'm afraid if we leave, I'll never see him again. As hurt as I am that he hasn't shown his face, I can't imagine him not knowing where to find me if he does want to someday.

Thomas and Clara Mae are coming to the house tonight. They stayed in town and Mama says they've been worried sick. Mrs. Owens has called several times to check on me. I can tell by my mother's side of the conversation that they're trying to talk us out of leaving.

Last week, Ruby told me the house Leroy and Les used to stay in has had several "accidents." Bricks were thrown in the windows; someone tried to start a fire, but another neighbor put it out. She whispered about the Klan and I shuddered to think those men were out there trying to fight my cause. I didn't ask them for help. I despise everything the Klan stands for. Even Nellie and Grandpaw don't agree with the things the Klan does, although I think Grandpaw would like to nail Leroy's and Les's hides to the side of a cliff…actually he'd like to do a good many more things than that, but that's what he goes around saying…with tears in his eyes.

I asked Sadie about it when she came. She had heard about the Klan incident and said Les's aunt owns that house and one of her little boys was injured from one of the bricks coming in the window. That has eaten me up ever since. Between thinking about everything that happened to me, I'm horrified thinking about what harm is being done, all in the name of justice. I can't believe what an ugly world this can be.

But Sadie and Ruby…when they're here, I feel loved.

I've been surprised by Sadie's affection. I knew Ruby loved me, but Sadie has treated me with such care. Her eyes take me in, really seeing me for who I am. She listens to everything I say and tells me fun stories to help pass the time. It feels as if I have known her forever. I can't bear to think of not seeing her again.

We talk about everything *but* Isaiah. She has only mentioned him twice. The first time was when she gave me the note. All she said then was, "Isaiah wanted you to have this."

On her third visit, she mentioned him again when telling how they found me and everything that happened that day. I had asked her each time, but she would shake her head. I told her I needed to know—how did they know where to find me?

ISAIAH WAS OUT working on his bike that afternoon. He was pumping air into his tires and polishing the chrome. He heard some commotion in the street and it was Leroy and Les. They were laughing and reaching out to give each other high fives across the handlebars on their bikes.

Isaiah heard Leroy say something (Sadie won't tell me what he said) that let him know they were talking about me and then he saw blood on both of them.

He ran in to tell Sadie what he had seen and she wouldn't let him go without her. They went to my house first and when I wasn't there, they began looking for me, calling my name…

Out past Talbot's pond, they heard moaning and searched until they found me.

The tears didn't stop coming when Sadie recalled seeing me lying there in the dirt. What scared them the most was the cut in my neck and the bump on my head. I lost a lot of blood. They were scared to even move me, but knew they had to get me to the hospital fast.

"But you're a fighter, sweet Caroline," she said. "I've never seen someone so determined to live."

My blood pressure dropped dramatically and when I didn't wake up for a couple of days, it seemed like I might never come back around.

I listen as if I'm hearing a story about a stranger. It feels surreal. It's as if I'm standing on the outside of a cloudy window, trying to peer in, because this surely did not really happen to me.

Here I am, though. The aches and pains in my body and the mess going on in my head are proof that it did indeed happen. I go over the details all day, over and over. *Was there something I could have done differently? What if I had fought harder? Why did I give up? How could they do that? What's wrong with me?*

And then...*Isaiah will never look at me the same again. Everyone is going to think I'm dirty. I deserve this. My friends are going to hate me now. No one will be able to treat me like a normal person.*

Then I cry. And we start the whole cycle over again. I cry myself to sleep...dream...wake up to the reality of this cold room.

Mama's right. We have to leave.

MY MOTHER COMES in with a new outfit. I can count on one hand the times I've had store-bought clothes, so this should feel like a special occasion. It feels a little silly putting on these nice clothes just to get in the car and go home, but I'm happy I don't have to go home alone and that my mom seems to be trying to make a nice gesture. I'm trying to be grateful for that.

"Today's the day, Caroline. You ready to get home?"

"Yes, ma'am."

She helps me step into the pale blue jumpsuit. Yes, pants! She *is* trying to make an effort.

She smooths down my hair as I button the last button. She hasn't mentioned my frizzy curls. Maybe I'll even be able to keep it like this. The pink foam rollers are just not going to happen.

She picks up my bag and we step outside the room. On each side of the hall, the doctors and nurses who have taken care of me are standing, smiling, and wishing me well. Dr. Niles is beaming most of all, and my nurse, Valerie is wiping her eyes, smiling her huge grin.

When I step outside, the heat is stifling, and it hits me how long it has been since I've been outside. I feel a wave of grief and I stagger for a moment, overcome with emotion. Then I remember everyone is watching me and bidding me farewell, so I lift my shoulders, turn around and wave, get in the car, and we go home.

❀ 14 ❀

GETTING OUT

MY MOTHER IS awkward on the drive home. She doesn't know what to say to me now. She didn't really know what to say to me before, so I realize it won't be any easier for us to talk now. I take a deep gasp of air, realizing as my ribs ache that I've been holding my breath. I don't want to be alone with her. I wish I could be with Ruby or Sadie—or pretty much anyone other than my mother.

We drive down our road. The peach trees are waving in the breeze. I try to look at them and not see the scenes of that day playing in my head, but it's hard to concentrate on what is really before me. I'm reliving those moments in this very field.

You're getting what you deserve. You're white trash ...I'm gonna teach you a lesson...

On and on, the record plays in my head. Words I don't even recognize coming out of Leroy's mouth—the meaning becoming clear as he wracks my body with hate. The shadow of Les's ugly face, not looking at me at all, but hating me and himself more with every movement.

I don't realize I'm shaking until we're stopped in our

driveway. My mother is in front of me, fanning me, saying, "Caroline, Caroline…do you hear me? Do you hear me, Caroline?"

"I can't breathe." The tears are rushing down my face.

"You can, you can breathe. Just try to get one good, deep breath."

She begins taking slow, deep breaths and in a few minutes, I do feel calmer. My heart is still beating in frantic beats, but the more breaths I take, the slower my heart races. I have sweat dripping off my head and back. Everything in me wants to turn around and go back to the hospital. Why did I think I could come back here?

"Let's get you in the house. You'll feel better inside."

She pulls me out of the car and I lean on her as we walk into my house. I look around, wishing my Dad would walk out of the kitchen and surprise me, but he doesn't.

Mama leads me to the couch and I lie down. Everything feels so heavy. My arms are weighing me down. My legs are heavily anchored to the couch. If I wanted to lift my head, I could not. I'm overwrought with weariness. My mother talks in the distance, but I can't listen anymore.

A FEW HOURS later, Mama's hand is on my shoulder. She pushes my hair back. "Caroline," she whispers, "Thomas and Clara Mae will be here shortly. Why don't we freshen you up a little bit."

"No, I don't want to see them. I can't get up, I'm too tired."

Mama doesn't know what to do with this. She has a little crease between her eyebrows. She doesn't know whether to push me or not. I turn over and go back to sleep.

An hour later, she wakes me again. "Caroline…" This time she speaks a little more forcefully. "They're going to be here any minute. Let's at least wash you up with this washcloth and spray a little perfume on you. And here, you can brush your teeth right here."

"No. I said I don't want to see them. Tell them I'm sleeping. I can't…"

Her jaw clenches and she wavers for a moment, trying to decide what to do next. I've never told her no. Finally she makes up her mind and leans down by my ear. "They're on their way here and you're going to see them. You need friends like Thomas and Clara Mae. After what's happened to you, no one will want to have anything to do with you. At least they're making an effort, and you're going to do whatever you have to do to maintain some sort of dignity."

She grips my arms and the pain shoots through me as she lifts me up. It takes all my will to not just limply fall back. I have no strength to fight her. I let her fluff my hair, brush my teeth, and pinch my cheeks. She smooths down my collar and plumps the pillow behind me. Once she's satisfied, she stands up. I lean back on the pillow and fall asleep again. I don't know how much time passes, but I wake to the sounds of talking around me.

"She looks so beautiful lying there," Mrs. Owens says.

"Is she feeling okay?" That's Clara Mae.

I open my eyes and stare back at them.

"Oh, Caroline. It's so good to see you. I'm sorry I didn't come to the hospital. Well, I did come to the hospital in the beginning, but you didn't know I was there. And it was just so scary. The police were everywhere and you looked just awful, Caroline...so bad. I couldn't even tell it was you at first. Mama thought it would be better if we waited until you came home so we...wouldn't bother ...you." Clara Mae pauses and looks at her mother for reinforcement.

"Yes, Caroline, we've been keeping up with your progress through your mother. You can imagine how difficult it was for Clara Mae to see you like that."

I nod.

Thomas is standing behind everyone. I glance at him, but he doesn't look at me.

Clara Mae sits on the side of the couch and takes my hand. "Your mama says you're leaving. Is that true?" Her eyes look ready to spill over.

"I think at least for a little while," Mama speaks up. "Until all of this is resolved."

"I've missed you so much," Clara Mae cries. "And I can't believe you're leaving."

Everything goes silent. I can't think of anything I want to say, so we just sit quietly for a while.

Mrs. Owens—won't you please call me Suzanne— leans over and pats my hand. Thomas is over at our bookshelves, fingering the books. Clara Mae begins nervously chatting about their vacation. I nod at the appropriate intervals and she's satisfied. The night will seemingly never end. It's too hard to be normal. When they finally leave, I go to my room, shut the door and cry.

Thomas didn't look at me once.

OVER THE NEXT two days, I sleep a lot. It's the only thing in life I really want to do. When I'm awake, my mom is asking which things I want to take. We're leaving our furniture here because Dad doesn't want to sell the house, and Mama doesn't want to take any of this 'garbage' with her. There really isn't much to take, other than books and clothes. My mom tries to talk me out of the books, but that's all I care to take.

We're leaving day after tomorrow. My mom has gotten a job in San Antonio and you would think it was Washington, DC, for how she is going on about it. She keeps muttering about how Grant was good for something, so I think he must have pulled some strings to get her this job.

Mama hasn't talked to me about her conversation with Daddy, other than to say he's sorry he can't be here. He says he'll come see us when we're settled. When I hear this, it sinks in that we really are leaving. I don't bother hoping Daddy will really come.

Knowing I may never see Isaiah again, I feel a sudden panic. I try to devise ways to sneak out to see him. Maybe if I call him, he would meet me somewhere. But as I'm planning, I know that I'm too scared to do anything outside these four walls. It's a helpless feeling.

I'm still angry with him. It washes over me like a dark thunderous cloud. It stuns me, the depth of anger I feel toward him, and yet, it's a relief. The anger slightly lessens the ache. If I didn't love him so much, I could just hate him and walk away from here and never think about him again. That would definitely be easier.

Mama walks by my room as I'm standing by my bed. I want to be pacing, but it just tires me out. Mama knocks lightly on the open door.

"Everything okay, Caroline?"

"Would you take me somewhere, Mama?"

"Okay. Where is it you'd like to go?"

"I need to go see Sadie and Isaiah."

It comes out before I can stop it. Even angry, I have to say goodbye to him. I can't leave this way.

Mama's face darkens a bit when I say this. She appreciates what they did for me and was polite when she saw Sadie at the hospital, but I know she hoped it would end once I came home.

"Do you really think that's a good idea, Caroline?"

"I need to see them, Mama. I can't leave without telling them goodbye."

"I'm just not sure it's even safe. I mean, they know those boys' families. They're probably friends with them."

"They're *not* friends with Leroy and Les, Mama."

"How do you know?"

"I just know."

"Well, I don't know about going to that side of town."

"It's just the other side of the fields and down the street. It's so close."

"Yes, but we don't belong over there, Caroline. It'll just stir up trouble for two white people to go in that neighborhood, especially you right now. If anyone sees us going in their house—I just don't know what they'd say."

"You think I care what people say?" I yell. "Look at me. Take a good long look at me." I point to the scar on my neck. "There's no hiding this. The whole town knows

131

what happened. Do you know how humiliating that is? You think I care if someone sees me going inside Isaiah's house? I just need to see him. I *have* to see him."

"Why, Caroline? What does that boy have to do with anything—besides finding you?"

It's all too much. I explode.

"He came looking for me! He knew I was in trouble. He saved my life. Isaiah is my best friend, Mama. For years, he has been the person who cares about me the most. I love him. If I didn't live in this crazy place, I would marry Isaiah Washington."

I didn't really mean to say all this, but once it comes out, it feels pretty good. I take a deep breath.

"He was there when no one else was, and I have to tell him goodbye," I finish quietly.

For once, my mother is stunned speechless. She stands there with her mouth open and stares at me for a full minute. I stare back, daring her to object.

"Do you mean to tell me you've been hanging out with these black boys?" The anger drips off her words.

"No, I haven't been hanging out with these 'black boys'," I mimic. "I've been hanging out with Isaiah."

Her face gets red, with a white line around her lips. She looks angrier than I've ever seen her and I've seen her angry plenty. She walks up to me, grabs my arm and drags me in front of the mirror. The motion sends a sharp pain to my ribs.

"What do you see when you look in the mirror?" She spits out. She begins crying; she's so mad.

I stare at her through the mirror. I won't look at myself.

She grabs my chin and tries to force me to look at my

reflection.

"What do you see? Because I'll tell you what I see…I see a beautiful girl who doesn't know the beginning of the mess she's created. I see someone who could have anything she wanted one day, she's that pretty and smart. And she'd rather throw it all away!" She jerks her hand away as if I'm contagious. "How dare you! After the way I've raised you! How dare you. Let me tell you something, you stupid, worthless girl. You can't go traipsing around with the likes of them. You think you're in love? You're a child. You don't know love. You want to know something? You asked for what happened to you. Do you know that? You asked for this."

I turn around so fast, it startles her. The slap rings out like a whip on a racehorse. My cheek stings when she slowly lowers her hand. I place my fingerprints where her hand has just been and walk out my bedroom door.

I'm an open wound with her. I ooze and bleed. Scab over. Heal. She picks it open again.

Scab. Heal. Scar.

I pick up the phone in the kitchen. I hear someone saying, "Hello, hello?" before I can dial anything.

"Hello?"

"Caroline?"

"Who is this?"

"It's Thomas. Please don't hang up. I need to apologize."

"Will you come get me?"

He pauses for a second. "I'll be right there."

WE DON'T SPEAK for the first five minutes. Thomas drives to the river and stops in front of a clearing. He hops out of the car and runs around the other side to open the door for me as I hobble out. No mention is made of my red-rimmed eyes or sniffling, but I know he took note as soon as he saw me.

We walk to the water and I sit down on a log. I pick up a few rocks and throw them in the water.

"You didn't look at me the other night," I start.

"I know. I'm sorry. It's difficult seeing you like this."

"Like what?"

He looks up at me for a moment. "Hard."

"Oh."

"And…I think I've been a little mad at you too. I was angry that you didn't like me back and then all this happened. I know it's crazy, but I thought if you'd been with me, this wouldn't have happened. I'm mad at you."

"Oh. Well, why did you call to apologize?"

"I can't stay mad at you. You were right to be upset with me. I'm sorry I was such a jerk."

"You're not a jerk…well, not a *complete* jerk."

Thomas laughs. "Yes, I have been. Look at me, Caroline." He tips my face up to his. "I'm sorry I didn't look at you the other night. I don't know how to make this better. I feel so bad about what happened to you. I want to kill those guys, I'm so angry. I wish I could make it all go away."

"You can't."

"I know and I hate it. I hate what they did to you."

He picks up a stone and hurls it across the water. He turns around to look at me again.

"I'm glad you asked me to come. Is everything…are

you feeling all right?"

I take a deep breath and look out at the water. "I don't know. Everything is so messed up. I don't know how anything will ever be right again. I had to get out of the house —fight with my mother."

I wince thinking about the horrible things she said… and the fact that she slapped me. I don't know how to get past that.

Thomas notices my wince and waits for me to say more.

"When I picked up the phone to call Nellie, you were already on the line. It helps that you have a car." I thump his arm, trying to lighten the mood.

"Hey! So that's all I'm good for, huh, a car?" He softly thumps me back.

"Pretty much."

"Well, now I know where I stand."

"Yeah, about that. You were just making me nervous …with the whole persistent thing. I needed a friend. I *need* a friend."

"I can do that. Well, as much as I can be since you're moving about a thousand miles away."

"Oh yeah," I sigh, "that might be a problem."

WE SIT THERE in playful conversation for a while, feeling more comfortable around each other than we have in a while. My stomach growls and Thomas smiles over at me.

"How about we go to Harriet's? They would be so happy to see you there."

I bite the inside of my jaw until it stings. "Well, I would love to see Ruby and Miss Sue. Maybe Miss Greener will even be there...this is her day to go to Harriet's."

I'm nervous, but when we arrive, all my favorite customers are there. I'm bombarded with hugs and greetings before we sit down. Ruby comes out of the kitchen when she hears I'm there.

"Well, as I live and breathe. You grow another foot since a few days ago?" she says as I stand up to hug her.

"Hi, Ruby." I can't stop hugging her.

"You look good, sugar. You feelin' any better?" Her eyes search mine.

I nod.

"I been so worried about you...and missin' you. I got attached to seeing you every day."

"I've missed you too." I hug her again. "Are you going to write to me, Ruby?"

"Girl, you gon' be piled up with letters. You know I ain't got no life 'sides Harriet's." She beams at me with those beautiful white teeth and it takes my breath away.

"I can't stand to leave you, Ruby." I hug her again and the tears fall.

"Oh honey, I know, I can't even think about it...let's not start all this ballyhoo 'fore you even eatin'." She lifts my shoulders back and pats my hair. "Now, I got just the thing for you..."

She cooks a feast for us, and we eat every bite. Delicious fried chicken with sweet potato casserole and collard greens. While we're eating, Leroy's brother, Tuck, walks in. The restaurant goes still. I feel all eyes on the two of us while he walks to the counter. He turns around and sets eyes on me. He saunters over, looking more like Leroy now.

He leans over into my ear, but talks loud enough for those close to hear him.

"You need to call the police off my brother and Les. Tell 'em what really happened...you makin' up stories tryin' to get attention. You need to call the dogs off 'em."

Thomas and a few other men jump up and pin Tuck to the wall. He raises his hands and they walk him outside. Before he's outside, he yells, "This ain't fair. You know it's just 'cause she's white. She says whatever she wants and you take her word for it. My brother didn't touch her."

My breathing becomes shallow. If I could just catch one good breath. Panic. I shake and sweat and the room goes black. When I open my eyes, I'm in an ambulance with oxygen on my nose and mouth. They ask me a bunch of questions, and I feel silly for even being here.

I'm wheeled into a room and Dr. Niles finds me. "What are you doing back here? I thought we'd gotten rid of you," he says lightly, peering into my eyes with a flashlight.

"I'm fine. I don't need to be here."

"Really. Well, I hear you passed out."

"I just couldn't breathe well for a minute there..."

"Well, let's find out what that's about."

He asks tons of questions and runs a scan. Everything looks normal. The next time he comes in, he talks to me in a soft, kind voice. His tone suggests he's doing everything he can to keep from upsetting me. He also gives me a new medication and says I need to stay on it for a few months. I tell him I'm leaving Tulma, and he says to find a good doctor in San Antonio. I get the feeling he means a psychiatrist.

When he leaves, my mother comes in the room. She comes timidly to the bed and puts her hand on the sheets.

"How are you feeling?"

"Fine."

"Dr. Niles says you can go home if you'd like."

"I don't want to go back there. I can't stay in that house. Just going down the road…it's too hard. I can't stop seeing…"

She wrings her hands. "We're leaving tomorrow morning, Caroline. It's just one more night."

"I have to see Sadie and Isaiah before I go."

Her eyes stare at me with steel. "You know where I stand on that."

"It's the only way I'll go anywhere with you."

❁ 15 ❁

GOODBYE

AS I WALK up the driveway, I see Sadie washing dishes through the window. My mother sits in the car and when Isaiah opens the front door, she drives away. Before I got out of the car, she said I had fifteen minutes to say everything I want to say. She'll be back in fifteen minutes on the dot. She can wait until hell freezes over, as far as I'm concerned.

My hands begin to shake when I see Isaiah. If he's surprised, he doesn't show it. His eyes slowly take me in, and he moves toward me as if he might hug me but then stops himself.

He says, "Hello, Caroline," and it's then that I hear the slight tremor in his voice, letting me know he isn't as calm as he appears. I step inside. Instantly, I've entered a warm haven. I've always wanted to be right here.

The room is small, but inviting. Quilts layer the couch and chair; the colors dark plum and green. On a hutch, a couple of Francie and Crissy dolls stand in glamorous pink outfits. It makes me smile that Sadie has these. I have the white versions at home.

Pictures of Isaiah at all ages line the wall. One particularly endearing photo is of him around two years old, holding a bunny. His eyes stood out even then; a light brown with flecks of green. He was one of the prettiest babies I've ever seen.

"Caroline, it's lovely to see you. We've been thinking about you 'round the clock." Sadie gives me a hug before getting ice tea for the three of us. We sit down in the living room.

"We've been staying close to home since you got out of the hospital, just in case you called," Isaiah says. "Mama heard you were…leaving soon and we were hoping you would…call before you left—" His voice breaks and he shakes his head. "I was scared you wouldn't, but Mama said you would."

"I couldn't leave without saying goodbye. We're leaving in the morning."

The lump in my throat is growing, and I will it to go away. It doesn't.

"We're so glad you came, honey. I've wished I could come see about you, but have tried to let you get settled back in at home. We've been so worried. You look so much better. I know you must still be in a lot of pain." Sadie dabs her eyes with a tissue and then hands me one as my eyes begin spilling over. "Oh honey."

She holds me close, and I try to get a grip. "Is there anything we can do to help, Caroline?"

"You've done so much. It's been a long couple of days. I saw Leroy's brother, Tuck, today and passed out— woke up in an ambulance."

Sadie keeps her arm around me.

"I'm fine now. I had a fight with my mother. I asked

her to bring me to see you. I told her—" I look at Isaiah. "I told her about us."

I look at Sadie then to see if she knows what we're talking about. She doesn't seem surprised.

"I mean…I know we're not talking anymore or anything, but I still…well, you know…I still needed to see you."

"Caroline…"

I can't look at him. The anguish in his voice is so thick I know it will haunt me.

"I'm so sorry," Isaiah says. His face is in his hands, and his voice sounds muffled. "This is all my fault." He looks up at me then, and says urgently, "Caroline, please. I don't know how you can, but please forgive me. You needed me and I wasn't there for you. I could have kept this from happening if I'd been there for you. Please don't leave. I'll make it up to you. I will *never* let anything bad happen to you again. I…I promise you I won't…"

We're both crying. Sadie just keeps handing both of us tissues as we need it. The anger I felt toward him earlier has completely faded.

"This is *not* your fault, Isaiah. There's nothing you could have done. You can't watch over me twenty-four hours a day. I'm not your responsibility."

"You are. You're everything to me, Caroline. Everything."

I look at Sadie again, a little embarrassed that she's hearing us talk like this. She doesn't seem bothered, so I relax a little. She smiles at me and pats my face.

"You're mighty special to my boy, honey. I'm gonna leave the two of you alone for a few minutes. Say what you need to say. Your mama is probably gonna be here any minute." She gets up and goes into the kitchen and begins washing the dishes.

I look over at Isaiah and he leans forward, his elbows on his knees. I've never loved anyone or anything as much as I love him. I try to memorize the way he looks at me. The way his lips tilt up when they see me. The way his eyes crinkle when he laughs at something I say. The way his eyes turn a darker shade of beautiful when he cries. I will love him until the day I die. I know this.

"I'm sorry I wouldn't talk to you at first. It was just too...awful. And I was angry with you...so angry. I never thought you'd walk away..."

"I'll never forgive myself for that, Caroline." He comes over to where I'm sitting and sits on his knees, taking my hands in his.

"When you came to the hospital, I was so humiliated that you knew. I can't believe it, really—I can't believe that any of it happened. But it did and it's not your fault..."

"It doesn't change the way I feel about you. If anything, I love you more," he whispers.

I feel my face go hot with those words. I lean my head down and touch my forehead to his.

"But Isaiah, you know—you said yourself it'll never work. You were right. Look at all the trouble we've caused. There's no way we can ever make it. They'll kill us first."

He shakes his head. "I'll kill them first."

"No. Isaiah, look at me. No. They're not worth it. You can't waste your life going to jail because of them. Please tell me you won't do anything crazy." I lift his chin up and force him to look me in the eyes. "Promise me."

"I'm not going to let anyone hurt you ever again."

Fear clenches my heart. I'm afraid of what he'll do. I know he means he'll kill them if he has to. Mama's right. I have to leave. He can't worry about protecting me. The best thing would be for him to forget all about me and have a nice, safe life. He can't do that if I stay here.

I look outside and it's dark. My mom is sitting out front, and I'm sure she's been out there for a long time. She's too afraid someone will notice her, so she doesn't honk or come to the door.

"I have to go, Isaiah."

"No, Caroline, please. Stay with us—we'll have supper. We can take you home. I'm afraid—I'm afraid if you go out that door, I'll never see you again."

I touch his face and lean over and kiss him, our salty tears mixing in with the kiss.

"I love you, Isaiah. I always will."

"Caroline, you can't go. I love you too. You belong here with me."

"I wish I did, Isaiah. You know I do. You don't belong to me, though. I wish you were mine, but you're not and you never will be. There is nowhere we could go that would accept us. I want you to have a good life."

"I will only have a good life if you're in it."

I stand up, knowing that I can't convince him tonight. He'll come to this conclusion when I'm gone. He's known before that we couldn't survive together; he'll know it again.

"Sadie, I have to go now. My mom is here."

Isaiah stands up and has his arm on my back. His face is panicked. I feel calmer than I have in weeks. I know what I have to do.

Sadie comes out of the kitchen and hugs me. "If you ever need us, honey, you just say the word. We will come wherever you are. Write us; call anytime. I hope you'll stay in touch. And hopefully, when those boys are caught, you can come back."

I nod, not trusting my voice.

I hug Isaiah, hard and tight. I try to pull back and he doesn't let go. I give in to the embrace for a moment longer and then pull away again. This time he lets me go.

"Caroline, I nearly forgot…stay right there one more minute."

Isaiah goes in his room and comes back with a small box. He hands it to me and watches as I lift the lid. Inside is my "C" necklace.

"I thought this was gone for good," I whisper.

"I found it that night…got a new chain for it. Want me to put it on you?"

"Yes. Thank you, Isaiah. So much."

He lifts the necklace out and it takes him a minute to get the clasp closed. When he's done, his fingers linger on the back of my neck.

He puts his arms around me and I close my eyes, savoring this one last moment. And then I move away before I'm unable to leave him at all.

"I can never thank you enough for saving my life. Words just sound silly when I try to tell you what you both mean to me…"

I turn to the door and look back at them one more time, my eyes settling on Isaiah. He looks back at me with defeat and despair.

This time I'm the one who walks out of the door and out of his life. Now I know how awful he felt.

NOT A WORD is spoken all the way home. I cringe when we pull down the road toward our house, but I made a deal. I'll stay here one more night, and then I'll never have to be here again. I feel nothing but hatred in my house, especially with my mother there. Everything and everyone in this house has let me down.

Miss Greener and George come over for a brief good-bye. Nellie and Grandpaw also come and stay for most of the evening. If anyone notices that my mother and I are not speaking, no one lets on. Nellie is weepy at the thought of us leaving, and I'm spent with all the emotion.

By the end of the night, I'm numb. I've cried more tears than I thought possible and cannot believe that I'm crying more as I lie in my bed, trying to sleep. The thought of not seeing my friends and grandparents on a regular basis is terrifying and heartbreaking. I've never even visited anywhere more than a hundred miles south. Good or bad, Tulma is mine, and I am inconsolable at the thought of leaving.

Crying just makes my ribs feel worse. I take some medicine and fall asleep with a wet pillow and heavy heart. I jerk awake some time later, groggy but awake. It can't be too late, maybe midnight. I know immediately that I'm not alone. I sit up in bed. There's a breeze coming from my window. It wasn't open before I went to bed. I always keep that window locked. As I reach for the lamp, my hands are yanked to each side of the bed.

I try to say something, but I can't speak, my voice is frozen somewhere down deep in my throat. I cry; I struggle. My wrists are tied to the bed with a heavy rope. I begin kicking and my feet are strapped down. Stretched out like an X.

They're here with me. Here in my room, not saying a word. Just getting ready to teach me another lesson. I begin to cry out just as my mouth is covered with a heavy cloth. It's too dark to see anything, but I hear them. Their ragged breath. Breathing hard from strapping me down. I vomit, but it has nowhere to go but back down.

He leans in, his breath hot and smelly. With a soft snarl, he says, "You call your little friends off me, you hear me? I don't want another visit from the Klan crazies, *do* you hear me? You should have died already, and now you're causin' me all this trouble. Listen, I will still hunt you down and kill you if I have to. I ain't afraid of them. And I sho ain't gonna let some little white bitch spread lies about me. I don't care how good you is at this. You got that? So change the little story you been tellin'. You want it as much as I do."

I nod my head. Whatever you say. Leave me alone and I'll do whatever you say.

I would know it's Leroy even if he hadn't spoken, by the weight of him. He's on top of me now and all the thoughts I had of killing him seem futile now. I'm paralyzed with fear.

You good for nothing coward. What are you going to do? Play dead and let him do it again? What's wrong with you?

I find my voice and begin yelling. It sounds muffled through the cloth, but I just yell louder. And louder. The realization hits me suddenly that my knees are free. I knee him in the groin, and it makes him mad. He punches me in the stomach with one hand and yanks my hair with the other. I butt my head into his, ramming it with a loud thwack. So much for getting over that concussion. It would be worth it to have another if I can hurt him.

A sound in the other room startles him.

"Caroline?" My mother is coming. Oh, thank God. Please come in, Mama. Please find me.

Leroy curses and rolls off of me. My eyes are adjusted to the dark now, and Les is by my window. He sounds scared. "Let's go. Someone comin' down the road. Come on! We gotta get outta here!"

Leroy pauses, but hears my mother again. They raise my window and jump out. The room goes quiet. I'm going to be sick again. I moan as loud as I can through the cloth. Please, Mama, hear me.

She opens the door and a beam of light fills the room. "Oh my God. Oh my God. Caroline. What happened?" She pulls the rag off my mouth and I vomit on the bed. She unties the ropes on my hands and feet. I curl up in a ball.

"Are they still here, Caroline?" She looks out the window and runs to get the phone. I hear her saying, "I thought I heard something and when I went in her room, she was tied up, and her window was open. The latch was broken on the window. I don't know. Yeah. It just happened. Okay. Please. Yes…"

She comes back in and I'm not sure what happened next. I remember her taking me to Nellie's and putting me in the bath there. Someone held me all night, I don't know if it was Grandpaw, Nellie, or my mother. Sometime in the early hours of the morning, Grandpaw came in the room.

"It's time, Caroline. Let's get you in the car. I love

you, sweet child. Everything's gonna be all right. We're gonna take care of it all."

I'm groggy and every inch of me is sore. Grandpaw carries me to the car, he and Nellie kiss me goodbye, and we leave Tulma for good.

16

NEW

WHEN I WAKE up, I'm alone in the car, parked in front of a weathered apartment building. I rub my eyes, and my puffy lids burn long after I've stopped rubbing. I try to figure out where we are. I have no sense of how long we were driving. The sun is shining brightly into the passenger side window. I'm hot and sticky and my mouth feels like sandpaper. My throat is positive it hasn't had a drink in years.

The windows are cracked but aren't letting in much air. I roll down the window more and look around. A little blonde girl runs outside and is flying her doll in the air. She doesn't notice me in the car. I watch her carefree play and envy her innocence. There are very few cars in the parking lot. *Amsterdam Villas* is written in curly letters on a large sign in front of the office. I open the door to see if I can cool off, and my mom walks out of the apartment closest to the office.

She closes the door behind her, and it barely shuts before it's opened again. This time my dad comes out. I'm stunned to see him. Relief floods over me. I get out of the car and start to move toward him. He stumbles as he walks to me. I get a better look at him and pause. He looks awful. His face is haggard and his hair is dirty. Even in his worst benders, he has always looked better than this. I get closer to him and his eyes are so bloodshot, I barely see my daddy in there.

He almost reaches me and is holding out his arms when my mom grabs my arm and turns me around toward the car. She walks quickly. I stumble as I look back, and Daddy has stopped and looks like he's going to fall over himself.

I swallow back tears and get back in the car. I'm torn about leaving. How can I possibly go when he's like this? The guilt rises to my chest and threatens to choke me. My stomach clenches. I can't do it right now. It's too much to see him like this. We barely get down the road when I tell my mom to pull over and I'm sick in the grass.

My mom and I don't talk as she drives. I see a few signs and surmise that we're in Memphis. The streets are full of traffic at this time of day. I watch all the people and try to forget about Daddy. Everything around me looks bigger and better here. The girls are wearing dresses so short that Nellie would keel over with a heart attack. Their hair is huge and I just *thought* mine was frizzy. This gives frizz a whole new meaning. Both men and women have on pants that have so much extra material, I try to imagine what my pragmatic Nellie would have to say about such waste. I've never seen anyone dress like this in real life…nothing even close to this.

Mama pulls into a motel parking lot and stops under the awning of the office. A flashing sign says, "Kitchen-ette, TV and Telephone." She goes inside and comes back out five minutes later with a room key.

"This will work for a few days…it's cheap enough. I don't have to be in San Antonio for a few weeks. We'll see if your dad can pull it together."

We pull around to room 149 and park in front of the door. There's only one other car in the parking lot. A Shoney's Restaurant is across the street and a busy gas station is on the corner. A group of three guys with bell-bottoms and shiny sunglasses are leaning against their Pontiac, laughing and looking like they have nothing better to do than look cool.

Tulma seems like an entirely different continent.

MAMA OPENS THE trunk and pulls out her suitcase. I grab mine too and we haul it inside. The room is spacious for a motel, with two double beds and a small kitchen and bathroom. It's not too bad, but the thought of staying in this small space with Mama for even one night is already making me claustrophobic.

Mama claims her bed and sprawls out on top of the bedspread. I unpack my suitcase, hanging up a few things and putting the rest in the bottom two drawers of the dresser, leaving the top two for Mama. She's asleep by the time I've emptied my suitcase. I decide to take a shower, the only place inside that I can go to have any privacy. The water pours over my face, and I let the hot tears fall. I cry for the daddy I've lost. I know now the one I loved is gone for good. I cry for Isaiah and the hurt I've caused him. I see his bleak eyes pleading with me to stay, and I wish that

I could have more than anything. I cry for the girl who is forever gone and wish that no one had found me in the fields. I could have just closed my eyes and let the dream carry me up to the clouds forever.

I HAD HOPED the dreams would fade once we were out of Tulma, but if it's possible, they've only magnified. Every night is an ongoing nightmare of Leroy and Les, Les and Leroy, Leroy and Les, Les and Leroy...their voices are distorted and their eyes taunt me. I feel myself passing out over and over and I wake up throughout the night gasping for air. I wake up feeling like I didn't sleep at all.

One day fades into the next and the next; each day worse than the last. Mama wants to pick a fight about everything. She tries to be the same controlling mother she's always been and I'm having none of it. I won't do anything for her. The days of me ironing her underwear are long gone. I don't ask her to lift a hand for me either, but it wouldn't matter—she'd be mad either way. It's beneath her to be somewhere she doesn't want to be. She drinks all day and moans about how her life was supposed to be so much better...how she should have just stayed with Grant and that Daddy never amounted to anything and never would. I put the pillow over my head and shut her out while she yells. On day four of this, I've had enough.

I begin to yell back.

"Just leave me here. I don't want you. I don't need you. I stopped needing you a long time ago. You make me miserable and I obviously make you miserable. Go! Just go and leave me the hell alone! Get out of my life. GO!"

She turns away from me, toward the wall and a cloud of red fury consumes me. I begin to shake violently and am too angry to care. I step in the space between the wall and her bed and lean down until my face is a foot from hers.

My teeth clench tightly and in a voice I didn't know was in my arsenal, I mutter, "You're not a mother. You're an emotionless lump of nothing. All you do is make everything worse than it already is. I can take care of myself. And I don't need someone else to tell me what a worthless person I am—I've already figured it out on my own."

Her eyes widen and then blink fast the longer I talk. I think I see her tears coming, but I'm not done.

"I'm not listening to you anymore. You lost that right the first time you left me. It's just taken me this long to not want you. You need to go. I'm better off without you. In fact, I'd be just fine if I never saw you again for the rest of my life."

My face is on fire and my throat burns from unshed tears. Unable to stand one more minute in a room with her, I walk out the door and go across the street to Shoney's. I ask if they're hiring and they say they actually do desperately need help. I tell them about my experience and perkily add that I am the right person for the job. They hire me on the spot and I'm so relieved, I feel lightheaded. Joann, the manager, asks if I can stay for a couple hours to train and then do a full 8 hours the next day. Oh blessed distraction. My tasks are so similar to the ones I did at Harriet's, I learn the job in no time. The other waitresses are friendly enough and the customers treat me well as I follow Linda, the waitress training me. I feel confident I'll be able to do this job well.

When I cross the street later that night, the car is still in front of the room and I take a deep breath before I go in to face my mother.

The room is empty when I enter. None of her things are there—no clothes, no suitcase, nothing. She's gone. On the kitchen counter, the keys are sitting on top of a note, along with four twenty-dollar bills.

Caroline,

Grant came to get me. I'm sorry you don't appreciate the sacrifices I've made for you. I feel bad for what has happened to you, but you have to live with your part in that. There are consequences to every action. It looks like you'll have to learn that the hard way.

You've always been able to take care of yourself and will do fine now. I don't know why I thought you needed me. You never have, not really.

I'm leaving the car for you. I know you've never driven much, but it will get easier the more you do it. Someone will let you know when it's safe to come back to Tulma. I'm not sure yet if I'll be in Tulma or if I'll go ahead to San Antonio. Until it's safe, stay here. I've paid for the month.

Mama

I put the money and keys in my purse. I open the dresser and take out my crowded clothes, spreading them out among the four drawers. I have a month and a job. I can do this. I won't shed a single tear over that woman again. She's not a mother. I'm thrilled she's gone. I'll never have to live with her again—and I won't be going back to Tulma. Ever.

I'm hollow with missing Isaiah, but every time I picture his sad eyes, I remind myself that I'm doing what's best for him. Having my mother around was torture, but as unwelcome as it was, it did keep me from thinking about Isaiah at least a small part of the time. Now, I'm completely alone in my anguish.

I'm still happy she's gone.

THE TIME GOES by quickly the next day at Shoney's. I don't really like the brown uniform, but it makes things simpler to know what to wear every day. Before I know it, a week has passed, and I've worked 40 hours. I'm ready for a day off and grateful to finally have one. I walk across the street and eye the car. Tomorrow will be the day I learn to drive it. Joann said there's a large school parking lot closeby that should be empty tomorrow since it's a Saturday. She doesn't know that I'll be teaching *myself* to drive, but what she doesn't know won't hurt her.

I cross the street, feeling exhausted, but pleased with the check that will be coming in another week. The sun is starting to set and I enjoy the wind on my face. I don't see him at first, but when I get closer to my car, he stands up.

His eyes crinkle at my surprise, that smile of his that I love—the one that makes his entire face shine.

"Isaiah!" The breath is knocked out of me.

"Hi, Caroline. How are you? I've missed you." He

seems a little reserved.

"I've missed you too. What—is everything okay?"

"Everything is great—I have some good news."

I look around and make sure no one is watching us as I unlock the door. We step inside, close the door, and we look at each other shyly for a full minute. He laughs and takes me in his arms.

"I'm so happy to see you," he whispers in my ear. "I haven't stopped thinking about you for a second."

I look at him and can't help but smile, even though I'm not sure how I feel about him being here. "What are you doing here, Isaiah? How did you ever find me?"

"Come here, let's sit down." He grabs my hand and we sit down at the table. He doesn't let go of me. I don't think I've ever seen him so animated.

"What's going on?"

"Aren't you happy to see me?" He grins and leans forward to kiss my cheek.

"So happy." I admit. "I never expected…to see you today."

His joy is infectious and I allow myself to just be happy he's here, for whatever reason. Any amount of time I might get with him, even if it's just for an hour. He's here. I thought I'd never see him again.

"You don't have to worry about Leroy and Les ever again, Caroline. They've been taken care of and won't hurt anyone anymore." He runs his finger along my jaw line and watches my reaction.

I stand up and clinch my hands together. "What happened, Isaiah? Tell me everything." My heart is pounding, and I'm terrified by what he'll say.

"I can't tell you everything, but trust me, it's all been

taken care of. You have a lot of friends in Tulma...more than you even know...and..."

"What do you mean by that? What part did you play in this? Or was it the Klan? I didn't ask for that. I don't want any part of them! Leroy and Les should be in jail, no one needed to "take care" of them for me!" I begin pacing the room. "I don't agree with how the Klan operates. And I certainly don't want anyone I love going after them and going to jail! If anyone should have killed them, it should have been me!"

The craziness of what I've just said hits me and I have to sit back down.

"Slow down. They had it coming, Caroline. They pushed too far. They went on a little spree after they left your house that night and were taken out. It wasn't the Klan, but I can't tell you who it was. Just trust me, it all worked out. The police were glad to get that trash off the street."

I stand up and begin pacing again with Isaiah on my heels. I trip over the carpet and Isaiah grabs me and holds me still. He takes my face in his hands and speaks softly.

"Please don't worry about me or anyone else. I know you'll have to deal with everything that happened to you for a long time, maybe forever, I don't know...but you never have to be afraid of those two ever again. That part is over."

He bends down and leans his forehead against mine. I close my eyes and imagine Les and Leroy going down with a thud. The weight of the world leaves my shoulders, and I take a deep breath that actually reaches my lungs.

It's over.

WE STARE AT each other for a long time, taking each other in, neither of us saying a word. For the longest time, we don't move, just feel the luxury of being able to look at each other without anyone else interrupting the moment. There is no one around to hide anything from, nothing to hurry off to, nowhere else to be but here, together. Finally, Isaiah moves. He winds his fingers through my hair and the other hand traces my jaw. His touch is so gentle, so very careful—as if I might fall apart like a dying rose, petals falling off one by one. Impulsively, I draw my mouth up to Isaiah's and kiss him...hard. He kisses me back at first, and then when I lean into his body with the weight of mine, he unwinds my arms from around his neck and takes a step back.

"Caroline..." His eyes are tentative. He takes another step back and holds my hands, bringing them up to his lips, one knuckle at a time.

I don't even know what I want. I want to forget; I want to remember. I want Isaiah back and all that we had before it was all destroyed. I want to forget all the ugliness and remember the good. I want to remember who I can be and forget the scarred girl who has no one. Hearing that it's finally finished is intoxicating. And it seems like a lifetime that I've been looking over my shoulder for one reason or another. No more. I don't want to be fragile another day of my life. I'm desperate to have some life sparked back in me again.

"Isaiah..." I say and close some of the space between us.

He nervously smiles at me, confused by my boldness. I know he doesn't want to make a wrong move with me. I'm sorry that he has to deal with such a conundrum. A teenage boy in a motel room with the girl he loves, and all outside influences completely out of the picture should feel like an opportune moment to seize.

"I need to wipe the visions of...everything...out of my mind." Tears burn my eyes and I angrily swipe them away. "Every time I lie down at night, they're all I see." My voice cracks. "I used to see you and that's what I want..."

"I'm just not sure you're ready for this, Caroline. You know I want to. I always want to be with you." He pulls me in and places his chin on my shoulder.

"I need new memories of us," I whisper.

I know it doesn't make much sense when I say it out loud, but for me, tonight, it's the only way I can imagine putting Les and Leroy out of my mind.

Isaiah takes a huge breath. "I just don't want to do anything you'll regret." He leans back and stares me down. "I couldn't take that. Just make sure that if you start changing your mind, you'll tell me." He grins his stop-my-heart grin and tugs on my hair. "I'm happy just looking at you."

"You are all that is good, Isaiah."

IT REALLY DOES help.

I was afraid I would never want to do that. Ever. But with Isaiah, it's just right. The hollowed-out hole that's been residing in my chest fills just a little and I feel almost like myself again.

Much, much later, when our eyelids finally begin to droop, Isaiah looks at me tenderly and tells me how much he loves me.

"I love you too." I sleepily smile back.

"Are you sure you're okay?" he asks for about the tenth time.

All through the night, he has made sure I'm not hurting or uncomfortable and that I want to continue with every step we take.

"Yes, I'm sure."

And I mean it. If he'll just hold me every night like this for the rest of my life, I will be okay.

I SLEEP A deep, dreamless sleep and wake up feeling I have slept for twelve full hours, instead of the actual four. My legs are tangled around Isaiah's, and he's watching me, holding his breath. I smile at him and sigh when I see the immediate relief wash over his face. He must have been worried about the emotions the morning light might bring. I move my head onto his chest and try to reassure him that I'm right where I want to be.

We finally untangle ourselves from each other and decide we have to eat sometime. We take a long shower and get dressed, stopping to kiss each other again before we go out the door.

Isaiah groans. "You keep kissing me like this, I won't need any food ever again."

Suddenly I don't want to share him with anyone, so I put my hand on his arm and say, "How about we drive through somewhere and bring it back here?"

He nods and backs me against the wall, kissing me. "Sounds good to me."

Eventually we get in his car and drive through a McDonald's, something we never get to eat at home. His hand is on my leg while he drives and when we stop to place our order, we can't take our eyes off of each other. We order and as soon as we get our food, we head back to the room and spend the rest of the day and night intoxicated with each other. Every minute with him heals me.

THE NEXT MORNING, we walk to Shoney's. I'm starving and have a hankerin' for their pancakes. I smile brightly at Joann when I see her. "I was just missing it over here." I shrug, thinking she will laugh.

She doesn't say anything, but seats us near the back of the restaurant. I don't think much of it, just that she must not be in a great mood. When I see her walk over to the waitresses and say something and then they all look over at us, I get an uneasy feeling.

We sit in the booth, memories of the time in our room making us shy with one another in the daylight. I think surely there must be a sign blinking over my head, letting the world know that I've been misbehaving for two days straight.

Isaiah smiles over at me. "You look like you have a secret," he whispers.

"It's a good one," I whisper back with a huge smile.

I didn't know I could feel this lighthearted. Hope is crawling its way back into my guts.

My stomach is rumbling, and Isaiah's is too. A half hour passes and still no one comes to take our order. I see several opportunities when Joann seems free, but she doesn't come. Isaiah doesn't complain, but I can tell he's noticing the stares. My joy is beginning to fade as I realize none of them want to come wait on us.

A tall man with a burly beard that I hadn't even noticed walks up to our table. He stands over us, glowering. "I don't know where you two are from, but around these parts we don't do this." He wags his finger back and forth between Isaiah and me. He leans down and gets in Isaiah's face. "You need to get out of here, boy…before I show you what we do to niggers like you who think they're white." He walks over to the booth across from us and stares us down. I guess he thinks he'll do that until we get out of here.

I start shaking and Isaiah holds onto my hand tight. Joann comes to our table then and quietly says, "You're making some people uncomfortable in here. I'm going to have to ask you to leave. Sorry, Caroline."

I'm in such shock that I don't even say anything back. I wish I had. I wish I'd told both of them to stick it where the sun and moon and stars and comets and everything else…don't shine.

I stand up and hold my hand out. Isaiah takes it and we walk out. Our mood subdued, we walk hand in hand to the edge of the street and wait until there's a chance to cross it. The guy in the car takes a double look at us and begins yelling awful things out the window. Isaiah grips my hand harder, and we cross the street in a hurry. We make sure no one is watching as we enter the room and close the door, locking it behind us.

"This is crazy." Isaiah walks to the window and peeks out. "I've gotta get you out of here. Let's go to California. Things are different there."

"How would we get there? We have to work to get enough money for that. I'm gonna have to get a new job now. And what about Sadie? You can't leave her in Tulma. That would devastate her."

"She knows I'm not happy without you. We'll get there. Let me worry about the details."

Shaken and upset that the whole air in the room has shifted once again to turmoil, I sit on the bed and feel exhausted. Isaiah comes and sits on the bed beside me. He takes my hand in his. "We're hungry. I'm gonna go get you something to eat. I saw a Popeye's just a street over."

I nod.

He kisses me and says, "I love you, Caroline Carson."

"I love you, Isaiah Washington."

He grins. "That's enough for me," he says as he walks out the door.

❀ 17 ❀

ANCIENT

HE'S GONE FOR a minute and I start piling my clothes into the suitcase and hurriedly write a note.

Dear Isaiah,

I love you. Never question that.

The last two days are something I'll never ever forget. I'm so grateful to you for showing me what love really is. You've always had my heart and you always will. Always.

I can't do this to you. I can't, Isaiah. It will ruin your life to be with me. I love you too much to let that happen. Go home. Be happy. Find someone that you're meant to be with...I know it will happen. You have too much love in you to not make someone so happy. It can't be me. Deep down, I know you realize this is true.

Please don't look for me.

Love,

Caroline

I practically run to the car and pull out of the parking

lot, tears running down my face and neck. I don't even think about where I'm going, I just drive and drive and drive and don't stop until I have to get gas. It's a good thing there's hardly anyone else on the road. I couldn't say if I swerve or not. I'm just moving forward. I try not to think about how Isaiah felt when he realized I left. I try to only think about how much happier his life will be without all the sorrow that I've brought into it.

I go through Nashville and find myself in Kentucky. Spotting a motel ahead, I pull off the road. There's a young girl in the office and I ask if there's an available room. She studies my face and takes in the splotches, puffy eyes, and red nose, and quickly hands me a key. She catches herself staring and smiles sweetly at me and says in a slow, thick drawl, "We serve a little breakfast from 6-9. Come on back here and we'll fix up your day."

I nod and head out the door, quickly pulling up to my room. My bag is heavier than a hundred-pound barbell. I close the door and lock it behind me. I go to the bathroom and crawl into the bed. *I am ancient.*

I look at the clock. It has been an eternity since last night when I was thinking the world had turned right side up with Isaiah.

My bones are tired. Aching. It's taking over, suffocating me. My body is slowly atrophying from every injustice it has suffered. Every grief, crippling. The pleasure from the last two days plays topsy-turvy in my mind, and it doubles me over that I will never see Isaiah again. I've lived a thousand deaths and can't live through another one.

Please, God, don't let me live through another one.

IT'S MORNING BEFORE I fall asleep. I hear a faint knock on the door and someone saying, "Housekeeping" but I can't shake the sleep enough to answer the door. They knock a few raps more and then go on their way.

When I wake again, it's dark outside. I doze back off and it's morning again the next time I'm awake. I want to go back to sleep and never wake up, but I'm too hungry. My stomach is so empty, it turns over and I think I might be sick. I shower and decide to see if I can still get breakfast from the motel.

The girl lights up when she sees me walk in. "Hello! I hope you've been enjoying your stay. Would you like some breakfast?"

She leads me into the side room and there's a small kitchen with a bar and stools. I sit down on one of the stools and watch her work. She's so happy to have a guest that she chats the entire time she prepares the food.

"How long are you in town?" She uncovers a pan that has rising biscuit dough.

"I'm not really sure." I watch as she places the biscuits in the oven and stirs the sausage gravy on the stove.

"Oh well, where are you headed?"

"I'm not sure of that either."

"Oh…" Unsure of where to go next with this one-sided conversation, she doesn't let that stop her for long.

A few minutes later, she pipes up, "Well, Bardstown is a very nice place to live. It's beautiful here. We just need a few more young people."

She laughs and her eyes disappear. She cracks two eggs into a frying pan and I watch the bacon grease sizzle around the eggs.

I wonder how old she is. She looks young—my age, maybe even younger. It's hard to tell though, if she might just be trying hard to look older. She's petite and has her blonde hair sitting on top of her head. Her nails are painted red and she has blue eye shadow piled on thick.

I decide to jump in since she's trying so hard. And I'm curious. "Have you always lived here?"

"Yes, ma'am, I was born and bred right here. My family opened this motel twenty-five years ago and we've grown up running this place. Wantin' to turn it into apartments to have something steadier, but...we'll see. My sister ran off to Louisville a year ago and I've been working in here full time since then." Her voice softens and she reaches across the counter and hands me a plate of eggs and biscuits and gravy. "My dad passed away five years ago and my mama hasn't been well for a while now."

She turns around and begins filling the sink with soapy water.

"This looks delicious, thank you."

"You're welcome! I love it when we have someone staying here. It gets lonely sometimes. Sure don't see girls your age around here very often."

I take a bite of biscuit and it's just right. "Mmm...so good."

"I'm glad you like it. My mama is the best cook this side of Kentucky. She wouldn't let me do it any way but good." She pauses a minute. "So where are you from?"

I hesitate before answering. "A really small town in Tennessee—Tulma?"

She wrinkles her nose. "Never heard of it, but that don't mean much. I don't get out any."

I blink back the tears that threaten to start. The lump in my throat grows with her simple kindness. I concentrate on the food and try to swallow the ache away.

"Sure would be nice if you'd stay a while," she says shyly.

Before I have a chance to think about it, the words are coming out of me. "Well, I think I might. You don't know of any work available around here, do you?"

Her ears move up, she smiles so big. "I sure do. Just yesterday, Shelby, from across the street," she points out the window and I turn around to see a small restaurant, "tried to convince me to come cook for her. I told her I had my hands full running this place, but she's been runnin' all over hell's half-acre."

I smile at the expression. Nellie used to say that.

"Shelby *stays* busy, a lot busier than us." She bites her lip as she finishes the last swipe of the counter and pauses before setting the rag down. "And I'd be willin' to give you a good deal on a little bigger room that you could stay in as long as you needed."

I think about this and nod my head. "Thank you. I think I'll go over and talk to her in a little while and then I'll let you know if I'll need that room. Shelby, you said?"

"Yes. Tell her Brenda sent you." She smiles then and holds out her hand. "I'm Brenda, nice to meet you."

"Caroline. It's nice to meet you too." We shake on it.

I START WORKING at Shelby's the next week and my days fall into a routine that isn't too different from Harriet's, except now I'm doing a lot of the cooking, as well as waitressing. Fortunately, I spent so much time watching Ruby as she cooked for me, I'm able to catch on to the cooking quickly. She'd be proud.

Brenda and I have gotten surprisingly close in the short amount of time I've been here. I did change to a larger room that has a kitchen, but I'm hardly ever in there. I eat with Brenda or at the restaurant and stay busy until I fall into bed at night.

She knocks on my door one night before I go to bed and when I open the door, she has a bag. I let her in and take the bag—it looks almost as big as her—and is as heavy as all get out.

"Whatcha got in here?" I ask and look down in the bag. There are tomatoes, cucumbers, onions, and peppers filled to the brim.

"I thought you might like some fresh vegetables. Picked a bunch from the garden today and have so much, I don't know what to do with it all." Brenda stretches and grins. The girl is always happy.

"Thank you. I'd love it. My grandma puts cucumbers, onions and peppers in vinegar and eats it with everything. I've been missing that. I'll get some vinegar and make it tomorrow."

"Good! I hoped you could find a use for it all." Brenda plops down on one of the two chairs in the room. "Wanna watch something on TV?"

"Sure." I turn it on and sit in the other chair.

The Waltons' theme song is just starting and Brenda sits up taller.

"I love this show. John Boy is so cute!"

I smile and keep my thoughts to myself. He doesn't do a thing for me. I like that he's a writer, but that's about it.

We get lost in the show. It's a nice break to see how problems are resolved in less than an hour. I wish real life were so simple. I think Brenda probably wishes the same thing.

"How old are you, Brenda?"

"I'm eighteen. How old are you?"

I'm caught by surprise—she looks way younger.

I hesitate before answering. Should I tell her the truth? "I'm fifteen."

The shock sets in before she can hide it.

"Fifteen?" she sputters. "But you look so much older! What are you doing on your own?" Her face flushes and she looks more serious than I've seen her yet. "Caroline, are you a runaway?"

"Well, not exactly. It's kinda complicated, I guess."

She looks so concerned and interested that I can't help it—I start talking, and once I start, I can't stop. I tell her everything. I figure I must need to get it out to someone, but when I finish, I'm embarrassed beyond belief.

Brenda sits quietly when I'm done. She's cried, held my hand, curled up into her chair with her hands on her knees—I thought I might see judgment in her eyes when I told her about Isaiah. And waited for it again, when I told her about Leroy and Les. But it never comes.

She clears her throat and leans forward to take my hand in hers. "Thanks for tellin' me your story, Caroline. I don't think I've ever known anyone as brave as you. If my mama ever…well, I don't know what I would have done if

I'd been alone the way you have. I'm just glad God saw fit to lead you here. I don't never get to church like I ought to, but I know the Lord understands. He knew that we needed each other." Tears roll down her cheeks and the tears start rolling down mine too.

I hug her and when we're wiping our faces a few minutes later, I say, "I'm a little confused about God right now, to tell you the truth. But there have been some people in my life that have seemed almost better than God has ever been to me. Or maybe if there is a God, he's sent them my way. Sadie, Isaiah's mother…Ruby and Miss Greener—good people who have been better to me than my own family. And now you. I guess I have to believe someone might be watching out for me after all."

"Well, I needed you just as much. I've wished for a friend for such a long time." She smiles and gives me another hug. "And I feel like I've known you forever."

She stays until we're both yawning and struggling to stay awake.

"Well, I better get to bed. I'll see you in the morning? You workin' tomorrow?"

"I have a later shift, so I'll come see you at breakfast."

I watch her walk toward her apartment in the back of the motel. She gives me a wave and blinks the outside light a few times to let me know she's in safely.

When I go to bed, my heart feels just a little less empty.

❀ 18 ❀

ISAIAH

THE MILES BACK to Tulma are endless. Driving to Memphis, I'd driven as fast as I could go, knowing the sooner I saw her, the sooner I'd be complete. I'd eavesdropped on Caroline's mom when I saw that she was back in town and heard her tell one of the other tellers at the bank that she'd been to Memphis. I was glad that her plans must have changed about San Antonio, otherwise, I could have been searching for Caroline forever. I immediately went home and told Mama that I needed to go find her in Memphis. Caroline needed to know about Leroy and Les, and she needed to be back home. I would bring her back home and we'd be happy.

I couldn't believe it when I spotted their car in front of the motel. I looked inside and saw one of Caroline's pencils—she likes to write in her journal with pink pencils —and knew I'd found her. I didn't even have to wait long before I saw her crossing the street toward me.

I'm still in shock that everything went so wrong. When Caroline left Tulma, I thought I'd die from the heartache. It was nothing compared to what I feel now.

172

Now I think I really *won't* ever see her again and the thought fills me with such panic and despair, I briefly consider driving off a bridge somewhere and ending my misery. The thought that I just have to find her again spurs me on. I can't give up.

The nights we spent together were better than anything I could have imagined. Her silky skin, her beautiful hair, her mouth. Her love staring back at me. God, I love her more than life. She *is* my life. I don't think I can live without her. The lump in my throat feels permanently lodged, choking the life right out of me.

I pound on the steering wheel. I never dreamed she'd leave. After finally feeling like we were going to survive, she'd given up. Searching all over Memphis, hours of driving through the streets surrounding the motel—I even went back in the restaurant and demanded to know if she'd been back in there. They threw me out and threatened to call the police, but I didn't care. I just wanted to find her.

The note is crumpled and smoothed back out. It sits on the seat next to me. I stare at it with contempt and try to be mad at Caroline. But I can't. I know what she did was out of love. After all, I did the same thing to her not too long ago. But I will pay for that mistake for the rest of my life.

I have to find her and make her see that we can't fight it any more. We deserve a chance like anyone else.

When I pull into my driveway, Mama runs out and without a word, she hugs me and helps me inside. It feels like I'm sleepwalking into the house. She prepares hot milk with butter and honey, but I can't touch it. I know she wants to hear what happened, but I can't get the words out just yet. Too exhausted. I lean over and kiss her cheek and head to my bedroom. I crawl into my bed and try to figure out what to do next. Where do I even start to look for her?

———————————— ❀ ————————————

OVER THE NEXT several months, I make multiple attempts, driving to places we'd talked about together. I go to Memphis four times. I hide outside her house, hoping she'll sneak back. Look in her mailbox to see if there's a message for me. Stalk her grandparents, her mother, even Thomas…nothing. Ashamed of my behavior, I still can't seem to stop myself.

My uncles threaten to fire me if I don't get my head on straight. The thought of Caroline coming back one day and me not having anything to offer her scares me into holding onto my job.

"Son, you're gonna have to let her go," Mama says one afternoon when she catches me staring into space yet again.

"I can't, Mama—" I give up trying to explain my feelings and put my head in my hands.

"She's gonna have to come back on her own, Isaiah, and I don't really see her ever doing that. Unless you hear from her, which for your sake now, I hope you do. I just don't see how you're gonna find her."

I know she's right, but I don't want to hear it. Without Caroline, my life feels worthless.

There has never been any doubt in my mind that I'm in love with Caroline Carson. I was sure as a boy, and when I made love to her, I was even more sure as a man.

Finally, I do something I should have done as soon as

I realized she'd left. I go back to Memphis and begin the search for her father. Caroline told me all about seeing her dad and what bad shape he'd been in. I don't know if she'll be with him or not. I kinda doubt it, but I have to try. Looking through the phone book to see if I can remember the name of the apartments, I pray that if I do ever find it, Mr. Carson will still be there.

Amsterdam Villas…that jogs a memory. It's worth a try. It's a little off the beaten path, but I find it. The mail-boxes have the last names matched with the right box. *There he is.* I run to the right building and pound on the door. No one answers, so I sit out there, hoping to catch Mr. Carson coming in. I have to wait quite a while.

MR. CARSON WALKS by, weaving and smelling strong of liquor. He doesn't notice me sitting there in his hall and jumps a mile high when I speak.

"Mr. Carson!"

"Oh, goodness sakes, son," he slurs. "You tryin' to kill me?"

"We'll see. For now, no," I joke back, then quickly hold my hand out and introduce myself, so he knows I'm really not trying to mess with him.

"Whatcha doin' all the way from Tulma?" he asks.

"Lookin' for Caroline."

That gets his attention. He stands up tall and gets serious. Mentioning Caroline was like an instant cup of coffee dousing his system.

He leads me to his apartment and I cringe when I

walk inside. Caroline would be mortified at the shape his place is in. Seeing the mess, I know for sure she's not here. I step over the bottles and dishes. It smells to high heaven. It's sad to see what he's done to himself. I hope I can get some answers from him, but as soon as we sit down to talk, he's opening another bottle.

❀ 19 ❀

THIS CHANGES EVERYTHING

ANOTHER MONTH DRAGS by. At first, I'm looking over my shoulder, halfway expecting Isaiah to miraculously find me again, but he doesn't. Things are going fairly well, until I get sick. For weeks, I can't keep any food down. Dark shadows circle my eyes. I think about sleep a lot and even when I get plenty, it doesn't feel like enough.

Brenda invites me over for Sunday dinner right before Thanksgiving. Her mom has gone to visit her sister, so it will just be the two of us. Brenda goes to church and I enjoy a leisurely morning off of work. As I walk to her place, my stomach lets out a huge growl. I think I might be able to eat this time without losing it. I'm feeling a little better. Until she opens the door and I catch a whiff of the turnip greens. I barely make it through the door and I'm running to the bathroom. *Maybe all my wishes of dying are coming true*, I think with some optimism.

"Caroline? You all right?"

I rinse out my mouth and open the door. Brenda stands there looking so concerned, I try to give her a reassuring smile.

The smell wafts through again and I close my eyes, willing myself to not throw up again.

"Do you mind if we eat outside?" I ask, leaning against the wall.

"Sure, we can eat at the picnic table. Are you up to eating?"

"Oh yeah, I'm starving."

Brenda studies me as we dish up our plates. I don't make any apologies for passing on the turnip greens. It's my fervent hope that I never have to see or smell them ever again.

The weather is stubbornly warm; the fall leaves haven't even fully come out yet.

Brenda says the blessing and we eat. Conversation between us has become so comfortable that usually there is never a lull in topics. She's quieter than usual today, though. When two minutes go by without her saying anything, which is highly unlike her, I set down my fork.

"You sure are quiet today. Everything all right?" I ask.

She finishes her bite of mashed potatoes, licks her lips, and takes a sip of sweet tea. When she sets her glass down, she looks at me, so serious it scares me.

"Caroline, I've just been thinking about you and how sick you've been. Have you thought that maybe you might be—pregnant?"

I choke on my tea and dab my mouth before it drips onto my skirt. No. No, I hadn't thought of that. At all.

"I-no. It never crossed my mind even once that I could be. I don't know why. My-my monthly is never regular, never has been." I lean my head into my hands and think about how long I've felt off. Somehow, I just know that it's true. "Oh, Lord have mercy. Why didn't I think of this? Good grief, how dumb am I? What am I gonna do?" My voice becomes higher pitched with each question.

This time I don't think it's the greens that makes me lose my lunch.

I LIVE IN the land of denial for the next few weeks. It isn't like I'm not aware of what's happening every day with morning sickness. Or when my clothes suddenly become too tight, even when I'm still getting sick at least a few times a week.

Brenda and I haven't talked about it. She just seems to know I haven't been able to yet. But when we get together on one of our Saturdays off and I ask if she'd like to go clothes shopping, her eyes do a sweep over my body. She clears her throat and I know it's coming.

"We need to get you to a doctor, Caroline. See how far along you might be—"

"I'm afraid once people find out, I'll have to leave. I might lose my job at Shelby's."

I take a deep breath.

"We'll figure it out. What if we tell everyone your husband is in the service? I know—he's in Vietnam…"

I cringe. "That's an awful thing to do, but…it actually might work. I stay to myself pretty much. I can't talk about it because I'm sad he's not here, and I'm not wearing a ring because he wanted to buy me a nice one, so we're waiting till we can afford it," I say, getting more into the story now.

This really might work.

"At least until the baby is born. And then I'll have more to explain."

"So you've accepted that you are?" she asks.

I think about it a moment. The tears I haven't allowed myself come then. "Yeah, I'm certain I am."

We sit on the couch, her arm around me.

"It's gonna be okay, Caroline."

"Brenda, I told you about what happened with Leroy and Les, but I didn't tell you that after that...after I left Tulma, when Isaiah found me...we-we were intimate then."

"You think it could be *his*?" she asks, shocked.

"It's the only way I can get through each day, thinking there's a possibility that it is."

"Are you gonna tell him?"

I think about that long and hard and never answer her.

MY THOUGHTS ARE tormented. The reality that I'm not married and expecting, is horrifying in itself. I've let go of some of the worries about what everyone back in Tulma would think, but the fact is, it's going to be a problem anywhere. It's a good thing I've been by myself, because people sure won't want to stay with me now.

I'm fortunate to look older. But what's really making me crazy is wondering who the father of this baby is. I want it to be Isaiah's so badly, but I know that's probably too much to wish for. It makes me pray to the God I'm not sure about…I plead for him to give me this one thing.

In my new swing shirts and high-waisted clothes, I look pregnant. One morning, I go in early and talk to Shelby before the customers start arriving. I tell her the tale that I rehearsed with Brenda. I feel terrible lying to her, but I just don't want to risk getting run out of town. Chances are, once they see this baby, I will be anyway, but I need to keep a job for as long as possible.

She believes every word I tell her, which makes me feel even worse, even though I'm also very much relieved. My husband was sent to Vietnam just a few weeks ago, out of Fort Knox. I visited him every chance I got before he left and have been quiet about it because I just miss him so much. She wipes a tear from her eyes and reaches over to give me a hug.

"You just say the word, sweetheart, whatever you need. I'll do whatever I can. Where is your family, dear? Are you sure you don't need to go be by them until the baby comes?"

"It's just me," I tell her sadly, leaving her to assume the worst. And she does. It's the most honest thing I tell her.

"Bless your heart, what a hard time this must be. And you're such a good worker, too. You just tell me what you need, okay?"

"Thank you, Miss Shelby. It helps me to keep busy—working here helps."

She gives me another pat on the shoulder. "Well, I certainly love having you here, and the customers sure appreciate your cookin'. Why, I get compliments on your pies every single day!"

I give her a big smile and get to work.

AT NIGHT, I put my hands on my growing stomach. The little bitty ball is firm and beginning to absorb my thoughts. A fierce feeling comes over me. This baby is mine.

I whisper, "You're my baby and I'm going to love you and take care of you. We're going to love each other most. I'll never leave you. I'll protect you from everyone and everything that comes against us. I'm not gonna let anything bad happen to you ever, I promise."

I love the way my body is filling out. I've always felt so gangly; everything on me is long and skinny. The curves are softening all my features and I feel like I fit in my body so much better.

The more my feelings grow for the baby, the more I miss Isaiah. I feel an urgency to see him again. Maybe I should tell him. Even if the baby isn't his, which I don't even want to consider as an option, I just want him to know.

The thought nags me for days. On a whim, I go to Shelby and ask her if I can have an extra couple of days off around Christmas time. She reminds me that she'd said to let her know whatever I needed. I thank her, and then I go tell Brenda my plan. The relief on her face is almost comical.

"Oh, Caroline. I've been hoping you'd do this. I'm so glad." She clasps her hands together and helps me get my things packed.

I'm able to afford a bus ticket to Tulma. At the crack of dawn on the Sunday morning after Christmas, I board the bus. Hours go by with me staring out the window, dreaming of seeing Isaiah, what I'll say to him, what he'll say. The excitement and nervousness builds with each mile. We stop a few times, and I freshen up in one of the restrooms. As we get closer, I nearly lose my nerve and turn around to go back. But the thought of being with Isaiah drives me forward.

When we finally arrive in Tulma, I'm the only one to get off at the stop. I walk through the bus station quickly, hoping I won't see anyone I know. Taking the back way, I walk to Isaiah's church. He should be getting out of church soon. Hopefully I can see him right away.

The breeze from the river picks up. It feels good to be home. I wish I could see everyone, but my bulging stomach kinda ruins that plan. I wrap my sweater tighter around me. Finally I wind around the corner and lean against the tree by the church. It's large enough that I can stand behind it without anyone seeing me.

I hear the organ playing and know they're almost done. About ten minutes later, people begin filing out. Almost everyone leaves and then there's a lull where no one else comes out. Then Sadie comes out and I feel like a little kid playing hide and seek. All of a sudden, I wish I could find a restroom.

Just when I start thinking he might have stayed home, there he is! My heart thumps in triple time. He looks so handsome in his church clothes. I can't take my eyes off of him. Except…I realize he's not alone. He looks back and a beautiful girl in a pale green dress steps forward. Her skin matches his, and for the first time I know jealousy in its truest, vilest form. She has everything I want.

They look so perfect—like they belong together. It

knocks the wind right out of me.

They walk to a car I don't recognize. She says something and Isaiah's head rears back and he lets out the laugh that I love. The one I haven't heard in so long. He opens the door for her and it's then that I see the look on his face. Looking at her. The way he used to look at me only a few short months ago.

I double over, the pain staggering. It sends me to my knees. Grateful for my hiding spot, I stay there until everyone is gone, my sobs becoming more forceful. Eventually, I make my way back to the bus station, my plan crushed back in the dirt by the tree.

I GET BACK on the bus and ride back to Bardstown, no one in Tulma the wiser.

SWOLLEN, PUFFY MESS

I HIDE OUT in my room. Everyone thinks I'm gone, so I don't bother letting them know otherwise. After becoming a huge, swollen puffy mess from tears and feeling every possible emotion toward Isaiah Washington, I feel the finality of losing him. Every hope I'd been hoarding the past few weeks, months, years…it's completely gone.

I never thought of Isaiah as fickle, so the thought that he could have feelings for someone else this quickly is a shock. I did tell him to go find someone else, after all. I just didn't expect it to be practically overnight. I can't wrap my head around it. Hours and hours of contemplation lead me to the conclusion that he never loved me the way I love him.

Which seems to be a recurring theme in my life.

What seemed like a beautiful memory in Memphis— our time together in that motel room, just the two of us in our hideaway—now has an ugly tarnish to it. It's just like staring through Nellie's dresser mirror, everything is blurry and the edges are completely worn away. Nothing is clear anymore. Now I don't believe that I was meaningful to Isaiah at all. Or maybe being with him in that way opened up something in him that he can't be without.

Mama always did say boys were pigs when it came to s-e-x and to never give one the upper hand by letting him take that part of me. The phrase 'damaged goods' was thrown around. I never did fully understand what she meant until now. Except the difference is I've managed to become triply damaged, all before the age of sixteen. The reality of this unhinges me. I just want to disappear. Please, God. Put me out of this hell.

The days drag in despair. I have to force myself to eat. It feels really strange when I go too long without eating, only further proving that I'm growing someone. At some point—I think when I've eaten all that's left in the cupboard—I start chanting vows to the baby. Like a crazy person. Ranting.

I will never make you wear pink foam curlers.

I will never lie to you.

I will teach you responsibility.

I will spoil you with affection.

I will iron my own clothes.

I will love you even if you're ugly.

I will love you even if I hate your father.

I will never leave you.

You will be my person, my blood, the one I know best, the one I admire most, my baby.

My purpose in life will be to make you shine.

I will be your mama. A real one.

And again from the top. Again and again. Until I'm pacing and crying and blubbering and falling back on the bed and snotting on the pillow. The words rush out of me like a waterfall, promises plunging into the deep. One hope is dying and another is rising in its place.

WHEN I WAKE up the next morning, the sun is shining. It's a new year. My baby will be born in 1972. Feels so strange to say—all of it. I get out of bed and devise a story to tell Shelby soon, about my dead husband.

I pat my stomach. "It's just you and me, baby."

Saying that aloud reminds me of the dream I had in the night. I was holding my baby and she was a perfect little girl. I could see her as clear as day. I grin for the first time in days.

"Okay, baby girl. We're in this together."

Before I go to work, I stop by and hug Brenda, avoiding her eyes. She sees my face and knows.

"Oh, Caroline. I'm sorry. Are you okay?"

"I'll tell you everything later, I really will. I have to get to work."

"I'll come by your room tonight." She gives me a tight hug and looks like she's going to say more but stops herself.

It's a quiet day at Shelby's. A few regulars stop in, but I think most everyone is with their family on New Year's day. We close earlier than usual. I go back to the room wiped out and sleep through the night. In the morning, a note is taped to my door. It's from Brenda. I must have slept right through her visit.

When I do finally tell her the details of my visit to

Tulma, she cries with me. She also says it might not be what I think, but I tell her how he looked at her and she sadly accepts that I'm probably right.

Over the next few weeks, Shelby's is busy, and it makes the time go much faster. I find myself taking more time with the customers, investing in longer conversation, getting to know people better in one sitting than I have in the previous weeks of waiting on them. It takes my mind off my heartache, and also, I think I've accepted that I'm in Bardstown to stay. At least for the time being. And when this baby is born, I'm going to need some allies.

I have a pile of money growing. One day I'll have a house of my own somewhere. With no history but mine with my baby. I hope it will work here—I like this place. But if not, we'll search until we do find a place to make it work.

THE DAY I kill off my pretend husband, I meet ol' Dr. Harrison for the first time. He's been retired for years and besides coming to Shelby's, seems to stay to himself. No one seems to know exactly how old he is. I've heard everything from seventy-five to ninety-two. He's old enough that everyone tacks that ol' on the front of his name.

I've just told Shelby my horrible news and feel like a lily-livered goat of a person when I tell her I need to keep working that day to stay sane for the baby. She cries more than I do and keeps saying I must be in shock or something. I know I'm going to hell.

Usually Shelby takes care of Dr. Harrison because she's says he's an old coot with a toothy bite. She's in the back when he comes in and I don't even think about it—I walk right up to Dr. Harrison's booth to take his order.

"Hello, what can I get for you today?"

He looks up at me as best he can under his huge mound of bushy eyebrows. They're white as meringue and I can't take my eyes off them. I've never been this close to him before. I come to with him snapping his fingers under my nose.

"Pardon me, what was that?"

"I said, I'd like my reg'lar."

"All right. Would you mind telling me what that is?" I look at him and smile, holding a pencil over my small tablet.

"Well, I've come in here every day for years and I've never had to tell anyone my reg'lar." He huffs and I notice his blue eyes finally, since they're glaring at me.

"Yes, but this is the first time I've waited on you."

"I know it. Whatcha got against an old coot like me?"

I guess he's heard his title. I can't help it, I laugh. And not just a little laugh, but a long, loud hysterical laugh—the kind that comes after you've cried far too long. He huffs and blows little Pffts out of his mouth, but as I'm wiping the tears from my eyes and still giggling, I see something shift in his eyes. A softening.

"How far along are you, girl?"

"I'm not sure," I whisper.

His eyebrows collide in a huge V and I get tickled again. He is the cutest old man I have ever seen.

"Well, I've delivered plenty babies in my day and I'd say you're near 'bout five months? That sound 'bout right?"

I hope and pray I'm only five months. With everything that is in me, I wish for that, but I know that I might just be smaller than some.

"Yes, sir," I answer. "That's probably right."

"You and your husband excited 'bout the baby?" he asks.

Shelby comes up then and says, "That's okay, honey, I can take over from here." Her eyes are huge and she tries to shake her head at Dr. Harrison without me seeing but doesn't know subtle from her backside. She gently shoos me off.

"Hey, I want the girl!" Dr. Harrison scowls at Shelby, and she backs away, looking at me with her doe-eyes.

I smile at her. "He'll have his regular, please."

Shelby nods and hustles off to the kitchen.

"Now, what were you sayin' 'bout your husband?" he continues.

I bite the inside of my cheek and take a deep breath before answering. "My husband was a soldier and I just got news that he didn't make it..." Oh God, forgive me, I don't wanna go to hell.

Dr. Harrison blows a big breath out and shakes his head. "I'm so sorry to hear that," he says softly. "So many boys, gone. Generations lost. I lost my boy in the first war...and my beloved grandson in the second." His eyes get even bluer with the tears that fill them. I reach out and take his hand and give it a squeeze. The gesture seems to shock him. He pats my hand and I let go.

"Thank you, girl," he says quietly.

"Caroline," I tell him.

"Thank you, Caroline girl."

HE'S MY CUSTOMER from that moment on. And when he comes through the door every day, Shelby excuses me being with him just about as long as he desires because she's so happy to not have to wait on him anymore. She says I've brought out the nice in him, but when she tries to come around and get friendly with him, he pulls out the grouch act again, so she's given up.

Every time he leaves, I can't wait to see him again. He makes me laugh and seems genuinely interested in knowing what I think about things. Brenda laughs at all my Dr. Harrison stories, and we both swoon over the way he talks about his wife, Eileen, who passed away twenty years ago. He still talks about her like she's right there.

"Caroline girl," he says one Saturday morning, "I brought you something." He holds up a handful of daisies and hands them to me. "I picked them from my garden just before I came and remembered you saying you loved daisies."

"Oh, Dr. H. Thank you," my voice gets caught in my throat and to my embarrassment I get tears in my eyes, "I haven't been given flowers in a long time."

Memories threaten to wash me away, but I squelch them down. Every last caramel-skinned one.

"Well, I've got a garden full. You should come over for iced tea sometime and pick all the flowers you want."

"I would love that!" I tell him and mean it with my whole heart.

I've missed gardening. It's probably a good thing I don't have a yard or the space to grow anything or I'd just miss Miss Greener and home more than I already do. But when I walk into my little place from work, especially when Brenda is working, the time drags on endlessly.

"When would you like to come?" Dr. H asks.

"I'm off tomorrow. After you get home from church maybe?"

He throws his head back and barks out a laugh. We tease each other about our lack of church attendance every chance we get, trying to one-up the other on how non-spiritual we are in a town of spirituals.

"Well, I'll probably beat you there then, since you seem to hightail it away from the altar when the prayer time comes." His shoulders shake as he says it.

"I bet I can be at your house before the offering plate has even reached the third row," I chime in.

"That's doubtful since I will still be seeing the back of my eyelids at that point."

"Pfft. You're an early riser and don't you dare deny it." I pour his third cup of coffee and it's not even eight o'clock yet.

He looks up at me and beams. "I guess that means I'll be seein' ya before nine? I'll let you make the coffee, and if you stay long enough, we'll get to that iced tea!"

That afternoon I ask Shelby if I can make a pie after the restaurant closes. She's fine with me using whatever I want, so I make Dr. Harrison's two favorite things—coconut cream pie and blackberry cobbler. As I'm rolling out the dough into strips for the cobbler, I think about Ruby and all the times I spent in that kitchen with her at Harriet's. I miss her so much, my heart physically aches. The tears roll down my nose and I try to catch them before they drip into the blackberry mixture. I finally lean back on the counter and have a good cry.

All of a sudden, the baby gives me a walloping kick. I've felt little taps here and there and it never ceases to fill me with wonder—that there really is something alive in me, growing in there. This was no tap, though, this one means business. I press on my stomach where I felt the kick and get another jab. I start laughing, along with the tears.

"Hey, little one. I love you. Everything's okay. Mama's gonna be okay. Don't you worry." I cover my stomach with both hands and she shifts. "I'm gonna worry about you, not the other way around, so you just settle on down in there, baby girl." And she does.

THE NEXT MORNING I wake up with new purpose. I put on one of the few things that still fits me—it's time to go get some new things, I'm definitely growing steadily now. I have the desserts set in a box and place it on the front seat next to me, as I head over to Dr. H's house. I haven't been much of anywhere besides across the street, so venturing off the only road I know in Bardstown is already an adventure. I look at the little map he drew for me on a napkin and remember he said it would take about twelve minutes to drive to his house. That's quite a trek around here, where everything is within a couple of minutes, at most. I guess I'd expected it to be closer, since he comes to Shelby's just about every day in his truck. I take a turn here and there, loving the pretty scenery, when I finally see his house down a long road lined with trees on either side.

Spring has already arrived, far earlier than usual, and it's fully apparent on Dr. Harrison's property. He didn't tell me he lived on a plantation. I clamp my gaping mouth shut and slowly creep down the driveway, taking in the beauty. The brick estate is something out of a storybook. I've certainly never been inside such a place. Nellie has told me stories of going through plantations in Louisiana on one of their vacations, but I've never seen one up close myself.

Land sakes.

Seeing a place like this I would have expected roses, rather than daisies, and sure enough, they're blooming in abundance. Peonies, daffodils, tulips, and forsythia are sprinkled throughout, too. Clematis winds over two iron arches on either side of the house. Hydrangeas and roses and even magnolias are everywhere I look.

Once I've gathered my senses, I pick up the box and walk toward the front door. Dr. H opens the door before I've even knocked.

"Caroline girl! Right on time. I couldn't wait—I made some coffee without ya!" He hurriedly takes the box out of my arms and peeks in. "Heavens, girl, what have we got here? Did you do all this?"

I bashfully nod and go inside. Oh my goodness, it would take me all day and then some to see all the pretty things in this house.

"Come on, let's get you inside. I think it's gonna rain out here pretty soon." He shuts the door and looks out the window at the clouds. "Have a seat. Well, first, come, let's get started on these things you made. They look good enough for Jesus."

And just like that, my nerves disappear.

21

MOVIN'

AFTER THAT FIRST visit with Dr. H, I go all the time. Every day off and some afternoons when I get off early, I head over and help him in the garden. Or make supper for him. Or read a book while he reads his. Sometimes when his eyes get tired, I'll read the paper to him. He seems to love me being there just as much as I do, and I feel so much better when I'm around him.

I take Brenda over there once in a while, and she loves it there too. He's never grouchy with her either. I'm starting to think he just didn't care for Shelby. He's taken me through all the rooms now. There are eight large bedrooms, one large kitchen and a smaller one off of the servants' quarters. Dr. H lives in the servants' quarters, which still shocks me to no end. I think about it for days after he tells me that. I just can't believe he'd have all those rooms and stay in the tiny stark room off the kitchen.

"Once the children grew up and moved away, there was no use for all this room. And then when Eileen died …I just didn't even want to try to stay in the same bedroom any longer. But this home meant everything to my daddy. I don't want to leave it."

All three of his children died long ago, even most of his grandchildren. I get the impression he regrets not having a close relationship with his boys or with the rest of his grandchildren. It sounds like he was always working so hard to keep the plantation afloat after his father died, that he missed out on a lot of years with his children. When we talk about his family, he gets sad, so we rarely talk about any of them but Eileen.

I still haven't gotten the nerve to ask just how old he is, but I'm thinking he has to be over 90.

One night in early April, I'm visiting Dr. H and feeling particularly tired and huge. He asks me to come sit with him. I set the drying towel over the sink ledge and go sit on the couch by his chair. I feel the beginnings of a waddle coming on and I'm trying to avoid it with every step. My back hurts. I worked a long shift at Shelby's and had already said I'd come see Dr. H before I knew I'd have to work such a grueling day. He hasn't been in the diner for a few days, feeling a little under the weather. It feels good to sit down. I must let out a huge sigh or something because Dr. H turns to me and chuckles.

"You work too hard, Caroline girl. You're in the last stretch, aren't ya? Needin' to take it more easy now, hear me?"

"I hear ya. I just have to keep workin' as long as I possibly can."

Dr. H looks at me with his watery eyes and studies my face and my stomach. "I don't know why you don't just come stay here. You know there's more than enough room."

He brings this up now at least once every visit. I

would love nothing more than to stay here with him, but as long as I'm working, it's handy to be across the street from the diner. And I don't know how he'd really feel about having a baby in the house later on. It's one thing to say that I'm welcome now, and another when there's a baby crying in the middle of the night. Although as big as this house is, he probably wouldn't hear a thing.

"You drinkin' enough water?" he asks.

"Yes, sir, I think so."

"Taking vitamins?"

"I started once you told me to."

"What has your doctor said lately about everything? You on schedule and all? You never do tell me what the doctor's sayin'." The way he looks at my stomach, I can tell he's assessing it with his medical eye.

I usually avoid the topic of the doctor and specifics with my due date like it's the plague, but for some reason, tonight the evasions don't come quickly for me. I stare back at him and my face crumbles. Shoot, fire, save the matches.

"What is it, dear?" He leans forward in his chair and lays his leathery hand on my arm. His eyes look so concerned, it makes the tears start flowing.

"I never went to the doctor, Dr. H," I confess.

I put my face in my hands and try to wipe the tears as fast as they're coming, but there's no catching them all.

"Child, why ever not?" he asks in alarm. "You're saying you haven't been at *all*? Is it money? I don't know why you're fighting me on that."

I know without looking that his eyebrows are doing that thing I love where they're all bunched up in one big fluffy white mess.

"Well, we're going tomorrow and that's that. I can call Dr. Mansfield first thing in the morning and he'll fit you in." His voice softens. "You've already proven you are quite independent, my dear. Let me help you. I don't know what you're trying to pr–"

"You know I can't take it, Dr. H," I interrupt. "I'm doing fine. I'm saving money even, it's just–"

The sob gets stuck in my throat and I can't gulp it away. It comes gushing out.

He gets up and sits next to me on the couch, leaning my head over onto his shoulder. I sit there and cry for I don't know how long. He pats my head gently and makes soothing sounds until I catch my breath and stop wailing.

"I haven't been honest with you, Dr. H," I whisper.

"Oh? Well, I reckon we all have secrets we want to keep," he says. "But you ought to know, I have a few of my own. Maybe we have some surprises left in us after all?" He laughs. "I've lived long enough that I don't think I have a judgin' bone in my body. That left, along with my pride, a long, long time ago. Whatever you say here won't go past these walls."

I look over at him and pat his hand that rests on my arm. Distractedly, I push along the old man veins on his hand and arm. When I push down, with barely any resistance, the skin indents and stays that way for a few minutes. Slowly, with lots of starts and stops, I tell him my story. Just as when I told Brenda, he doesn't react like he wants to hang me by the toes when I tell him about loving Isaiah. I have a feeling he knew the story about my husband wasn't true. Tears slowly roll down his cheeks when I tell him about Les and Leroy.

"I'm scared to know," I whisper. "I want this baby to

198

be Isaiah's more than anything, but...I'd rather just not even know. I'm gonna love this baby whether it's his or not." I blow my nose in the hankie Dr. H hands me. "Oh, and I'm not quite sixteen, but I will be next month," I finish. "And that really is everything—pretty much all the secrets I've got."

"Fifteen?" He shakes his head. "Mercy me."

He pulls another handkerchief out of the end table drawer and gives his nose a good honk.

"Caroline, listen to me." He turns my head to face him and makes sure I'm looking in his eyes before he continues. "Even though you've only been in my life a short time, we've covered more ground in one day than I ever have with any of my family, besides Eileen, of course. And it's that way every time we're together—was right from the start." He grins at me. "You feel more like family than any of my grandchildren or even my own children ever did, and that's worth more to me than I can even tell you."

He leans his forehead over on mine for a second and I sniffle.

"Now," he says in his gruff voice that I know isn't really gruff, "here's what we're gonna do. I want you to move into this house...the sooner, the better. I'm not gonna take any more arguments about it. You don't need to raise a baby in a tiny motel room, I won't stand for it. And I might be old, but maybe now I can finally learn how to be a proper grandfather." He chuckles and gives me a wink. "Or Papa—do I look like a Papa?"

I wrap my arms around him and squeeze him until he squeaks out a cough. "Oh, sorry!" I half-laugh and half-hiccup. "Yes, you do look like a Papa. And I like you far better than my own," I admit.

He pats my leg before getting up and walking to his desk across the room.

"Well, we can just keep that to ourselves, in case I ever run into him," he says. "Although, I do have some things I'd like to say to all of your family!"

He shakes his head sadly. He rolls back the top of his desk and pulls out a little key to unlock one of the compartments. I see his mouth shift when he finds what he's looking for. He brings it back to me, opening my hand to give me a key.

"This is a key to the house. It's yours now."

I stutter and don't know whether to laugh or start crying again.

"Thank you, Dr. H." I hug his neck. "It'll take a little while before I get used to calling you Papa, but know that's what you already are to me."

He smiles so big, his cheeks nearly reach his eyebrows. "You can call me whatever you want to, child. Now, how about you get going to that room of yours tonight, rest, get packed up and tomorrow after your appointment with Dr. Mansfield, we'll bring your things back here to stay."

I nod, too overwhelmed to do anything else.

He gives my hand another pat. "I've been wishing you'd say yes for a long time. It's gonna be real good to have laughter in this house again, Caroline, real good."

THE NEXT MORNING, Dr. H calls with the time for my

appointment and fifteen minutes before we're supposed to arrive, he pulls up in his pickup truck to take me to the doctor. I barely have anything to put in the back. A suitcase and a couple bags of food are pretty much all I own.

It's handy to not have to crouch down to get in a car. I can just lean sideways and sort of fall right into the truck. I feel like I've grown overnight, so any little bit of help is appreciated. Spring has already jumped on ahead to summer, even though it's not technically due for another couple of months. Apparently you can't tell that to Kentucky, just like you can't in Tennessee. Sweat rolls down my back and my dress sticks to my skin. My hair is pulled up in a high ponytail. If my mama could see me now. She'd be throwing out a comment about me looking like something the cat dragged in. I'm too pregnant to care.

"Let me get this air working for ya, Caroline girl. You look downright miserable."

"I don't know what I'd do if I were short. A lady came in the diner last week and she was a petite little thing and her pregnant belly looked like it went right up to her neck, like she was choking with baby."

I shudder just thinking about it. I don't think I've ever been so grateful to be tall as I was when I saw her trying to catch a breath.

Dr. H lets out a laugh so loud the windows of the truck give a tiny rattle. "You do say the funniest things, child."

I grin at him lovingly. In such a short amount of time, he has become the happiest part of my day. When he calls me *child*, my gut aches for Ruby, I miss her every single day. I don't know how I would have survived without Dr.

H. When I'm away from him, all I can do is pine for Isaiah. I'm still angry with him and so heartbroken, but I miss him so much, it hurts. Every night, I go through a grieving process that I know needs to end soon. I can't keep mourning the loss of Isaiah or I will be no good to this baby.

I sure wish Isaiah could meet Dr. H, though. He'd love him too. Thinking of Isaiah sobers me up quick. I look out the window and wish for the day that Isaiah isn't always the one my thoughts lead to…

The first thing Dr. H says to Dr. Mansfield when we get inside the small office is: "I'd like you to meet my granddaughter, Caroline. She's had a hard way to go— husband di—" he keeps talking, but it's all mumbled and then comes back strong with, "—carrying this baby by herself. She's a young little thing, but tough as my Aunt Euler. I want you to take good care of her, Joseph, ya hear me?"

Dr. Mansfield nods his head gravely and looks at me with sympathy. I blush from head to toe. When Dr. H leaves the room and throws a wink over his shoulder, I get a mad case of the giggles. I try to get a serious face back, to at least match Dr. Mansfield's sorrowful expression.

After answering a million questions, Dr. Mansfield does an examination and takes measurements. It's appalling enough to convince me to never have another baby ever again. He pulls his hand out of me and I look everywhere in the room but at him. He clears his throat.

"Everything feels good. You have the perfect birth canal for having a baby."

I confess to tuning out to whatever he said after *perfect birth canal*, but my ears perk up at this:

"Given that you don't know the date of your last cycle, I can't give an exact due date, but I'd say you're measuring about right for late May to early June."

I want to ask if he can tell me when that would mean I conceived, but I don't have the nerve. His answer doesn't tell me anything. I still don't know. But I'm not as upset as I thought I would be.

Brenda would say it's a blessing because she knows my mind has been all-consumed by knowing who the daddy is. But today, it's enough to know that my baby is okay. I have a place to call home now. And as odd as it may be, I can be happy that even though it's small, I even have some semblance of a family.

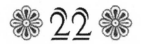

NEW ROUTINES

ONCE AGAIN I have another new routine that I've fallen into, except this is one I love. Dr. H—my beloved papa— and I get up every morning, have a cup of coffee together, and then he drives me over to Shelby's. He stays there for a little while, chats with some of his friends, and then comes back to pick me up in the afternoon. In the evenings, Brenda will come visit and we listen, enraptured, to Dr. H's stories about the love of his life and their romance.

Not long after I move in, Dr. H comes and finds me outside, working in his garden. I can't really get to anything too low or I'll never get back up again, but everything higher is properly deadheaded and pruned. He comes along behind me and does what I can't reach.

"Come here, love, I want to show you somethin'," he says, standing at the end of the roses.

I wipe my head and pull off the gardening gloves. He holds out his arm and I hook mine through it. We walk past the gardens, past the grapes that have kept the plantation going for years, and around the curve of an outbuilding. Taking my hand, he helps me inside the barn and leads me to a spot in the floor that looks like any other. He bends down with a grunt and lifts the slabs of wood one at a time. Underneath the wood, I see steps leading down into a dark room.

"Now when you've had this baby and are feeling spry again, I'll bring you back here. But I wanted you to know about this place, Caroline. And you'll see why, even though I jest about not settin' foot in a church and all, you'll know I believe God brought you to me for a reason."

He has my curiosity fully wrapped by now. I look at him, waiting to hear everything.

"Right down there is a tunnel. It leads all the way back to the other side of town and comes out at the railroad. Imagine the worst horrors you've seen of people being mistreated, and that's what my daddy saw when he was a young man. He helped many, many people get to freedom through this tunnel, and as a boy, I helped him. Not so many years ago, I'm sad to say there was still a need for it. I'll never understand why people see color as a dividin' line." His eyes look pained as he says this. "Now, I show this to you because I want you to know the history that's here. The fact that you're bringing your baby into this home is not small or irrelevant to me. I like to think it's a way of the heavens thankin' my family for what we did and blessin' us with a new life to carry on here." He wipes his face with his handkerchief and shakes his head, moved at the thought. "No small matter, a'tall."

I wipe the tears from my eyes, something I've had to do non-stop since being pregnant, it seems, but this is finally something worthy of a river of tears. I stand there taking in all that he's just told me.

"I'm honored to know you, Papa," I tell him.

"No, we only did what every decent person should have done. I'm glad we were able to find a way." He puts his arm around my shoulders and squeezes. "I'm not naive about what might happen though, when people see that baby of yours…which is the other reason I showed you this, Caroline. You need to know how to get out quickly if it were to ever come to that."

He looks at me gravely and I swallow a hard lump. I know he's right, but hearing it out loud makes it all the more real. He lowers his head, closes his eyes and we're silent. I'm imagining all the people who have come through here, scared, possibly leaving everything they've ever known to find safety and acceptance.

I rub my stomach, thinking I will always do all I can to protect this child from knowing that pain, but wondering what challenges will face us. It feels like we've got an uphill battle before we've ever even begun.

THE END OF May will mark another birthday coming and going. Sixteen. Hard to believe. I feel like an old woman already. Lugging this massive stomach around makes me feel about thirty. They throw a shower/birthday party for me at Shelby's a couple weeks before my birthday. As I blow out the birthday candles, I feel a mixture of melancholy and genuine happiness. I've eased into a new life that has been, in some ways, far more wonderful than anything I've known. I still cry when I get in bed, remembering my last birthday with Isaiah, but I can't even be angry with myself for still caring. I'm accep-ting it's just the way it is and the way it will probably always be. It's just proof that my heart is unwavering. I wish he'd deserved it, but I can't help that.

I wake up about three in the morning after my party cry, feeling very uncomfortable. I sit up and ease my feet over the bed, trying to get up. I stand up and double over. Something has changed with the baby. Everything feels lower, a *lot* lower. I shuffle to the bathroom, still doubled over, and before I open the door, my abdomen hardens. It hurts. I make it to the restroom and contemplate getting in the tub and washing my hair, just in case this is it. I stand there long enough to feel another pain and decide to just go lie back down.

It eases when I get settled on my side, but I still don't feel quite right. I watch the sun rise through the lace curtains in the room I'm staying in. I can't say it's my room just yet, but I do know it's the prettiest room in the house. I study every beautiful line on the furniture, the pretty arched door frame, and out the window at the magnolia tree that's in my line of vision. Anything to distract me from what might be happening in my body.

Around eight o'clock, Papa knocks gently on the door. "Caroline girl, you okay?"

I'm normally up by seven with him.

"Come in, Papa. I'm not feeling too good."

His forehead is etched with deep grooves of worry when he walks through my bedroom door. He comes over and puts his hand to my head, checking to see if I have a fever.

"You feel a mite warm. What's been happenin'?"

"It feels like she's dropped and is just sittin' right on my bladder. I've been having pains, too, but they're a little better right now. Earlier the pains were coming every three minutes, but in the last thirty minutes, they've stopped."

He nods his head. "I wish you'd called me, dear. I thought I was letting you sleep in." He gives me a sweet grin. "We'll just keep an eye on this. It's possible you're in the early stages. I can call Shelby for you, tell her you won't be in…I think you probably need to be done with workin', Caroline. Shelby will understand. She knows you're close now."

I nod. I haven't wanted to stop until the very last possible minute, but the thought of being on my feet with the baby hanging past my drawers sounds awful.

"Tell her I'll call her later this afternoon to give her an update, but I think you're right, I'm gonna have to slow down, if nothing else."

He scoffs and I can hear him muttering about me 'slowing down' as his feet patter out the door.

"I'll make you something to eat!" he hollers when he reaches the end of the hall.

"Thank you!" I holler back.

That whole day I stay in bed. Every time I attempt getting up, it feels like the baby is just gonna slip right out. Shelby ends up calling me in the afternoon, beating me to the punch.

"Now you listen here, Caroline, you stay home from here on. You hear me? We've known it could be any time and we're gonna be all right. You just take care of you and that baby, okay?"

I thank her and take a nap. Now that I'm horizontal, I realize how worn out I've been.

The next morning I feel a little better and am able to get up and do a few things around the house. I mostly sit, though, and work on sewing baby pajama sacks. I resist making any in pink, even though I know this baby is a girl like I know my name is Caroline. Sewing makes me miss Nellie and sometime during the course of the day, I decide to write her a letter to let her know how I'm doing.

Dear Nellie and Grandpaw,

I'm okay. I've found a nice place to settle down and it's starting to feel more like home each day. I've made new friends, so I'm not as lonesome for Tulma as I thought I might be. I do think about you often and hope that all is well with you. Please don't tell anyone that I wrote. I'd just as soon everyone there forget about me, so we can all move on, but I did want to let you know that I'm doing just fine. Know that you are always in my heart.

With loving thoughts,

Caroline

I didn't expect it, but I feel better when I write the note…like I've just been released of a lifetime of expectation. I love my grandparents, but there's never been any doubt that I see the world so differently than they do. They will never accept the baby I'm carrying, no matter the circumstances in which it might have come into this world. In fact, it's just another strike against it, if it is—well, I can't even think about that right now. I'd rather remember my grandparents with fondness than hate them for the injustice I know deep down would occur if they were around my baby. I could never do that to any child of mine. It's best that I got out of there when I did.

THE REST OF the week is a seesaw of stops and starts. I feel awful. I feel okay. I hurt. I'm fine. I think I'm in labor. I'm ready to clean the entire house. We get to the actual week of my birthday and I'm tired of crashing hard on the pendulum. I go for a long walk, determined to go ahead and get this baby out. No more pussyfootin' around. Maybe we'll end up sharing a birthday.

I walk and walk and in the last ten minutes of the walk, the pain intensifies about a hundred notches. When it eases up somewhat, I walk faster, realizing this wasn't the smartest idea I've ever had. As Nellie would say, my brain is rattlin' around like a BB in a boxcar. To make matters worse, I don't see Papa's truck out in the yard. I think he had a meeting in town and start a prayerful intercession that he will come home soon.

As I set foot into the kitchen, I have to lean onto the counter for several minutes. A pain comes sharp and fast. I grip the edges of the sink and slowly breathe in and out. Just then a little trickle runs down my leg and I panic, thinking it's going to be a gush. As soon as my pregnancy started showing, the horror stories began, particularly at the diner. I've heard more than I ever needed to know, and have been terrified since, that my water would break in some sort of horrifying and embarrassing situation. I'm shocked that this tiny trickle is all there is.

The pains feel like they're coming quickly, but I think they're still five minutes apart. I've always thought I could tolerate pain pretty well, but holy cripe, this hurts. Sweat is pouring out of me. I make it to the bathroom and run the shower, determined that I'll go in the hospital clean. It takes all the willpower I possess to be in the water for a minute. I'm in just long enough to rinse off the sweat, and when I get out, I bite down on a towel during the contraction. I put on one of the few dresses that still fits, grab my overnight bag, and sit by the door, waiting for Papa to get home. The contractions get closer together. The only sound in the house is my ragged breathing. I swipe the tears off my cheeks and when I think I can't take anymore, I pick up the phone and dial.

Thankfully, she's the one who answers. When she hears it's me, she cries out and says, "Darlin', as I live and breathe, I was just thinkin' 'bout you!"

"Can you come? Can you please come?" I gasp out. I tell her where I am and as soon as it seems she has it straight, I hang up.

It might be hours or it might be seconds. It feels like an eternity.

Surely I am dying.

The pain, good God and Lucifer, it hurts so bad.

How could this happen to me?

I hate everyone I have ever known.

I want to be shot.

Now. Just take me now, Lord. What did I ever do to you? I really want to know.

Kill me. Please.

Get this creature that is clawing me inside out—get it out.

I hate Eve. Stupid Eve and that stupid apple. What in the world was she thinking, eating that stupid fruit and causing all this affliction on womankind for the rest of forever.

I get on the floor, desperate to find a comfortable spot, and am there when Papa comes home. He's frantic. He calls the ambulance and they arrive quickly. They put an oxygen mask on me and several pairs of worried eyes look down at me. We get to the hospital and I'm wheeled directly to the delivery room. The contractions are making my eyes roll back in my head. I feel like I'm losing all sense of reality.

I push when they tell me to push. And vow to myself that I will never ever let another man get near my nether regions to do this awful thing to me ever, ever again. Never in a million years ever.

"Okay, Caroline, this should be the last push! Get a deep breath and when I say go, you push. Ready?"

"I CAN'T WAIT," I yell.

This baby wants out of me and I want it out so bad. I bite down on a towel my nurse has given me to clutch and push until I can't push anymore. Every cell shakes as the blaze ignites every crevice of my body. God, it hurts.

And then she's out. I hear a lusty cry and they flop her tiny body on my chest.

IS THIS WHAT love is? I look at Gracie Mae and feel like my heart is going to burn right out of my chest, it's so full of love for her. She's smaller than they expected. Just barely over 4 pounds. I look in her eyes and know the reason. I would have loved her no matter what. There is no doubt in my mind. Before she was even born, her love began healing me. But when I see her face, I shake as the sobs overtake me.

She is, without a doubt, Isaiah Washington's daughter.

23

SAVED

A YEAR LATER

GRACIE IS GOING to be a year old tomorrow. In some ways, it's gone much smoother than I expected. It's true that having a child so young has made me ancient before my time, but I'm pretty sure I already was before Gracie ever came along. Maybe she's the reason I had to grow up so fast.

RUBY ARRIVED THE night before we came home from the hospital with Gracie. As soon as she heard the anguish in my voice over the phone, she left Harriet's and packed everything she'd need to come stay awhile. Once she was here, we knew we couldn't ever be apart again. She's gonna go wherever I go and vice versa.

Ruby was the angel I saw as we pulled into the driveway with Papa, bringing Gracie home for the first time.

Standing out front, her white apron blowing in the slight breeze and her hand up to her mouth, she watched for us.

Before I could get out, she was opening the car door for me and holding me tight. I don't know whose tears fell more, hers or mine. I'd never been so happy to see someone in all my life. She saved me. Ruby and Gracie and Papa. They saved me.

AFTER I PUT Gracie to bed, I help Ruby make the cake for Gracie's birthday. We're having a party tomorrow, just something small to break the monotony of all the busyness that's been going on around the plantation. I say small—the party keeps getting more elaborate every time Papa goes into town.

"I just can't resist giving her this one more thing!" he says.

I just can't resist anything he does. He is crazy over my girl and me. The love he and Ruby shower over us has been enough to make up for a lifetime of neglect. Every day I wake up excited to see my Gracie and happy to face a day with this family.

It hasn't all been easy. I don't take Gracie into town very often because of all the looks people throw our way. The older she gets, the darker her skin turns and someone inevitably makes a comment. Her hair is getting longer, and it's the most perfect shade of caramel. I like her curls wild and don't want to have to tame them for going into town. I do, though, because it seems to invite trouble when I don't.

Miss Shelby bit her tongue many times from what I knew she was dying to ask, until finally, when Gracie was about four months old, I came out with it. I figured we'd worked together long enough that I should tell the truth and let her decide what to do with the information.

Once I told her the full story, she was quiet for a long time. I apologized profusely for lying to her. I felt horribly guilty for my soldier story. She ended up saying she understood why I'd done it.

"Truth of the matter is, I wish you hadn't told me," she said.

She quietly admitted that she might not have given me the job if she'd known I was having a 'colored baby'. By that time, though, she loved Gracie.

"You can barely even tell she's black," she said. Like that was a good thing.

It's those little backhanded ways the people have here that makes it challenging. Painful. Jarring. On the one hand, they are kind and do care; and on the other, there are still prejudices that run deeper than the Mississippi River. Here we might as well be back in 1950. I know it would be that much worse in Tulma.

I can't shop at the corner market next to Shelby's. Or go to the gas station across the street from the doctor's office. More than once I've come home clutching my baby and whispering loving words in her ear to ward off all the evil that's just been spoken over her. It was one thing when she couldn't talk, now she's starting to understand way more than anyone thinks. Just last week, I stood up to a woman in Shelby's. When Papa came in with Gracie and she ran up to me to pick her up, saying *Mama*, the woman got a grotesque look on her face.

"That baby yours?" she practically snarled.

"Yes, ma'am, she sure is," I said, kissing Gracie's face. I took napkins out of my apron pocket to set on the woman's table and as I was walking away, the napkins all scattered to the floor.

The woman had shoved them off her table.

"I aint gonna be waited on by no nigger lover," she said.

I covered Gracie's ears, picked up the napkins off the floor, and said, "Well, I guess you better keep moving on outta town. Don't settle here. I'm not gonna let my daughter be surrounded by people like you. And we're not goin' anywhere."

I acted tough, but I shook for about an hour after the encounter.

It's one of the reasons I've agreed to open a bed and breakfast at the plantation. Papa is the one who mentioned it first, once he tasted the heavenlies, otherwise known as Ruby's cooking. In a month, we're having our grand opening. I've already set it up with Shelby to quit working at the diner a week before we open the Inn, so I can help finish up the last-minute preparations.

We talked it over with Brenda too, not wanting to take any business from her. But all her rooms are now rented out for longer stays, and she likes that better anyway.

I'll be able to have Gracie with me all day. We won't have to go into town as much, and we'll hopefully make a little money to keep everything running. According to Papa, we don't need to do a single thing, he'd be just fine if we sat in the living room reading all day, every day. But he's learned that Ruby and I don't know the meaning of not working, so he's just trying to be accommodating with us at this point, I think. And I'd venture to say, he admires our drive to do something worthwhile.

He strolls into the kitchen with a glass of scotch. I hold out a spoon of cake batter for him to try and he rolls his eyes back in his head when he takes a bite.

"How did I get so lucky to find you?" he asks.

"You're easy to please." I laugh and reach out to lay down some stray brows that are covering his eye.

"That's not the truth. I didn't even like cake before y'all got a hold of me."

"I don't blame ya! I tasted what they's eating at Shelby's and that ain't good for the soul," Ruby claims. "Not using enough vanilla over there," she whispers to me.

"Well, when we open the Magnolia Inn, everyone is gonna be clamoring to taste your cooking, Ruby." I lean over and kiss her cheek. "They can't help it that they're not as good as you."

"Honey, you is getting to be every bit as good a cook as me." Ruby shakes her head and tries to tone down the smile that takes over her face every time I love on her.

I WAKE UP to little girl kisses on my eyelids. Gracie knows how to climb out of her crib already, and she dives into bed with me every morning. We cuddle for a while and then we go to the bathroom. I set her up on the toilet and she tinkles. She's been doing this since she was nine months old. Nellie always said you just have to learn a child's schedule. Take them every half hour when starting to potty train, until you learn when they go. She was right. It works like clockwork—either that or my little girl is just brilliant. However, Nellie had her brothers and sisters potty trained long before nine months, so I think she might have been onto something.

Gracie is an early talker, too, like I was. I never believed my parents about all the things I was supposedly saying before I was even a year old, but now I've seen it's possible.

"Happy Birthday to you," I sing as I run Gracie's bath water. She hums along with me and happily splashes around in the bubbles.

We hear Brenda before we see her. She comes in the bedroom, saying, "Where's the birthday girl?"

"We're in the bathroom," I yell.

"Baffwoom," Gracie echoes. "Buffday, Mama, buff-day."

She wants me to keep singing, so I do. I've been sing-ing her birthday song for a week. She's still not tired of it.

"There she is! I hear the birthday girl." Brenda comes into the bathroom holding so many balloons, we can't see her face.

Gracie lets out a huge gasp and we get tickled at her. "Boooon," she shrieks.

"Oh, that was worth it." Brenda laughs. "You like these 'boons'?"

"Ont boon!" Gracie tries to get out of the bath as fast as her chubby little legs will take her.

"Slow down, Gracie. They're not going anywhere!" I help her out of the bath and dry her off.

Brenda hands her the balloons while she's still naked and I give Brenda a mock glare.

"What?"

"I'll never get her dressed now!"

"Oh, oops."

Sure enough, Gracie takes off flying with the balloons, streaking through the house like a banshee. There's lots of squealing and giggling, and then a single pop.

Everyone freezes.

And then the wail comes.

"Boooooooon," she cries.

"Come on, little nekkid jaybird, let's get you dressed." I pick her up, balloons and all. We navigate back to the bedroom, careful not to pop another one, and get the birthday girl ready for her big day.

THE BOONS, THE cake and the wrapping paper are Gracie's favorite gifts of the day. Among other things, Papa's big gift to her is a tricycle, which looks huge next to her. She crawls up on it and then wants help getting off when it moves. It's gonna give me a heart attack, I just know it. Ruby made her some pretty little dresses. How she found the time to do it without me knowing, I'll never know. I save her present from me for last and give it to her right before she goes to bed. Her sweet face lights up when she sees it.

It's a baby doll, one that has a soft body and eyes that open and shut. She plays with the eyes for a long time in her crib. Open, shut, open, shut.

When I lean over to kiss her goodnight, she wraps her arms tight around my neck and squeezes. I give her a butterfly kiss by her eyelashes, an Eskimo kiss by her nose, a monkey kiss with our cheeks, a giraffe kiss with our necks, and a Mama kiss on the lips.

And then I have to do the whole thing with the baby doll.

WHEN I GO back into the kitchen to start cleaning up, Ruby and Brenda stop in mid-chatter. They give me a guilty look and then try to start up a conversation that was obviously not what they were talking about before I entered the room.

"What are you two sayin'?" I call them out. "You both look like you done swallowed a canary whole."

Brenda is the first to confess. "I was just telling Ruby that Charlie has a friend from Elizabethtown who has been coming over some weekends. He's cute, Caroline! *Really* cute."

She looks at Ruby again and lets out a nervous laugh. Ruby gives her an encouraging nod.

"I think you should go out with him," Brenda says super fast.

I groan and start shaking my head while she continues to rattle off facts about him. Ever since she started dated Charlie, she thinks I have to be with someone too.

"How long have you been doin' inventory on this guy, Bren? Doesn't it bother Charlie that his girlfriend is so knowledgable about his friend?"

She grins wider. "Charlie's the one who told me all of this. He thinks *Robert* would like you so much and wants you to give him a try."

"Robert, huh. Well, does *Robert* know I have a little girl?"

I already know the answer. It'll be the same answer she gives me every time she tries to talk me into going out with someone.

"Not yet, Caroline. But…"

"But what? Why would I waste someone's time when I already know they won't be able to handle me already having a little girl?"

We've gone round and round about this and Brenda usually backs off, but this time she does a little stomp with her foot and turns pink.

"Once someone gets to know you, they won't care! You're seventeen, Caroline. It's time for you to have some fun."

"Did you just stomp your foot at me?" I grin and then get riled up. "My life is never gonna be the typical, Brenda. I gave up wishing for that a long time ago. And— I'm not gonna like anyone anyway. That's what you don't seem to understand. I fell in love already. I had someone who was everything I wanted. I didn't get to keep him. And I'll never get over him."

Brenda and Ruby share another look, and I brace myself for what else they've discussed without me.

"You need to tell him, Caroline."

I move to the chair and sit down, the wind knocked out of me. My eyes blur and I grip the edges of the table-cloth to keep my hands from shaking.

"Isaiah would want to know, honey, you know he would. I've been tryin' to give you time, but…our baby girl is a year old. Look at all he's already missed out on,"

Ruby says so softly I have to strain to hear her.

I lay my head down on the table and the tears all drip onto the table. When I raise my head back up, I have to grab a paper towel to blow my nose.

"You think I don't think about this? Every single day. It's *all* I think about. I feel so guilty for keeping it from him. He would love her so much. I just—I can't go back to Tulma. I can't. *Gracie's* life is good here. It would be harder for her in Tulma, you know it would, Ruby. I just haven't been able to put her through that, not even now when she's too little to understand it. Everyone there knows my history."

"If you'd been there, it would have given everyone time to come around to the idea of you having Gracie. All your customers at Harriet's—they's not all bad people. They love you there. And they eventually would Gracie too."

"I was nearly killed there. Les and Leroy might be gone, but their families haven't forgotten me. I feel like I'd be putting Gracie at risk there and myself too. And I can't leave Papa," I whisper. "He has changed my whole life by loving me. I can't leave him."

Ruby walks over and stands behind my chair. I lean my head over on her stomach and she strokes my hair.

"I don't want you to leave Bardstown!" Brenda's voice wobbles across the room. She finds the softer tissue and gives her nose a big honk. "But at least give Isaiah a chance to know about his baby girl. I think the guilt is killing you. You're never without a smile, but I see the shadows around your eyes and the way you drift off into your thoughts after Gracie has just done something adorable."

"She's right, darlin', you's needin' some closure to

move on with your life. And that baby girl in there needs a daddy."

We hash over it for hours.

Papa comes in and adds his two cents, which is, "Tell him."

They've all said it at one time or another, but now the three of them ganging up on me all at once is a bombardment. Darts all flying with single purpose straight into my heart and not letting me recover before shooting another, I heed their words.

AT TWO IN the morning, I begin my letter to him.

Dear Isaiah—

It seems trite to start this letter off with any small talk. We were never about that, were we? But I do want to ask the questions that could seem like small talk if you didn't know how much I cared to know the answers.

How are you? That would be at the top of my list. What's new with you? is another. I really, really want to know. Every day I think about you and wonder these things. I wonder if you've found love with the girl I saw you laughing with one Sunday after church. I wonder if you kiss her and have forgotten my kisses...

I crumble it up and start over.

Isaiah—

I have something to tell you and I am so sorry for not

telling you sooner. You will hate me and you will have every right to.

We have a daughter.

Her name is Gracie Mae and she is the most beautiful child you've ever seen. She has your eyes, Isaiah. That's how I knew she was yours. She's so smart, further proof that your blood is running through her veins. She is so full of life. It's impossible to not smile when you're around her.

I came back to tell you I was pregnant. I knew you'd want to know, even if the baby wasn't yours. I saw you with a beautiful girl outside your church. You walked with her and laughed with her...and you looked at her with the same adoration that you used to look at me. I just couldn't ruin your life anymore, Isaiah. I couldn't do it.

I also couldn't stay around to watch you fall in love with someone else. You will always have my heart, Isaiah. I'm not too proud to say it. When I fell for you, it was for keeps.

The fact that I haven't told you about Gracie has haunted me. Please know that it has never been out of anger that I've kept the truth from you. Our love was never without complication, and I've wished to spare you from any more of that. But that's just not real life. And I know that I can't keep our baby in a bubble for much longer. God knows I've tried.

I'm just outside of Bardstown, Kentucky. At the old Harrison plantation. In a month, we'll be opening up a bed and breakfast here called The Magnolia Inn. If you ever want to see her, I will never ever deny you.

Caroline

❀ 24 ❀

BLESSED DISTRACTION

THE MAGNOLIA INN is thriving. We've filled all five of the Inn bedrooms for the last twelve weekends. And some of those have been filled throughout the week, too. I keep it spotless and help check people in and out. When I've done the cleaning and laundry for the day, I work on the garden with Papa. The guests are raving about the dishes Ruby makes. She swears that the vegetables and fruit from our garden are what makes everything so tasty. She cooks a fancy breakfast every morning and also supper Friday and Saturday night and Sunday afternoon.

Our flowers fill every room. I do a huge arrangement for the living room and dining room every five days or so. Ruby says that might be my calling.

Gracie floats in and out, charming everyone with her sunshine. She stays by my side most of the day, dragging Dolly along as "we" clean.

Papa and I usually enjoy an early breakfast to ourselves each day, out on the screened-in porch. We like to have this time together, before all the strangers start coming out of the woodwork. Although, we get a kick out of seeing them long enough to see if they're crazy or not. Most are on the eccentric side—I don't know if that's common for bed and breakfasters or what, but they give us lots of material to laugh over each morning.

After a second cup of coffee, Papa clears his throat. "Caroline girl, I've been worried about you."

"Why, Papa?"

"You just haven't been your perky self for a while now. Everything okay? You regrettin' doin' this Inn? Is it too much?"

"No, I'm loving it. I really am. Does it seem like I don't?"

He just studies me.

"I'm tired is all, that's probably it," I assure him.

"You sure? Nothing else?"

"Well," I take a deep breath and try to keep my voice from shaking, "actually...I did write him a letter, Papa. I told him all about Gracie and even that I still love him…"

I can't say his name out loud. Papa takes my hand and pats it, waiting for me to come out with it.

"And nothing. Not one word." I study the ceiling intently. *I will not cry.*

Papa exhales a large gust of air and reaches up to smooth his eyebrows. It's what he does when he doesn't know what to say.

"I sent it the day after Gracie's birthday, before I could lose my nerve."

"That was three months ago!" He looks as shocked as I've felt all these months.

"I know. I never dreamed he wouldn't respond. It's so—unlike him. I don't even know what to think."

"From all you've told me about him, I have to admit

that it shocks me too," he says. "You're sure he got it?"

"I guess so. I mean, it hasn't been returned or anything."

"Yeah, it would have surely been returned had he not been there to get it."

Our conversation sits in my chest all day, nagging me. It's been hard to get away from it all these months. I've been so glad the Inn has been keeping me so busy, otherwise, this would have crushed me. I'm not surprised that Isaiah has moved on, but I never expected him to not want anything to do with his daughter. The more I think about it, the angrier I get.

That night I write him again. I don't send it until another month passes where I still don't hear from him.

Isaiah,

I expected you to be upset with me, but I never expected this.

You're not who I thought you were. You don't deserve the privilege of knowing my little girl.

If you wanted to shut off my love for you, you've succeeded.

Caroline

I didn't think it would help, but it does. I'm so angry with him that it propels me into a whirlwind of motion. I get things *done*. And I don't cry a single tear for him again.

WE'VE HAD SOME real characters at the Inn. This week Hal Manning arrived. He had only been here half a day and we were wishing he'd pass on through. Yesterday was his fourth night, and I check the roster as soon as I go downstairs to see how much longer he's planning to stay. I audibly groan when I realize we have three more nights with him and then I look around to see if anyone heard me. Nope, free and clear.

I have my breakfast early and then help with serving the guests. Hal comes past the time we've allotted and plops down in front of the only clean place setting while I'm still clearing off the table from our other five guests.

His polyester suit is at least two sizes too small. His neck fat bulges out over his collar, making me need to take deep breaths just thinking about being squeezed up in something so tight all day. He picks up his cloth napkin and wipes all the sweat off his forehead, upper lip, and neck, doing a final sweep up around his hairline.

I swallow.

"You've missed breakfast," I tell him.

It's happened the last four mornings and this morning Ruby huffed, "I ain't doing no mo favors for Hal Manning! He can get hisself up to eat when it's time or go down to Shelby's later!"

He just stares at me and pushes up his thick glasses. "I paid for breakfast and I want my breakfast."

"Breakfast ended at 10 o'clock, Mr. Manning. I'm sorry you've missed it today."

He grits his teeth and turns red. "I don't care if it's 11! If I paid for breakfast, I want breakfast!"

I mentally tick off how many times he's said *breakfast*.

"Shelby's down on Main will be serving breakfast all day."

"This is ridiculous. I travel fifty weeks out of the year and I can tell you, this is ridiculous!"

He gets up and throws down the sweaty napkin and hobbles off, mad. I know he'll be calling within the hour requesting more towels in his room (probably to wipe off all his sweat, yuck). I try to catch him before he gets to the stairs.

"Here are some extra towels, Mr. Manning. I know you li—"

"Extra towels does not equal breakfast," he spits out.

I'm aware of that. I think anyone with a brain would be aware of that fine fact.

Out loud I say, "Quite right you are. Have a good day, Mr. Manning."

Later, I tell Ruby about the whole exchange and we have a good laugh over coconut cream pie.

"I'd like a fresh white towel with cream, please," I say to get her laughing all over again.

She leans over and slaps her knee with her hand, laughing. "Extra butter on my towels…"

"Can I get some syrup with that towel?" I say between breaths. "And a towel sausage patty?"

Papa saunters into the kitchen to us howling. "What is going on in here?" He chuckles.

"Would you like an omelet towel, Papa?"

We lose it then, while Papa just shakes his head, looking amused. "Lord sakes, what did I miss?"

FIONA HAS COME once a week since the Inn opened. Every time she comes she says she just needs to get away for a night, but I think she's lonely in her big old house and likes our company.

"Caroline, this is the best coffee cake. I just can't make it like this."

"Ruby is the best cook in the whole wide world," I boast.

"I'm inclined to agree," Fiona says with a smile. "I'm bringing my grandson Bobby with me next time I come."

She says this every time. He has yet to come.

"Bobby would think you're a looker, all right."

She also says this every time. And I change the subject every time.

"Would you like some coffee to carry out to the garden? It's a pretty day out there."

"He always has a book on him, just like you."

And it never works.

"One can never have too many books." I smile at her.

"You think you'd go out with him, Caroline? He needs a good girl like you."

She studies my wild hair as she says it and I can see her mentally straightening it out once she has me hitched to her grandson.

"No, I don't really date," I tell her. "Now, I better get to work on that garden. Can I get you anything else before I head outside?"

"You better start if you want to have a family!" Fiona insists.

She slowly gets up from her chair and weakly pushes it to the table. She's a tiny thing.

"I already have one." I give her arm a squeeze. "In

fact, I better get to my daughter right now," I throw in for good measure.

"You have a daughter? I didn't know you were married!" Fiona looks shocked and dismayed. "Where's your husband?" She looks around, like he'll suddenly appear out of the crown molding.

"I'm not," I say quietly. "But I've got Gracie—you've probably seen her running around here, although we do try to keep her out of the guests' way."

I see it in her eyes when it registers.

"Oh," she says. "Oh." She takes a step back. "I thought she was Ruby's grandbaby or something," she says softly.

"Well, she pretty much is," I say.

Her lip curls up and she looks at me with disgust. "Well, first of all, I feel physically sick for all the times I've thought you would be a nice girl for my Bobby," she says. She shakes her head and looks like she just might vomit at the thought. "But second…you oughtta be ashamed of yourself—getting on with some colored boy like that, bringing a child into your sin…it's just wrong! What a horrible mother, to bring a child into a world that will just be confused their whole life of where they really belong…which is nowhere."

I double over when she says that. It physically takes my breath away and I can't get it back. When she walks out of the room, I slide onto the floor and hold my head in my hands, trying to make sense of what just happened. I wish I could say her words just bounced off of me, like a penny pinging off the sidewalk. Bounce, bounce, bounce. But they don't. Not the things she said about me—I left my pride in the fields long ago—but about my baby. God,

I hope she isn't right.

Gracie runs in the room just then or I might have continued my downward spiral. She sees me on the floor and crawls right in my lap.

"I love you, baby. Listen to Mama. You belong to *me*. You are just what I needed. And what Papa and Ruby needed. And I will always be helpin' you find your place. Do you hear me?"

I hug her until she squirms. She grins from ear to ear and pats my cheeks and then she's off again.

I finally get up and mentally shake off my shame. There's no time for that. There's too much to do.

Fiona checks out by 11 and that's the last time we see her.

I HAVEN'T TRIED to keep the truth about Gracie a secret, but I haven't gone out of my way to draw attention to her either. It's a sorrow that will always follow me, because I will never understand it. Never. And now I have a little one to protect. Every day I kiss her face and tell her I love her beautiful brown skin. I tell her she's beautiful and just the way God made her—perfect. And after the Fiona episode, I've added in that she *belongs*. Just in case she ever doubts it.

But it's a physical pain in my body that occurs every single time anyone says one word against my child. It hurts more than all the other painful things I've gone through put together…I guess that's what it's really like to be a mama. I never knew it would be that way.

The underground passageway Papa showed me that day serves as a reminder that there are people out there with twisted thoughts. And they might be dressed up in a nice suit or a pretty dress. They might be people at church or the old lady who works at the corner mart. Sadly, they might even be a friend.

But then there are people like Papa and Ruby, who have so much love in them. Their hearts are color-blind.

DAVIS JONES COMES looking for work one gorgeous October morning. I've never seen him around town before, but he says he's lived in Bardstown all his life. He looks to be around my age, give or take a year or two. We make small conversation and then he gets to the point.

"Do you have work, by any chance? I can do anything you don't want to do around your property," he tells Papa.

Papa looks at me.

"Those things *are* startin' to add up," he says.

We've been talking about needing to hire an extra hand for some of those things.

"I can fix anything, make it look and run good as new. Paint, uh…well, just whatever, I can do it," he stops awkwardly and clears his throat. "I added the new patio over at Shelby's…"

"Oh, that looks real nice!" Papa perks up. "*Real* nice. You did a fine job!"

I give Papa a subtle nod. I have a good feeling about Davis. I can tell Papa does too.

"Do we have enough work to keep him busy, Caroline girl?"

"Yes, sir, there's the doors in those two bedrooms that need to close right and some painting around the house. We've talked about extending our patio too, but we might need to wait until next spring for that," I tell Davis. "However…Papa—four-season porch!"

His eyes light up. He's been dreaming about turning the screened porch into a four-season porch since our first breakfast out there.

Papa throws his hand out to Davis and they shake on it.

"Job's yours," Papa says.

Davis does the outside tour with Papa and when they come back in they're ready for coffee. Ruby meets Davis then, and as soon as the cake comes out of the oven, Gracie's head pops out of the little playroom we've set up off the kitchen.

"Gracie, this is Davis. Can you say hi to Davis?"

"Hi-to-Davis," she says in one breath.

He leans down and shakes her hand. "Hi Gracie. I like your name."

"I yike yoah name," she repeats. Or maybe she means it. "Mama? I sit Todavis?"

We all laugh and then she does too.

"It's just Davis, baby, and yes, I think he will let you sit by him."

Davis shyly smiles at us both and nods. "I'd like that."

The five of us squeeze in at the kitchen table to have a bite of orange marmalade cake with our coffee.

I think Davis will fit in around here just fine.

TRUTH IS, I don't know what we ever did without Davis. It's only been a few weeks and already he has filled a void we didn't even know we had. He finishes projects quickly but not without precision. He takes pride in his work but doesn't seem to need validation or direction, he just sees what needs to be done and does it.

He's a guy of few words, but the kindness is evident in everything he does say. And Gracie is crazy over him, so obviously he's a good egg.

He's in the kitchen before me every morning. Ruby won him over with that cake and right away, she knew she had someone else she loved to feed. He might be the only one who can out-eat me, that remains to be seen. We haven't had a boiled shrimp dinner together yet.

This morning when Gracie and I come in, she hops out of my arms and runs to sit between Davis and Papa. They love on her and she eats it up.

I dish up some scrambled eggs and set the plate in front of her. I'm getting my plate ready and pouring coffee when I look back at the table. Papa and Davis have papers in front of them. "What are y'all workin' on?"

They look at each other guiltily and my eyes narrow. "What are you up to?"

"Well, I thought about just doing it as a surprise, but that's probably not gonna work since you're so nosy." Papa laughs and wipes his eyes. "Davis is gonna work on the attic, Caroline. I've had somethin' cookin', but want to know if you like the idea."

He has me all curious now.

"Spill it!"

"Well, what do you think about making that for you and Gracie up there? It would give you so much space and you'd have the ceilings you like so much."

He grins at me when my mouth drops open.

I poured over magazine after magazine with him while we were getting ready to open the Inn. Attic ceilings are my favorite thing in the world.

"I would love that!" Tears fill my eyes and I get embarrassed then. "*Thank* you. Are you sure?"

"Of course I'm sure. It won't take much to get it fixed up. It's already insulated pretty well. There's room enough for several bedrooms up there, so you and Gracie will have lots of space. And we can go through all the things up there in the next week or so before Davis gets started on the floor. That *is* gonna be a job."

I shake my head. "You're something else." I go over and hug his neck and wipe my tears before they fall in his hair. "Thank you, Papa."

"Oh, I'd do anything for my girls." He pulls Gracie into our hug.

Ruby pats my back and smiles at me. "Who woulda thought we'd find a family like this?"

I reach over and hug her. The tears keep coming. "God must have known we needed a do-over!"

"Speaking of Caroline's room, Ruby, I was thinking you'd probably like to move into that one…give you more room too."

Ruby looks at me and then Papa and back to me. And then she starts to blubbering.

"I ain't never had so much love in all my life. I am filled to the tips of my toes with all the goodness," she cries. "I love the room I's in. It's the most beautiful room I ever did have. I wouldn't know what to do with all that space in hers," she cries. "But the fact that you said it, Dr. H, that means the world to me. It do."

"Well, maybe if you moved to Caroline's old room, Davis here could move into yours…" Papa looks at Davis with his eyebrows raised.

Davis looks up with a stunned expression. His top lip gives a little tremble. Oh my, we're a mess this morning.

Papa says quietly, "I don't know your story, Davis, and I don't have to know…but I know you need a place. You're welcome here in this hodgepodge of a family."

Davis shocks us all by wrapping his arms around Papa and then grabbing me and Ruby. Gracie is squished in the middle, but she doesn't mind. She knows it doesn't get any better than this.

ISAIAH

"DO YOU HAVE that last kitchen box, Isaiah?" I hear Mama calling from the dining room.

"Yes, ma'am. Right here." I pass her and take the box to the kitchen.

"Thank you, son. It's coming together! Look at this pretty view out our window."

"Mm-hmm."

I look out where she's pointing but can't really focus.

We've moved again. Someone set our house on fire in Tulma a little over a year and a half ago. I wanted to be there in case Caroline ever came back, but Mama never felt safe there again. Everyone—even the police—knew it was Les's family, but they never found any proof, so we got out of there. We decided on Memphis after I brought Mama on one of my trips and she liked it, but it took time to find a house that we could afford. It's a lot more expensive here.

We like it here, far better than Tulma. I'm in my second year at the U of M, studying business, so I can run my own construction company. During the summers, I've worked with Dan Carson ever since he sobered up.

When Caroline first left, I didn't know what to do with myself. Anytime Tulma started suffocating me, I'd drive over to Memphis and check on Dan. That first weekend when I found him was hell. I didn't even know if he'd remember me when I went back the second time, but he did. He let me in the door every time. I raged against him for leaving his daughter. He agreed he was a worthless son of a bitch. I talked maniacally about Caroline, while he wept maniacally. We've been a mess together ever since. Except he's gotten so much better.

I guess I'm better too, but it's like she's looking over my shoulder, or just around the corner, just far enough out of my reach that I *feel* her, but when I look, she's not there. It's how I imagine it would feel to be haunted by a ghost.

"Isaiah?" Mama's hand is waving in front of my face.

I blink. "Sorry, Mama. What were you saying?"

She shakes her head and puts her hand on my arm. "It's time to move on, son. A new start. We're settled... doesn't it feel good? This is our home now, we don't have to look back or move in a few months...we can just look ahead. Right?"

I nod. "Yes."

"Why don't I believe you? You still have that distant look in your eye that lets me know you're not fully here with me yet." She lays her head over on my shoulder. "I know you wish you could find her...but...I don't think she wants to be found."

Her words burn a hole in my chest. I know she's right.

"Dan still looks for her too. He wants to make it right

239

with her."

"As he should…but you're a different story. He left her; *she* left *you*."

"But she thought she was doing what was best for me. She was scared. I know she needs me."

"She did do what was best for you. You didn't need the heartache of fighting with someone at every restaurant you go in or the glares you'd see whenever you held hands walking down the street. Neither one of you did. Neither one of you need to go through any more hardship. Life has dealt you both enough of that without having it every day, staring you in the face."

"I'll always have it every day, staring me in the face. I'm black, I can't change that. And I can't forget her."

"You're not even trying…"

"Because I don't want to, Mama," I say harshly and then try to soften my tone so I don't show her disrespect. "I don't want to forget her."

She pats my cheek and then turns to pull something out of one of the boxes. "I know. We'll never forget her." She's busy for a minute and then says, "What about that nice girl Nia told you about—the one who's coming to school here in January?"

My cousin Nia moved to Tulma right after Caroline left and we got pretty close. She never saw me with Caroline though, so she didn't see the connection we had. She's tried to set me up with someone new every time we go visit. The last time I was with her, she swore she had *the one* and my mom overheard. I wanted to kill Nia.

"Shanelle," I answer.

"Yes, Shanelle. She sounds like a nice girl."

I shake my head and walk out of the room. I need to

be done with this conversation before I say something I really regret.

I walk into my room and think maybe I should have moved into the dorm after all. Next year…

It doesn't take me long to unpack. Each move has gotten easier. I don't accumulate junk and only have what is absolutely necessary in my room. Not much. It makes for a sterile, but clean and depressing space. Suffice it to say, I probably won't be in here much.

I have one picture of Caroline. It's one I took with my Polaroid the day she left Tulma. She came by the house to tell me goodbye and as she walked out the door, I grabbed my camera off the coffee table and ran out. I said her name and she turned around. I snapped the picture and captured her beauty in a quick second. She didn't even stay long enough to see how it turned out.

"If it's not good, promise you'll throw it away and don't have that be the last way you see me." She smiled and walked away. Got in her mom's car and rode off.

When I couldn't see her taillights anymore, I looked down and saw the picture that had formed. Her eyes were the last to come into focus and when they did, I took the picture inside and studied it for the rest of the night.

I finally stopped sleeping with the picture, afraid I'd smash it in my sleep.

Every time I unpack it, I prop it up in front of the lamp on my desk. Caroline's eyes stare at me, summoning me…they tell me she loves me and that she doesn't want me to ever give up on her.

But that was a long time ago.

Who knows what she thinks by now. I may never know.

RENOVATIONS

I'VE GOTTEN REALLY attached to Davis over the last couple of months. He has this quiet, but playful way about him that calms me and is fun all at the same time. If I'm ever having a rough day with customers or if Gracie is being a handful, Davis smiles this slow, lazy smile that makes me feel like things aren't so bad after all. And Gracie is over the moon about him. The feeling is mutual.

Besides, it's nice having another young person in the house.

Over breakfast this morning, Papa said something about me only being seventeen. Davis has gone around all day shaking his head every time he sees me.

"Seventeen!" he says, like he'll never get over the shock.

Finally, after the umpteenth time of him saying it, I put my hands on my hips. "What's the big deal, anyway?"

"Well, you look a *lot* older, for one thing," he finally admits. He seems embarrassed, but I'm tired of him going on about it.

"Like an 'old woman' older? Or just older than

seventeen?"

I really want to know the answer because there have been times over the past year that I've looked at myself in the mirror and been appalled by how different I look. It's like the pain has all shown up on the outside of my face, while my insides have actually gotten a little bit lighter.

"Well, no, you don't look like an old woman. I did think more like twenty-four or twenty-five." He ducks his head. "You just look so...so...weary," he stutters. "And you have Gracie, so I thought..."

"Weary..." I nod. "Yeah, that pretty much describes it."

I can't even be offended because I know he's exactly right.

"You're still real..." His voice fades out and his cheeks turn a shade darker than I'm used to seeing on him.

There's a long, painful pause, so I jump in. "Whew, well, that's good to know. What would we do if I wasn't *real*?" I tease him.

He turns even redder.

"You're still real pretty, Caroline," he practically whispers.

For some reason, I go all splotchy. It's been a while since I've turned red. I've sorta stopped being so self-conscious the longer I've been away from Mama.

I look at my feet and he clears his throat.

"Thanks, Davis," I say softly.

He starts to walk away and I call after him. "How old are you?"

"Eighteen," he says before he turns the corner. And the smile he flashes me is a mixture of pure orneriness and something that looks like resolve.

CHRISTMAS IS GORGEOUS at the Inn. We find the perfect tree out past the vineyards on Papa's property. Davis cuts it down and straps it on the back of his truck. The tree is at least twelve feet tall and looks magnificent in the living room. Before we start decorating, Papa supervises by being the Taster of all the Treats. Brenda and I make eggnog, while Ruby and Gracie work on Christmas cookies. Gracie is standing on a little stool that Davis built for her, so she can reach the countertop. It has helped tremendously—before she had the stool, she would try to use the tricycle to stand taller. The girl has become surprisingly agile.

Davis wanders in and leans over to see how Gracie is decorating her cookies.

"I like that green on there," he says quietly and plants a kiss on her cheek.

Gracie turns around and puts her hands up on his face to kiss his cheek too. When she gets green frosting on his ear, she giggles.

"Mess," she says.

"You're a mess," he says and tickles her side.

She reaches up to hold onto him and gets even more frosting on him.

"Oh, now you've gone and done it," he teases and tickles her harder.

GRACIE STEALS THE show on Christmas morning. I

don't think any of us have ever had more fun than we do, watching her open presents. She does a little gasp and puts her hand to her mouth with every present. I can't get over it. She even gives each one of us a hug and a kiss—without prompting—when we tell her who the present is from. My little lady. She makes my heart explode with love.

After all the presents have been opened and the affection has been doled out, we sit down to a feast. Ruby has been cooking for days and it's worth every shooing out of the kitchen we've had to endure in the week leading up to the festivities.

I barely think about Isaiah, well…except long enough to wonder if he's spending Christmas with that girl, if he's happy, if he looks old too, and to ask myself if he ever still thinks of me at all.

WORK ON MY 'attic getaway'—as it has been dubbed—has been underway since the day after Christmas. Seeing that we had a lull in the Inn's schedule, we went ahead and closed the Inn and decided to have a little vacation ourselves. If you count completely remodeling the attic of a huge plantation home as a vacation.

Davis has put in more hours than I can count. He's done some of the work for the past month but avoided being too loud while guests were with us. Now he's going strong, day and night, and we're all pitching in to help as much as we can. There's giddiness in the air about how the space is shaping up—I can't stay out of there. It's so pretty. The floors are buffed to a fine finish, and the walls have been painted a buttery yellow.

A few days into the work, I lay Gracie down for her nap and head up to the attic to see the progress. Davis hears me coming and tries to block me from coming in all the way.

"I want to see what you're working on—I haven't gotten to come up all morning!" I huff.

"I know! I'm finally getting some work done!" He gives me as much of a steely glare as he can manage.

It just makes me laugh.

"Come on, let me in."

"No, I'm not going to let you back in here until it's finished," he says with a grin.

"Are you *smirking* at me?" I shake my head. "Oh no you don't. You're a perfectionist and it will take you *forever* if I don't get in there to help you finish."

I try to brush past him, but he grabs both my shoulders and holds me firm.

There's something different in his touch now than the hug he gave all of us in the kitchen that day with Papa and Ruby. Something about it reminds me of how long it's been since I've had physical contact with a boy. It's been about two years, three months, two weeks and two days, to be exact. I back up like I've been shot and run back down the stairs, all the way to the main floor, and out to the garden.

I STAY OUT of his way the rest of the week, telling myself that I'm just giving him space, not breathing down his neck and getting underfoot…but really, I'm still trying to process what happened, or more like what *didn't* happen between us the other day. Because nothing happened. And nothing will. Because I don't need a dumb boy latching on to my heart.

AFTER A BIG pork supper, collard greens, black-eyed peas and cornbread—the traditional food you have to eat on New Year's Day if you want to have good luck all year—Davis shifts in his seat and makes an announcement.

"After supper, I'd like everyone to come up to the attic," he says without looking at me.

It's then I realize he's been avoiding me too.

Ruby claps her hands together and I stare at her.

"Have you seen it already, Ruby?" I ask.

She shrugs, but by the way her lips are curling up, I'd say she has.

"Well, I never. Have you seen it too, Papa?"

He raises his eyebrows and gives a shrug too. His twinkling eyes give him away.

"I see it, Mama!" Gracie says loudly.

"*You've* seen it?"

"I see it!" she repeats.

"No, she hasn't seen it yet, Caroline," Davis says, still avoiding my eyes.

"Well, everyone hurry up and eat!" I start shoveling the collard greens and peas in my mouth. I'll take all the good luck I can get.

WHEN WE GET to the top of the stairs, Ruby covers my eyes and they lead me inside. I hear the gasp from Gracie and Ruby takes her hand off. Then I do a shriek of my own. Ruby has me turned facing the left wing. She opens my bedroom door first. A four-poster bed with sheer white curtains hanging from ribbons around it stands on the left of the large room. The bedding is plush and looks so inviting, I want to crawl in it and stay there. Next to my room is Gracie's, with a bed just her size. She runs right for it and does get in hers. In the open space outside our rooms, a window seat lines all the windows and pretty white wooden shutters filter in just enough light to make it feel airy.

"You made all this for us?" I ask Davis, my mouth hanging open.

He nods. "Yep."

"He's been working on the beds for a long time," Papa says. "We've had this idea brewing for quite a while. What do ya think?"

"It's so beautiful. Thank you." Tears roll down my face.

"You haven't even seen all of it." Ruby shifts me a little to the right.

It's even better on that side. Built-in bookshelves are filled with my books and a large plush floral chair sits next to a mini pink chair. One for me and one for Gracie. And a little further to the right, in the corner of the room, a wooden swing hangs from the ceiling. I run and sit in it, giving myself a light push off.

"This is the prettiest attic I've ever seen. A swing! Who puts a swing in a house? It's the best idea ever."

Davis smiles and points to the books. "You need another place to read all your books, when you're tired of just sittin' in that chair. And some days are too hot for you to swing on the one outside...I know you...like it out there..."

I hop off the swing and move in front of him, chewing on the inside of my cheek to keep from bawling. "Thank you, Davis. This is the nicest thing anyone has ever done for me. Well, besides Papa having me move here in the first place." I lean over and take Papa's hand and look back up at Davis. "Really—I don't even know what to say. Thank you."

He looks down. "I didn't want to make you cry, but I thought you might." He looks up and gives me a smile that makes my heart jump over itself just a bit.

He really is pretty handsome, now that I give him a good look. And I do give him a good, *long* look, noticing some of his features for the first time. His brown eyes are kind and warm, with eyelashes that might be longer than mine. His lips are full and always have a smile just hovering on the edge, ready to take off. His blonde hair is thick, and for a brief moment, I wonder what it would feel like to run my hands through it...

Okay, enough. I will not think about that.

I reach over and awkwardly pat his shoulder. I stare at him a little longer and everyone is quiet until Gracie yelps. In the corner across from mine, is her swing. She climbs up on it before we can even blink and tries to swing on it standing up. I rush over to her and set her on her bottom and give her a little push.

"I yove it," she says and I beam at her. "I vewy yove it!"

"I very love it too!" I grin at Davis over Gracie's head. "We'll never want to leave our room now!"

It's our very own little haven, mine and Gracie's.

Davis just stands there quietly, looking content and rather proud of himself. I vow to myself to make his favorite cookies *at least* once a week.

FEELINGS

AFTER THE GRAND gesture with my room, Davis is bolder. His shyness hasn't gone away, necessarily, and he's still quiet, but now there's a new confidence there. He looks at me, and all I know is that his eyes are trying to tell me something. He looks at me *a lot* more now. And I look back.

I'm trying to figure out what has suddenly drawn me to his attention and vice versa. How did I not see how cute he is until now? And his voice—it's like hot buttered rum on a cold night; every now and then it seeps through the ice that has taken over my heart and melts a tiny spot.

He doesn't really make any major move to let me know what he's thinking exactly...until Valentine's Day. I've been intent on making every holiday special for Gracie, but would just as soon ignore Valentine's Day altogether.

When I start getting sentimental in the days leading up to the holiday and pull out everything Isaiah ever gave me—dried flowers, his notes, the jewelry box—I know I need to just forget the whole day altogether.

I *have* made Davis cookies once a week, just as I

planned, but I haven't made them this week yet, because I'm so keen on not drawing attention to anything romantic.

But on the fourteenth, I open my bedroom door and find two boxes of chocolate—a big heart for me and a little heart for Gracie. A long red rose is laying on top of my box.

I lean my head over on the doorframe and let out a big sigh.

"Not what you were hoping for?"

I nearly jump right out of my clothes. "I-I didn't see you there," I stammer.

Davis is almost to the top of the steps, just outside my room. He smiles. "Or were you wishing they were from someone else?"

He's never asked me any questions, and unless Papa or Ruby has mentioned something to him, he knows nothing about Gracie's daddy.

I swallow hard before answering. "I'm not sweet on this day anymore, to tell you the truth."

He nods. And waits for me to say more.

When I don't, he says, "How 'bout we change that?"

My eyes grow wide and then I have to blink about six times because they get so dry. I lean down to pick up the chocolates, just as Gracie swoops out of the room. She sees the cute little box in my hands and knows it's for her. I hold it up for her to see and tell her it's from Davis.

He stretches his long arm out and takes the box, waving his hand for her to come sit by him. She ends up on his lap and as their heads bend over the box while he's opening it, another little trickle drips off my ice.

Gracie picks out a chocolate and while she's making fast work of it, Davis's eyes meet mine over Gracie's

252

head.

"Ruby said she'd cover for you later today. If you'd like, we could go out while Gracie's napping. Ruby will take care of the guests. Papa will listen for Gracie and watch her while Ruby's cooking. And she said she's good for as late as we wanna be out. As long as we're bright and cheery in the mornin'," he says, laughing.

"Sounds like y'all have it all worked out. This is a busy day for the Inn, are they sure about this?" My voice sounds a little shaky.

He nods. "Yep. All set. Ruby has actually been workin' ahead all week, so we could do this. *If* you said yes, of course…" he adds.

"Where are you wanting to go?"

His right shoulder tilts up and his eyes shine, as he says, "I had a little somethin' in mind."

"Oh, is that right?" Without meaning to, my tone went full-on flirtatious. I shake my head to try to stop myself. But it's not working. My heart thumpety-thumps.

Gracie is done with our conversation and she jumps up and takes the chocolates with her. Davis stands up and leans an arm above me on the doorjamb. He's standing far closer than he ever has.

"What do you say—will you go out with me?" he whispers, looking in my eyes and then down at my lips.

All I can do is blink and then I finally find my tongue. "I don't know, Davis. I don't really…go out…*ever*…at all."

"I've noticed," he says.

I study his face. Up this close, his eyes are so dark, I see the light bouncing off his eyes. No wonder they seem so bright.

"Do you—do you think you might could like me, Caroline? Eventually? You know, as more than just a friend?"

It's the first time his confidence has wavered and now he sounds tentative. He steps back and holds both hands up. "Wait, don't. Don't answer that. Be ready in an hour? Wear something warm. It's a nice day out there, but chilly…if you're up for it?"

I nod slowly. "You know, I think I might be."

He leans over and kisses my cheek.

My heart speeds up even more.

"Yes, yes, I'm pretty sure I am," I add.

He laughs at me and I can't help but laugh back.

"I'll come pick you up in an hour." He gives me one more grin before turning around and running down the stairs.

I can do a lot with an hour, so with fifteen minutes to spare, Gracie and I are both bathed and hairdos done. I study my closet as if something new will magically turn up, but nothing does, so I just put on my favorite patchwork maxi skirt with a red turtleneck. Nellie would be dismayed by my wardrobe. It now consists of jeans, a couple long skirts, t-shirts and two sweaters. I haven't gotten brave enough for a mini skirt and it wouldn't fly at the Magnolia anyway.

I take one more look in the mirror, trying to imagine what Davis sees. Not so lanky anymore, my body has filled out. Mama would be telling me I'd better watch it or I'm gonna resemble a fat piggy pretty soon. I smooth down my skirt and sort of like the curves. Once I've done all the primping I can stand, Gracie and I sit on our swings. She keeps licking off the lip gloss I put on her and wanting more.

"Yips? Mo-ah?" she asks.

"One more time," I tell her and we both hop off the swings and meet in the middle.

She puckers those pretty lips out and I have to kiss them first.

"Come on, let's go find Papa and Ruby." I grab her hand and we open our door.

Ruby is just reaching the top step. "Why, don't you look pretty!" she says before giving us both a hug.

"I'm having all kinds of company up here today," I say in her hair.

She laughs. "Sound like you got a fun day ahead of you, sugar." She pulls my head back and looks in my eyes. "This boy is a good one, Caroline. I believe you can trust him."

I bite my lip and nod. "I don't really know how to get over Isaiah, Ruby. I mean, I hate him, so that helps, but...I don't know..." I trail off.

She shakes her head. "You not gon' be able to compare Davis to Isaiah, darlin'. Or the other way around. It ain't fair to either boy. And Isaiah ain't *here*, so put him right outta that mind of yours and just be with Davis today. You don't have to make any promises or do anything other than *have fun*." She gives my cheeks two little pinches to accentuate those last two words.

I kiss her on each cheek and she takes Gracie from my arms. I lean over to kiss Gracie.

"Bye, Mama." She gives a little wave and doesn't seem fazed one bit that I'm leaving.

As their heads disappear down the stairs, I hear Davis saying hi to them on his way up. I guess he was serious about picking me up.

He stops in his tracks when he sees me standing there. His mouth goes into a tiny O. He better not whistle or this will all be over before it's ever started. You'd think he's never seen me, the way he's gawking.

"You look so pretty," he says shyly.

"Thank you. You look nice too." He actually looks *exceptionally* nice, but I can't quite tell him that. He's wearing a long sleeve button down shirt with his jeans instead of one of the scroungy t-shirts he's usually wearing.

He holds out his hand and I pause only briefly before taking it. Oh sweet Mary, he smells divine. I let go of his hand.

"I'm not sure if this is a good idea, Davis."

"Okay. Going out today? Or holding my hand?" He puts his hands in his pockets and waits for my answer.

"Either one."

"Why not?"

"Well, we live here together...and what if...someone gets hurt and then we have to be around each other all the time?"

"I'm not gonna hurt you. Are you gonna hurt me?"

I stare into his warm eyes for a full minute. The way his broad shoulders look like they could carry me for miles. The way he has been a steady, quiet presence in my life every single day for the last four months. The way he hasn't ever asked anything of me, but has already given me so much of himself in the little things he does. The way he adores my little girl...

I reach out my hand and he takes it. "No, I won't hurt you," I promise. And I mean it.

OUR FIRST STOP is to the carriage house next to the barn. It's been a couple of weeks since I've been out here. Since the barn is used more and we're full all the time now, Davis thought it would be a good idea to turn the carriage house into a place that people can come for longer or more private stays. I've gotten to pick out all the materials and colors. Papa says I have the eye for it and Davis agrees, so I'm happy to play. It's fun for me. Every time I've visited him out here, I've been amazed at how pretty it all is, but the last time I saw it, there was still a lot of work to have it ready for guests. When we step inside, I nudge his arm.

"You're just full of surprises!" I laugh. "It's so beautiful, Davis. I can't believe how talented you are. And the lights! I love the little white lights everywhere!"

"I would have never thought to put all these things together," he says, holding a pillow next to a picture I found. "I just build it. You're the one who makes it look like those magazines you like. We do work well together," he finishes quietly.

"I didn't pick out this table."

Davis has led me to an intimate round table that has china already placed on it.

"I made that," he shrugs like it's nothing, "and Ruby let me bring the dishes out here last night. I figure we can't get any better cookin' than hers anywhere within 200 miles, so we may as well eat here before we go."

"How do you have time to do all this work? Everything is always running so smoothly since you came, which is a job in itself, but no, you're out here building tables with intricate legwork and sturdy chairs. I don't understand how you do it all…"

"I don't sleep much. I've been staying out here, actually, and I get a lot done when it's quiet. I…it's good for me to be busy."

"Me too. I don't like to have too much time to think, which is what happens when I stop," I tell him.

"What keeps you awake at night, Caroline?" He gets right to the point.

"My past," I answer.

I fidget with the cloth napkin on my lap. Davis takes the lid off the white tureen in front of us and scoops Ruby's vegetable soup into our bowls.

We start slowly eating and Davis picks up the conversation again.

"What happened to make you leave home?"

"Are you sure you want to get into this? It's way more fun talking about decorating," I say.

"I think it's time, don't you?"

He says it so sincerely, I feel safe to answer whatever he asks.

I take a deep breath. "Okay. I was raped by two boys and they came back for more. I had to get out of there."

I don't think I've ever said those words out loud.

He sets down his spoon and his eyes go black.

"My dad is an alcoholic and disappeared before all this happened. My mom left me in Memphis…we weren't getting along. And my boyfriend found me and told me those boys were dead, but I still couldn't go back."

"That's…" He blows air out of his lips. "Whew. A lot. How could they leave-?" He shakes his head. "Okay.

Boyfriend, you said?"

"Gracie's dad."

"Oh. So…where is he now?"

"Tulma, as far as I know. I went back to tell him about Gracie but saw him with another girl. And then I didn't have the nerve to tell him until Gracie's first birthday, but I sent him a letter and he never responded. I sent him two, actually, but nothing…" I've said it all in one breath, saying it as fast as I can get it out.

I feel surprisingly numb.

"What's his name?"

"Isaiah."

"Wow," he says. "I-I don't know what to say. Wow."

"Yeah, it's not exactly a great conversation starter… but hey," I shrug, "it's what I've got."

I try to smile, but it's more like a wobble. He reaches out and holds my hand. I like his strong grip. Makes me feel ladylike. With my spare hand, I take another bite of my soup.

"This is my favorite Ruby soup."

"Now that I did know." He smiles.

"What about you? What horrid secrets do you have to tell me?"

"Nothing so horrid as your story. I'm sorry you've been through so much, Caroline. And I've been sorry for ever making you feel like you look anything other than beautiful…because that's what I really see. I should have never said that about you lookin' weary. I can't believe how you just go on like nothing bad has ever happened to you a day in your life. I've never heard you say one foul word to anyone and I've been around you approximately a hundred and thirty-five days now." He pauses when I laugh at that. "The fact that I didn't know this story until today…well, it's just not the norm. Most people have to share all their sad stories before they ever even get to know the person they're sharing with. You're constantly smiling, even when I know you've gotta be so tired."

"Well, I came here pretty beat up. But, I've never been happier than here with Gracie, Papa and Ruby—Brenda, too—she's been such a good friend. And now…you. Hopefully, I won't look old forever," I tease him.

"I think you're looking more like seventeen these days," he says. "Soon to be eighteen…"

"Pfft. You think I'm gonna believe you now?"

His face gets sober. "I mean it. I nearly lose my air every time I see you, Caroline. Even when you're not dressed all…cute." He waves his hand up and down around my outfit. "And I like that the world can't keep you down. You're formidable."

"Formidable," I repeat. "I like that."

"I like you," he says.

"What's made you start…thinking like this?" I ask. "And I haven't heard you talk so much at one time. Ever. Or using words like *formidable*."

He laughs. "My mom died when I was fifteen and she always used big words. I *am* being chatty, huh." He changes the subject quickly. "I guess I think I better get it all out while we have a chance. And Gracie is hard to deny. When she says, 'Come 'heah', I cannot refuse her."

We both laugh at that. She is always grabbing his hand and taking him off to show him something.

"I'm really sorry about your mom. Is your dad alive?"

He shakes his head no. "But I didn't miss him when

he went. My mom…she was…I just…I miss her a *lot*."

He swallows hard and his Adam's apple bobs up and down quickly.

"I kinda always have 'thought like this' about you… since pretty much the first time I saw how you take care of everyone around you. That was right around day one," he continues.

I gulp the lump that has formed in my throat.

"You seemed so capable of taking care of yourself. I didn't think you'd ever look at me. And then when I found out how young you really are, I thought just maybe I could have a chance to show you how you can be taken care of too."

"But you've never even really acted like you like me …like *that*. I mean, we talk and we've been friends and it's been fun, but I didn't even feel an inkling that you liked me. Until…"

"Yeah?"

"Until that day in my room."

Davis nods and doesn't say anything. We both sit there with the lights flickering across our faces, holding hands, and I think this is one of the most romantic moments I've ever experienced.

"I could stare at you all day, but I don't want to freak you out," he finally says.

I laugh nervously. I've been enjoying staring back.

"I want to show you something. You warm enough if we go for a walk?"

"I think so," I answer.

"Here, let's put this around you." Davis grabs a scarf from the couch and loosely winds it around my neck. He pauses for a moment and my breath stops.

I think he might kiss me.

His fingers linger on my scarf and then he lifts them up to my cheek. He traces my jawline and then his hand suddenly drops. He takes a step back and puts his fist up to his mouth. He stares at me like he wants to say something but just clears his throat instead. His eyes are shining as he smiles at me.

"Caroline?"

"Yes?"

He leans in closer and whispers, "I want to take away every sad thought that's behind those eyes..." He lifts a hand to touch my hair and then drops it again. "I-you're-well...I don't think you're quite ready for me yet, but I'm just gonna be right here, every day, showing you..."

"Showing me what?" I ask when he just leaves it hanging.

"Showing you I'm not going anywhere."

And with that bold statement he turns around and holds out his hand. "Come on, let's go before it gets dark."

We walk, quiet, commenting on a flower here and there or the way a squirrel seems to be keeping up with us. I'm not sure how long we walk, but I know that I needed this. The exercise feels good. And this feeling...it's like fresh air pouring into my lungs.

"We're almost there." We take a turn further into the woods and he points straight ahead.

There's a huge tree, the only one not affected by winter. Its leaves are green and the branches are heavy with the weight. It's beautiful. The sunlight is highlighting it, giving it a dreamy effect. I half-expect a fairy to fly overhead anytime.

"It's spectacular," I tell him with a smile.

"I think so too." He bends down and looks up at me. He points to the ground.

My eyes get wide when I see it. Eleven rocks all shaped like hearts are lined up in a row. Some are perfect, some are uneven, some are fat, some are little-bitty…I bend down and pick each one up, examining them all.

"How did you find all these?"

He taps his temple. "Once you find a heart, it's like it's all you can see." He smiles his sweet smile again then leans over and kisses my cheek.

My heart just fluttered back to life again.

❀ 28 ❀

HIGH EXPECTATIONS

THAT FIRST DATE starts a series of weekly dates. Davis and I see each other throughout the day, eat together, and sneak time together between demanding guests, with Gracie always basking in our attention. But every Monday night, after the crazy weekends and after I've put Gracie to bed, we go out, just the two of us. We've gone on long drives, been bowling, horseback riding twice, watched the sunset through our tree, and to the movies three times. Tonight we're going to eat dessert at this new little restaurant in town.

I never thought I'd find my place. Ever. I expected to always feel misplaced. On the outside. Wishing for more. Never having normalcy.

Each day is a new revelation. *This* is what it's like to be open. *This* is what it's like to be young. *This* is how life is supposed to be.

And with Davis, it's just *easy*. He doesn't have a moody bone in his body. He's laid back, fun and seems like he's just looking for ways to show me how good everything can really be.

I'm beginning to believe him.

My only complaint about him is that he hasn't kissed me yet. It's been two months and while it feels like more than just hanging out with my best friend—and that's what he's become—I'm starting to wonder if we're really attracted to each other in that way. I know that it *feels* like I am, and it seems he is with me, but I can't figure out why it hasn't happened by now. Sometimes the tension in the air is so thick it could pop. Davis studies my lips for the longest time—I just know it's going to happen—and then he'll smile and take a step back and start talking about wood or rocks or food or Gracie.

I made a new dress for tonight. I rarely get out of the house without him or Gracie, so shopping just doesn't happen. Every now and then I miss sewing with Nellie and pull out Eileen's old machine that Papa lets me and Ruby use. I finished this dress last night and love it. It's shorter than anything I've ever worn, but not as short as some of the others I see on TV or even on the women in town. It's red and black with a white pointy collar. The top half looks prim and proper like all the dresses I used to wear, but the bottom flares out several inches above my knees, making me feel like I'm living on the wild side. I did make sure it wasn't short enough to see all the way to the Promised Land, since I have Nellie perched up on my shoulder most of the time.

Davis comes to my door to pick me up, like always. I wave to Ruby, who sits with Gracie and reads when we go out. Davis's eyes bug out of his head when he sees me. I shut the door softly behind me and lean against the door. He puts an arm on either side of me, hemming me in, and leans close, so his face is not even a foot from mine.

265

"I've never seen your legs," he whispers.

"Of course you have," I say.

"Your ankle maybe…one time I think I saw a glimpse of knee, but…no. Not like this," he says emphatically.

I look at him out of the sides of my eyes and smirk. "Well, now you have."

"I'm gonna want to see them all the time now."

"Is that right? Had I known seein' a little leg was all you needed…I would have shown them a long time ago," I tease.

His brows crinkle together. "What do you mean, *all I needed*?"

I shrug and don't say anything.

His eyes stare me down and I think he must surely hear my heart pounding.

He puts a hand on my neck, high enough where it's appropriate and low enough that I know he can *feel* my heart pounding.

"That…feel that?" He waits for a moment and I know he's talking about my heart. "That's what I need. Do I have that?" He studies me, looking for the answer in my eyes.

"I think so," I whisper.

"What would help you know?" he whispers back.

I don't answer for a moment and when I do it's so quiet, I'm not sure he hears me at first.

"If you'd kiss me."

He tilts my chin up with one hand and with the other, winds his hand through my hair and brings my mouth to his. He doesn't go soft and gentle like I thought he would, he goes all in and claims me. Like he's been denied his whole life and is now making up for lost time. When he finally pulls back, I feel weak and deprived. I could kiss him forever.

"Well?" he asks.

"You have me," I whisper.

"Come on." He pulls my hand and we fly down the two flights of stairs and out the back door to his truck. "Do you mind if we skip the restaurant?"

I shake my head and climb in his truck.

We speed down the backroads and he pulls up to a large pasture not far from the house. He shuts the truck off and pulls me over to him and kisses me again.

It's a long time before we stop. My lips feel raw and puffy, but I can't get enough.

"I've been dying to do that for so long," Davis says.

"I was starting to think you never would."

We get lost kissing again.

When we finally come up for air, Davis reaches for my hand and puts it up to his lips. "Kissing you is even better than I thought it would be. And I had really high expectations." He grins.

"I thought you might just be feeling like I was your best friend and didn't want to go past that," I admitted.

"I thought that's how *you* were feeling." He presses his forehead to mine. "Now, what do you think?"

"I think I wish we'd been doing this all that time." I laugh and pull him in for more.

The next break, he says, "Caroline? What happened to you…I haven't known what you'd be comfortable with and I know we talk about everything, but we don't really talk about that…or Isaiah."

I shift uncomfortably in the seat. It feels wrong to talk about that…and them, *him*…in this moment.

"I haven't wanted to rush anything and I know that I kinda came on strong right off the bat, but…I've tried to hold back too. I couldn't help but tell you how I feel…I just haven't wanted you to feel pressured by my feelings. I've wanted you to come around to the idea of us in your own time." He puts his hands on my cheeks. "Tonight I realized that you might still not be sure of my feelings, and I couldn't have that. But, listen to me, Caroline, I will take it all as slow as you want to go."

"I'm ready to let go of all of it," I tell him. "You're my future, Davis. You are. I know it without a doubt now, and I don't want to look back anymore."

"I love you," he says and before I can respond, he kisses me. This time his hands roam up and down my legs, going higher each time. "Your legs are too much," he groans.

He holds both hands in the air and starts the truck. "I'm gettin' you home, lady."

I laugh and scoot as close as I can get beside him. Leaning my head on his shoulder, I look up at him and take in his features in the moonlight. He's beautiful and his heart is mine. I love him too.

When we get to the house, he walks me up to my room and gives me a chaste peck on the lips. I didn't know he had those in him anymore after all those steamy kisses.

"This has been the best night of my life," he whispers.

I hug him tight and when we let go and he walks to the edge of the staircase, he pauses and turns around. He looks so happy. He gives a little wave and starts down the stairs.

"Davis?"

He turns around to look at me.

"I love you too."

The beam on his face would light up a moonless sky. He nods his head, puts a fist over his heart and walks down the stairs into the night.

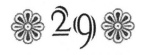

STEAL AWAY

OUR DAYS BECOME opportunities for a quick kiss here, a long session there. Papa has caught us kissing several times, tucked away in an alcove of the house, outside by the barn, in the kitchen pantry…he just laughs.

"When are you gonna make an honest girl out of her, Davis?" he teases.

Papa and Eileen got married when they were sixteen, so he thinks nothing of getting married young. "Why waste time when you know?" he says.

After my eighteenth birthday, I start thinking about marrying Davis. Brenda comes over with wedding magazines and we talk about Charlie and Davis and what it would be like to get married. I don't really have to marry Davis to be happy—I'm pretty happy right now. But I know he does want to 'make an honest woman out of me' and it's getting harder and harder to keep our hands off of each other, so as soon as he asks me, I will say yes.

We've nearly had sex many times, and every time, Davis has been the one to stop. Clothes have been on the verge of being shed and he'll say something like, "I want it to be right and…better than this for you. We're gonna wait, baby. I want it to be perfect." We're usually in his truck or in his room when this happens. Lately, we're spending a lot of time with everyone, instead of being alone together. I hate how much self-control he has.

IT'S A WARM August day when Papa asks us to sit down with him in the living room. We only have three guests, so I'm done with my work earlier than usual. We both sit on the couch, while Papa sits in his chair across from the couch. Gracie gives Dolly 'tea' at the coffee table.

"I've been thinking," Papa starts out. "When and if y'all decide to settle down…you could start out in the carriage house—we managed fine with just the rooms and we will again. You could stay in there while you're building your own little place."

Davis and I look at each other and back at Papa.

"There are several prime spots." Papa winks at Davis. "I think you know a few…"

Davis's cheeks tinge a few shades darker, and he looks at me again. "That sounds like an amazing plan, but I don't even know if she's ready to marry me," he says like I'm not sitting right beside him.

I feel both sets of eyes on me then. "Well, you're not gonna find out until you ask me," I huff.

"You can't even give me a hint of what you'd say?" he asks.

"Nope," I answer.

He looks at Papa. "See what I have to deal with?"

Papa laughs.

"We've only known each other ten months," Davis says to me.

"I know. I've kept track too," I say.

"Well, what do you think about that?" he asks.

"I think life's too short to waste time."

Davis's eyes widen.

Papa lets out another huge guffaw. It rattles the china in the hutch. "Sounds like you got your work cut out for you, boy."

Ruby wanders into the room then. "What's all that racket?" she asks.

"Davis has something to ask Caroline," Papa answers.

"Well, looks like I made it just in time," she says. She reaches in her apron pocket and tosses something to Davis. He catches it and smiles a huge grin at her.

He looks at me and holds up a ring. "Can't do it properly without this," he says. He gets down on his knees in front of me.

"Wait a minute. What have y'all done here?" I ask.

They just laugh at me and Gracie comes over to see why Davis is on his knees.

"I might have needed them for extra courage," Davis says. "Not because I'm not ready, I am so ready. But so I would be brave enough to ask. You don't have to say yes," he says.

"To what?" I egg him on.

"To marrying me."

"Was that a question?"

He shakes his head, confused. "What?"

"Were you asking me a question?" I tease him.

"Oh. Yes. I was. Am. Will. Am about to ask you

one…" He fumbles all over the place.

Gracie giggles.

"Davis?" I take his hand.

He just looks at me.

"Will you marry me?" I ask.

"Yes!" he answers.

"Is that what you were gonna ask?"

"Oh, were you not asking…"

"DAVIS! Ask me already!"

He nods, and the humor disappears as he looks me straight in the eye. "Caroline, will you marry me? I love you and want you to be my wife more than anything."

"Yes, I will," I say and grab his face to kiss him before he can say anything else.

Gracie jumps up and down. "Kiss!"

Papa hops up and pats us both on the back while we're still kissing. Ruby comes over and we all pile together in a hug, the way we did that day in the kitchen.

AND JUST LIKE that, we're engaged. I start planning a wedding, putting all the ideas Brenda and I have talked about in a big white binder. We've decided to get married on October 19th, a year after we first met. It will be simple, small, and I can't wait.

There's something about knowing that he wants to be with me forever—it makes me love him even more. No one in my life has stayed. No one in his life has either.

My mind has an inner war with itself as I try to push Isaiah out.

He might have left, but he came back.
But he left in the first place.
I left him last.
Maybe he would have stayed.

I squelch it down and remind myself that this is all for the best for everyone involved.

The carriage house is ready for us to move in, and Davis and I have walked miles over the property to find the perfect spot to build our future little house. We find it, just past the gardens and grapes, where we can still appreciate the beauty and see the main house, too, but far enough to have some privacy. Davis gets a few guys from town to help lay the foundation, and they've already started putting up a rough frame of the house.

There's a stone archway leading into one of the gardens in the back, more intricate than the other two, and that's where I want to get married. Right in the middle of my favorite flowers.

Davis and I are so busy, we fall asleep a lot after we put Gracie to bed...kissing and talking and then fading out. The Inn has been busy this summer. I've been working on the gardens and also making my dress. It's going to be beautiful, simple just like everything else, but beautiful. Papa let me go through all of Eileen's material and I found a cream lace that I love.

I'm pinning it all when Davis sneaks into my room. Gracie is swinging with Dolly in her corner and I hear her giggle before I feel his arms around me. I jump up and try to hide the dress.

"You can't see this. It's bad luck!" I spread my arms wide to cover it.

He leans down and nuzzles my neck. "Only if I see it

on you, this doesn't count." His hair tickles my neck and I shiver. Gracie runs over to us and he swoops her up.

"I can't wait to see your mama in this dress," he tells her.

"Pwetty Mama," she says.

"You've got that right," Davis says.

I nuzzle Gracie's head and then point to the door.

"Hey, you two, let's just scoot right on out this door and don't be sneaking any more peeks, Davis, do you hear me?"

I push them out and Gracie is laughing, repeating, "You heah me?" all the way down the stairs.

I roll my eyes, but I can't wipe the grin off my face.

THE NEXT DAY, just four Saturdays from the wedding, I wake up to loud thunder. I get up and look outside, hoping the weather doesn't get bad and ruin anything on the new house. We survived a series of awful tornadoes in the spring with minimal damage, but we were the few lucky ones. I jump when I hear a quiet rap on my door.

"You scared me," I whisper to Davis when I open the door.

"Sorry," he says softly. "I just wanted to see you before I head out. I've gotta get the coverings secure on the house and I need to go into town for some supplies... looks like the weather's gonna get bad today. Might take me a while to get everything done."

"Okay, be careful out there."

"I will." He leans over and kisses me and wraps me

up in a bear hug. "Just four more weeks," he whispers in my ear.

"I know," I smile at him and lean back in for another hug, "I can't wait."

GRACIE AND I eat with Papa and then I take care of the breakfast rush. We've had really sweet guests this week. A young couple and three sisters...they've been nice and easy to please. They check out around 11, and the Inn is quiet. Ruby starts canning fruit. Papa is snoozing in the darker than normal living room. Gracie and I play for a while and then I put her down for her nap. I feel restless and can't quite settle into anything. I work on my dress, it's nearly done. I read for a little while. I keep looking out the window. Davis worked out there for a long time and then I saw him drive off in his truck, so I watch for him to come back.

When Gracie wakes up a couple hours later, we go downstairs. Papa is with Ruby in the kitchen.

"Our guests for this weekend have all cancelled because of the weather," Ruby tells me.

"Really? It's that bad out?" I walk over to the back windows. It does look rough. The rain is coming down in thick sheets now.

"It's supposed to get worse."

"I wish Davis would get on home."

"I thought I saw him pull back in," Papa says.

My heart calms. "Oh good, do you know where he is?"

I just need to see him. I know he's busy, but I've been uneasy all day and he's the only one who can usually take that away.

"I'm not sure. I haven't heard him come in," Ruby says.

I go check to see if he's in his room. It's empty.

"Can Gracie stay with you while I drive out to the house? I just want to check on him."

"You know she can," Ruby says. "Tell Davis he needs to get inside, quit worryin' 'bout that house for today."

"Yes, ma'am…"

I put on a raincoat and lift the hood over my hair and run out to Papa's truck. I look at the state of my flowers and groan. They didn't need so much water. I pull around the back of the house and drive the short distance to our little place. His truck is parked out there, and I breathe a sigh of relief. Looks like he got the tarp completely up too, everything is covered. He's so efficient. I love how hard he's working on this place for us. Just another way that he shows me he loves me.

I get out and run to the house and lift up the tarp. "Davis?" I walk around carefully and look at what he's gotten done even in the last day. It's going to be so pretty. "Davis, are you hiding?"

He's not in here. I go out the back of the house and trip on something. I look down and it's Davis.

He is lying completely still, eyes wide and afraid. I bend down and touch him. His head has a trickle of blood coming from his hairline. Blood seeps out of his mouth.

"Davis!" I cry. The tears and rain immediately blind me. "Davis, what happened?"

He tries to say something and I can't hear him. I lean in as close as I can get and try to hear what he's saying.

"I-I tried...I tried to...wanted to make it right for you." He whispers.

"It's all gonna be all right. I'm gonna go get help. It's all—"

He closes his eyes and the rain and tears roll down his cheeks.

"Open your eyes, Davis. Stay awake, okay? I'll be right back. You just stay awake." Frantic, I stand up and look at all the blood around his head. His fingers touch my ankle.

He looks different. I bend back down and kiss his cheeks and my breath catches. He's not breathing. I feel for his pulse and can't find one. I lay my head on his chest and don't feel the slightest movement. I get by his mouth to feel breath and there's none. Nothing.

I can't comprehend it.

"No, no. No, you can't leave me, Davis. You can't. I love you. I can't live without you too. Do you hear me? Davis! No, you can't go. Please..."

He just lies there, perfectly still.

"Open your eyes. Come back to me. Wake up!"

I give his shoulders a little nudge, afraid to touch him too hard but wanting to stir him. He has to just be sleeping.

He doesn't move.

I scream and yell, my fists on his chest. "God, don't let this happen. You can't. Davis, please don't leave me!"

The rain beats on us. Thunder crackles over our heads and lightning slashes through the sky, making Davis glow for a moment.

He's gone.

Pellets of ice form back over my skin and circle my heart, closing it back up. I lie down beside him, close his eyes, and will myself to die too.

30

I'VE BEEN HERE

I WAKE UP in a hospital room and immediately flash back to waking up in another hospital room all those years ago. I half expect to see Sadie sitting by my bed, but it's Ruby. The second thing I think is, *Davis*...

"Davis! Where is he? I want to see him!" I tell Ruby.

The tears are already falling. The pain is suffocating. God, why didn't you take me too?

"Baby girl, he's gone. He's gone."

She shakes her head and her tears drip down her cheeks. She swipes them away with her hand.

"He fell off a high beam and they say he died immediately because of the impact to his head."

I don't want to hear this. I just want to be with him.

"I can't live without him, Ruby. I can't."

"I know if feels that way, but you 'gon have to, sugar. You got that baby girl and she need you. I need you. Your Papa needs you, Brenda..." she trails off after naming everyone in my life..

"But there's no one like Davis. He's become my whole world," I cry.

"I know, baby. I know."

"I thought he would never leave me…"

"That boy loved you more than anything in this world," Ruby cries. "I hadn't never seen a boy so in love with a girl as he was with you."

"He changed everything, Ruby. I can't…" *I can't do this again.*

The nurse comes in and takes my temperature. "Still over a hundred," she says. "We have antibiotics going in your IV, just to fight off infection."

"I'm fine, I don't have an infection," I tell her.

"You were in the rain for a long time, they said. And you've had a fever all night," the nurse says in a nasally voice. "The doctor would like to keep you here until that fever goes down."

She walks out of the room and I look at Ruby. "Where's Gracie? Does she know about Davis? I've been in the hospital all night?"

"We found you late last night. We thought you two were probably out there kissing, like you alw–" she stops mid-word.

I look out the window and it still looks grey and rainy. We probably would have stayed out there kissing, if he'd been inside like he was supposed to be.

"Gracie doesn't know yet. We wanted to get you home safe and sound before we told her, to not scare her even more."

"I've never spent a night away from her. Was she okay this morning?"

"She cried a little bit when she didn't see you *or* Davis. She's with her papa though and he's takin' good care of her."

"I want to go home. Don't make me stay here, Ruby. I'm fine. I just got too chilled out in the rain, that's all. I need to get to Gracie." I look down at the IV in my arm, attached to me like chains.

Suddenly the desire to hold her in my arms is all I can think about…

"I have to go home."

"Let's just wait and get you feelin' better. You won't rest if you go home. Get that fever down and you can go home," Ruby says firmly.

"Would you get me a cold washcloth, please?" The panic takes my voice up a few notches with every word.

Ruby presses her lips together. She knows me like the back of her hand.

"Yes, I will. But we're not 'gon rush this, sugar. I can't lose you too." Her lips tremble when she says it and I reach out for her hand.

"He loved all of us so much," I whisper.

"Yes, he did. Our lives will have a big ol' empty hole where he was."

She wipes her tears and pats my hand before getting my washcloth. When she comes back, some of my fight is gone. I don't have enough energy to get out of bed. She puts the washcloth on my head and I close my eyes. Hot tears trail down my cheeks and my head pounds from it. I turn my engagement ring around and around on my finger. I was crazy to think I could have everything. Davis came along just long enough to give my life some sunshine and make me hopeful. I won't make that mistake again. It's too hard to wake up to reality.

The nurse comes in and gives me medicine to make me sleep. She stands at the foot of the bed and just watches me for a few minutes, her eyes full of concern. I grip the sheets so I can still the shaking sobs that take over my body. Turning onto my side, I face the wall and close my eyes...like a child playing hide-and-seek. If I can't see anyone, they can't see me.

I SPEND ANOTHER night in the hospital and am sick with missing Gracie by that time. Papa too. Brenda picks me up and cries all the way to the house.

"I just can't believe it," she keeps saying. "I can't believe he's gone."

It's a sunny day, which just feels wrong. We pull up to the house and I avoid looking toward ours. His truck is probably still out there, and if I see it, I'll start wailing all over again. It doesn't matter. I thought it, so the tears come falling down.

Gracie runs out the door and when I bend down, she leaps into my arms. "Mama. I miss you," she cries.

"I missed you too, baby," I lean my head into her curls and a sob gushes out. I try to hold it in, so I don't scare her, but she pulls her head back and sees my face.

"Why you cwyin', Mama?" she says in her angelic voice.

"It's Davis, baby. He's had a bad accident and didn't make it. He's not coming back."

"Where he go?" She looks at me with her eyebrows scrunched together and her lips puckered up. Her eyes fill with tears. I don't know if it's because she sees mine or if she really understands what's happening.

"He went to heaven to live with the angels where he belonged," I tell her.

She looks up into the sky. "I wanna go up they-ah," she says.

"Me too," I whisper.

"He watchin' up they-ah?" she asks.

I look up to the sky again. The clouds look voluminous; big puffs to skip around on. I can just imagine him leaping from cloud to cloud.

"Maybe," I tell her. "Maybe."

"I sink so," she says. "I sink he's up they-ah watchin' us."

"Then you're right, baby girl. I bet that's exactly what he's doing."

I DON'T KNOW how I forgot that it was Gracie who kept me living that other time I thought I was dying. Being pregnant with her, knowing I had to be okay to take care of her, it got me through losing Isaiah. And even though it feels like I can't get past this, it's Gracie who helps get me through each day, minute by minute. There's probably not a second that goes by that I don't wish I had another baby in my stomach to take care of now…Davis's baby in me to love. A piece of him that could stay with me forever. It's my biggest regret.

OCTOBER 19TH COMES and many more tears are shed. I

drive out to our tree and hurriedly gather all the heart rocks that Davis and I kept adding to and move them all to his grave. When I'm done, you'd think I ran five miles. I feel all wrung out.

We talk about Davis a lot. It seems we all need to. Papa can hardly make it through a day without crying for him still. So I know I'm not the only one who is in immeasurable pain. I try to be okay for him and the others, but when I get in my bed at night, I die a little more. It's just too much.

LIFE CARRIES ON. It's hard to believe but Christmas is almost here. I'm just trying to ignore the fact. Everyone else has decorated and I just clean. Clean and play with Gracie.

I'm cleaning the bedrooms upstairs when Ruby finds me.

"You have a phone call, Caroline." She never says my name, so it makes me stand up and take notice.

"Who is it?"

"Your daddy."

I sit down on the bed and she comes and puts a hand on my shoulder. "Sugar? Are you all right?"

"But…how did he find me?"

And then I remember the letter I sent to Nellie. But that was years ago.

I stand up and follow Ruby to the kitchen. The phone is laying on the table and she shoos everyone out of there. Papa kisses me on the cheek before he goes out of the room.

I pick it up slowly. "Hello?"

"Caroline, is that you?" His voice sounds raspy and older.

"Yes, sir." My voice catches and I try not to cry. I'm sick of crying.

"I can't believe I found you," he says.

"How *did* you find me?"

"Well, Caroline, I'm sorry to tell you this way, but... Nellie...she passed away about a month ago and I...well, I just found your letter to her in one of her drawers." He clears his throat.

I sit down. I didn't think my heart could ache any more, but it can.

"I've been looking for ya, and finally talked to someone who knew you were at this number...I called every motel and hotel and apartment building I could find in the Kentucky phone book. I'm actually in Bardstown...a little diner called Shelby's? Once I talked to someone who knew who you were, I just got in the car and drove. Would you—would you be willing to see me?" He sounds tentative.

I can't believe he's at Shelby's. If I weren't already walking around in shock, I would probably feel something: anger, rage, sadness, maybe even a little joy. But as it is, I feel nothing at all.

"Okay. Just come on out here whenever." I give him the address and he thanks me, like we're strangers.

We *are* strangers. The old Caroline is dead.

I'M PLAYING ON the floor with Gracie when he gets there. It's only been thirty minutes since we hung up. I didn't expect him so quickly. I didn't tell Gracie about him and Ruby and Papa have given me space. Maybe I didn't even think he'd come at all.

When the doorbell rings, Papa comes around the corner and sees me standing up.

I take a huge breath. "That's my dad, I think."

Papa nods. "Okay. Would you like me to stay in here with you or do you need some time to be alone?"

"Stay with me and meet him. Maybe we can see what state he's in? He could be drunk, for all I know."

Papa nods again and kisses my cheek. "Okay, Caroline girl. Just give me the look and I'll find somewhere else to be right quick."

Gracie goes to the window to see who's out there. I pick her up and open the door.

We stare at each other, taking it all in. He looks older, lines around his eyes, a little grey in his hair, gaunt, but clear-eyed and sober. He looks like he's been living quite the life. He smiles at me sweetly and looks at Gracie. His eyes widen a little bit when he gets a good look at her. He looks at me again and then back to her in shock.

"Hi Daddy," I say. "This is Gracie, your granddaughter. Gracie, this is your grandpa."

"Hi," she says.

"Hi," he says to her and then looks at me. "Hi to you too."

He smiles his wide smile, and I see the handsome in his face again. The image is fleeting, but for a second I see the daddy who sat by my bed and told me Clovis the Bunny stories.

"She's beautiful, and so are you."

I don't say anything. I open the door wider and he walks inside. Papa is standing there, and he holds out his hand to shake Daddy's.

"Ivan Harrison," he says.

"Dan Carson," my dad says and they shake.

Ruby rounds the corner, her eyes looking wide as saucers.

"And did you ever meet Ruby? She lived in Tulma a long time."

Ruby isn't as warm as Papa. She stands next to him and folds her arms over her chest.

"About time you come lookin' for your daughter," she says.

My dad looks down and nods. "You're right," he looks back up at me, "I should have never left."

No one says anything for a moment and then Papa takes control of the situation.

"Why don't you come have a seat in here. I'll get you some coffee, if you'd like." He looks at me quickly when he says that, and I know he's regretting his offer to leave the room.

"I'll get the coffee, Dr. H, don't you worry about it. You go on and sit down," Ruby bosses and we all hop to.

Gracie seems to understand this is a serious meeting because she's as quiet as a mouse. Her normal chattiness has disappeared and she's just taking it all in. She doesn't miss a thing, this one.

The three of us sit on the couch facing my dad, who sits in the chair across from the couch. It feels like we're a team waiting to see if we should pick him or not.

He leans his elbows on his knees and looks up

earnestly at me. "Caroline, I know I've been an awful parent..."

You won't get any argument from me there. For about a second when I was a little girl, I lived in a make-believe world where I thought you were a decent daddy.

I say nothing out loud. I just wait for him to say his piece.

"I've been sober for two years now. I've driven up and down the southern states, looking for you. Made peace with your grandparents. I'm grateful that I was with your Nellie when she passed."

I feel a little twinge when he says that. I hold Gracie's hand tighter.

"I know I can never fix all the mistakes I made with you, Caroline, but I want to try. I love you. I've always loved you, and I'm so sorry that I was too caught up in myself and my problems to take care of you. I will spend the rest of my lifetime regretting that, and if you'll let me, the rest of my lifetime making it up to you."

The only sound is a bird squawking in the distance. My dad runs his hands through his hair and looks at me again.

"How old is Gracie?" he asks softly.

"Just over two and a half," I answer just as softly.

He smiles at her and I look down to see her smiling back at him. She looks up at me then.

"You daddy?" she asks.

"Yes, my daddy. Your granddaddy."

"That's Papa." She points at Papa and then looks back at me.

"Yes, that's our papa too."

She gets down and goes to stand in front of my dad.

"Up?" she says.

My dad looks surprised, but he picks her up and looks like he's about to cry.

She pats his cheek. "Gwanpapa," she dubs him and the tension in the room lessens somewhat. My dad laughs and Papa chuckles. I even have to smile a little bit at that.

Ruby brings in some coffee and I go with her to the kitchen to get dishes for the coffeecake.

"Are you okay, darlin'?" she asks, her dark eyes worried.

"I guess so. He says he wants to make up for everything. I don't know. I'll believe it when I see it, I reckon."

"He hurts you again, I'll hang him up by his drawers," she says with a vengeance.

A giggle comes out of me that shocks both of us. I don't think I've laughed since Davis…

Ruby grips my shoulders and hugs me tight. "You're gonna be okay, my girl," she whispers. "You are."

MY DAD STAYS the whole afternoon. I show him the plantation—the house, the gardens, the carriage house, the grapes. We traipse through the snow, the crunching of our feet making a racket out in the quiet. Step by step. I come to a stop when I look out at our house and see Davis's truck sitting out there. The tarp blows in the breeze. It's as if he's just right inside there, working.

I turn around and lead my dad back to the main house.

WHILE GRACIE IS still napping, I sit with my dad. Papa has realized it's okay to leave me alone with him and has gone off to give us some time. I ask all about Grandpaw and more about how Nellie was at the end. Then I broach a subject I haven't really cared to know about since I moved to Bardstown. I figure I may as well know the truth, it doesn't change anything.

"What about Mama? Where is she? Are you together?"

"No. Your mama and I were divorced about a year ago. She's remarried and living in Chattanooga."

"Mr. Anderson?"

He nods. "I think she's happy with him. Happy to be done with me, that's for sure." He laughs. It sounds hollow and false.

"I was supposed to get married…eight weeks ago." I look out the window and study the clouds, seeing if I can make out any shapes.

"What happened?"

"He died."

"Caroline!"

"He died building that little house behind the grapes. Fell off the roof. Four weeks before we were supposed to get married." It all pours out of me, but I sound like an emotionless robot. "He brought me back to life and now he's gone."

He comes and sits beside me and takes my hand. I let him.

"Caroline. I am so sorry. I-I can't imagine what

you're going through," he says softly.

We sit there and don't say anything for a long time.

After a while, I go check on Gracie. She's still sleeping, so I leave the door open and go back downstairs.

My dad is standing, looking at the pictures on the mantel. There's one of Davis and me, the night we got engaged. He has his arm around me, and we're looking at each other with huge smiles on our faces.

He holds it up when I walk in the room. "This is him?"

I nod.

"Good-lookin' guy."

"Yeah," I respond.

"So, Gracie…"

I've known this was coming, but he still manages to be the one to surprise me.

"Her daddy is the one who saved my life."

JUMBLED UP

MY STOMACH FEELS like it fell out at my feet.

"How do you know Gracie's dad? And what makes you think you do know?"

"I've gotten to know him pretty well, and she looks just like him."

He looks at me and puts his hand over mine. We're still standing at the mantel.

I stare at him, waiting for more.

"He found me when he came lookin' for you," he explains. "And I treated him like the scum on the bottom of my shoe." He shakes his head, remembering. "He kept coming back though, no matter how I treated him and I just got worse...he came back for more. He looked for you for a year and a half." He stops and looks at me. "He dragged me out of bed, stayed while I went through hell...withdrawals...we drove all over Tennessee looking for you. He has searched high and low for you, Caroline. He even went to California once, but got out there and realized there was no chance he'd find you with nothin' to go on. He dealt with me straight about the alcohol. He even knocked me out one time." He laughs, holding his nose like it's a fond memory.

"Does he know you're here?" I ask, afraid of the answer.

"No, he doesn't. I...I know he's finally trying to move on, and I wanted to see you first. You and I have never even talked about Isaiah Washington. I didn't want to surprise you by bringing him with me. I figured I was surprise enough."

"Yeah," I mutter.

I suddenly feel exhausted. I back away from the fireplace and put my fist to my mouth. My stomach turns and I run to the closest bathroom. I throw up and stay on the bathroom floor after I'm done.

Ruby knocks on the door. "You all right in there, sugar?"

"Not feelin' so well, can you let my dad know?"

"Sure will. You need to lay down?"

"Yes, ma'am, I do."

"Okay, sugar. I'll be right back."

Ruby's gone for a few minutes. I hear the front door close and she knocks on the bathroom door again. "He said he'll call and check on you shortly. I told him he could stay in the carriage house tonight if he'd like. Is that okay with you?"

I stand up and open the door. "Yes, ma'am, thank you."

"Oh girl, you lookin' a little green around the gills!" she exclaims. "I hate so bad you not feelin' good, what we 'gon do with you?"

"Put me out back and shoot me," I say half-heartedly.

"Now that ain't even funny, child."

She leads me up the stairs and to my room. Gracie is just popping up in her bed and rubs her eyes. Ruby pulls back the covers and tucks them up to my neck when I get in the bed. Then she goes and picks up Gracie.

"We 'gon let Mama take a nap," she tells Gracie.

"Mama nap?" Gracie giggles.

"I know, it is funny, ain't it. That mama of yours never do take a nap like a good girl!" Ruby winks at me and shuts the door behind them.

I'm too confused and weary to even make sense of my thoughts. I turn over on my side and sleep the rest of the day away.

MY DREAMS ARE a jumble of Isaiah and Davis and some weird combination of the two. Half the time, I think I'm dreaming of Isaiah and in mid-sentence, he'll turn into Davis. I wake up sweating, with all the covers piled over me like I've been hiding out in a blanket cave. It's the middle of the night. Gracie is asleep in her bed. The moon is casting shadows over her face as she sleeps. She does look just like her daddy. So beautiful it makes my chest hurt. Her eyes are his—the same color, same shape, same expressions.

I lie back down and think about everything my dad said. It's all finally registering that I actually saw him today.

Everything I knew of Isaiah and how my dad talks about him now…it doesn't make sense. None of it adds up. I go back over everything Dad and I talked about and think about the letter. I told him where I was. I sit straight up. *I told him where I was.* If he was looking for me, why didn't he come when he got the letter?

I look at the clock. It's 3:30. I'm tempted to go out to the carriage house and wake my dad.

What does it matter anyway? What would I have done differently if Isaiah *had* come?

I try to get comfortable with my pillow. I was happy. I thought Isaiah had moved on and I had too. What if he hasn't?

But my dad said Isaiah was *trying* to move on. I wonder if he's with that girl still…

My thoughts and emotions clash around…and then I feel bad for even thinking about Isaiah at all. If Davis hadn't died, I'd be happily cuddled up to him right now, in our bed. I know I would have been happy with him the rest of my life.

Even if I'd constantly wondered about Isaiah.

But what if Isaiah *doesn't* know about Gracie at all?

The thought nags at me all night. I doze on and off, but it's restless. I wake up to Gracie's fingers on my cheeks.

"Mama sick?" she asks.

"I'm okay, baby girl." My mouth feels like cotton.

She rests her head on my chest and I play with her curls. I take deep breaths and feel better, just having her near me. Her head pops up. "Gwanpapa?"

"You hear him?"

"I sink so," she says, her voice perking up at the end. "I go see him wight now."

"Well, how 'bout you get your clothes on."

"I yike my gownie," she says.

"I know. I like it too, but let's get one of your pretty dresses on. You can show Granpapa your tea set."

She likes the sound of that, so I get her dressed and she plays with her dolly while I take my shower. When I'm ready, we go downstairs together.

My dad looks up when we come in. He's at the breakfast table with Papa and Ruby.

"Mornin'," I say to everyone. "Sorry, I overslept, Ruby. I'll take care of the dishes once the guests are done."

"Don't you worry none about that. I'll take care of it today. You just feel better." She smiles and seems a little softer when she looks at my dad this morning.

Papa pulls out my chair. "How are you feelin', Caroline girl?" he asks.

"A little better."

"I'm sorry I upset you yesterday, Caroline," my dad says.

I shrug. "It's oka—you know what?" I take a deep breath and look him square in the eyes. "It's not okay. I don't need you coming here after all these years and acting like we can make a relationship out of nothing. We don't *have* anything to pick up where we left off. It wasn't working to begin with. Took me a long time to see that, but I see it now. I'm not gonna be 'nice' just to try to not hurt your feelings. When I was little, I thought you were my savior. Mama would be mean to me and you'd scoop me up," my voice cracks. I shake it off. "You'd hold me and tell me she didn't mean it. But she did. I thought you were on my side, though...that no matter what she said, you'd be there...even in your drunken mess, it was better than nothin'. And then you take off? I was raped, *Daddy*. I was raped and where were you? I was nearly killed and where were *you*? I was left with Mama and then she left *me* time and time again, and *WHERE WERE YOU*?"

I'm shaking now and Gracie reaches up to touch my face and I jump. She starts to cry and I pick her up.

"I'm sorry, baby. Mama's sorry. I didn't mean to scare you," I whisper, rocking her back and forth.

I walk out of the room with her and go up to our big chair in the attic. We sit there a while and then we swing in my swing, her facing me, sitting on my lap, while I pump my legs back and forth. Her arms are clutched tight around my neck and she doesn't let go.

Maybe I will never leave this room.

I might be losing it.

I VENTURE DOWN the stairs at suppertime. Gracie's hungry and Ruby brought lunch up, but by suppertime Gracie is antsy and tired of being pent up in our room. She's pulled out every book on the bookshelves. We've read them all a few times. Her toys are strewn all over the floor. Maybe I'll bundle her up and take her outside.

I find them all at the table, almost as if they never left, but I know Ruby would never sit all day long.

My dad stands up when I come in the room. "Caroline, I'm sorry. I'll leave if it helps. You're so right. I don't deserve any chances with you. I missed out on every chance you've ever handed me. But I want more than anything to be here for you now, in any way you'll have me. If you think you might be willing to try even just a little bit…someday…I will wait for that day."

"I'm sorry I yelled," I say.

I meant what I said, but I do still have some manners left.

"I don't know what we can have. I guess I'm willing to wait and see. See if you stick around. See if you mean what you say," I add.

He nods eagerly. "That's as much as I can hope for," he says.

"I do have some questions, but I don't think now is the time." I motion toward Gracie. "Maybe we can talk about it after she goes to bed."

"Okay. I'd be happy for that."

I listen to Ruby and Papa talk to my dad during supper. It's not exactly chummy, but certainly warmer than yesterday's reception. He seems more comfortable, and since I know them so well, I can tell they aren't just being nice for my sake anymore. He's won them over a little bit.

WHEN EVERYONE ELSE goes to bed, my dad and I sit in the living room. We both have a cup of coffee and a whole lot of baggage hanging around our shoulders. Our space is thick with sorrow.

I don't waste time.

"I sent Isaiah a note, telling him about Gracie when she was a year old. I had gone earlier to tell him while I was pregnant, but I saw him with someone. I didn't want to wreck his future with her. In the letter, though, I told him exactly where we were. He never came."

"Where did you send the letter?"

"His house in Tulma."

"Les's uncles burned down Isaiah's house, Caroline. Isaiah and Sadie finally went to Memphis."

I sit, stunned with this information. *He doesn't know. He didn't reject her. He didn't reject me.*

I ignore that last thought. I don't matter in this equation. I have to tell him about his daughter.

I don't know whether to be happy or to go throw up again. My whole body aches from being so tense and the coffee feels like lead in my stomach.

I shut my eyes and will my insides to stop churning.

"Do you know where I can find him?"

"The last time I talked to him, they were finally moving into a house, but I don't know where exactly…"

"They?" I want to hear her name.

"Isaiah and Sadie."

"He still lives with Sadie?"

"Yeah, he was gonna live with her until he finishes up school. He's going to Memphis State," he adds proudly.

"Why are you acting like you like him?" I shake my head. "All I ever heard growing up with you and Mama and Grandpaw and Nellie, was *black people belong with black people*…except Grandpaw and Nellie didn't say 'black'. It was disgusting. I hated it. You always treated every black person we knew like they were less than you. Like they were privileged to have your kindness. As if your measly droppings were a generosity…"

"I'm ashamed to say that Isaiah is the first one I've ever really gotten to know. He gave me back my life, Caroline. And he's the kindest, smartest, most compassionate man I've ever met, with the exception now of maybe Ivan Harrison."

"Doctor," I say.

"Doctor?"

"*Doctor* Harrison to you," I sass.

My dad grins. "Dr. Harrison, yes. Isaiah is a man of that caliber. I would have never known it if he hadn't forced himself into my life."

I think about that for a while. I can't believe Isaiah spent all that time looking for me. And then helped my dad, in spite of not finding me.

"Will you help me find him?"

"Absolutely."

ISAIAH

SHANELLE CLIMBS OUT of my bed and leans over to kiss my shoulder. Her fro tickles and I brush her away. I didn't mean to stay the night, but now that I'm here, I just want to sleep. She begged me to not leave and I felt bad for wanting to so bad. I look at the clock and groan. It's seven. Dammit, I'm gonna be late for my first hour.

We slept together for the first time last week during Christmas break. She's chased me for the last year and it's been flattering and even fun. I thought I was more than ready to have sex with her, but I already feel the strings tightening around my neck. I should be more than ready for this. I haven't been with anyone but Caroline, and I can't help but still wish it was her. I know I'm crazy. Twenty years old—I should be screwing everything in sight. All my friends seem fine with it. I just don't work that way.

Shanelle is a beautiful girl. She's nice. Not too deep, but not an airhead either. Her body is perfect and the sex is fine. She's *black*. On paper, we're supposed to work. But I can't stop comparing her to Caroline. I still remember how she smelled. I remember her funny expressions and how much I loved to make her laugh. How compassionate she was. Her body. It would have made me content to make love to her every single day of my life.

I get hard just thinking about her. I put my pillow over my head and groan.

I've gotta get out of here.

"Where you goin'?" Shanelle asks.

She eyes me as I put on my Jockeys, coming over like she's a lioness about to pounce.

"I need to get home and shower before class. I'm gonna be late if I don't go right now," I tell her.

"Come shower with me. I can wash you quick," she says.

"I gotta go, Shanelle."

She sticks her lips out in a pout and pulls me in for a kiss. I back up when she slips her tongue in. I don't have time for that.

"Call me tonight," she says.

I nod and get out of there before I make any other promises I can't keep.

MY PROFESSOR'S VOICE drones in and out. I sleep-walk through my day and can practically feel my bed as I drive home. I hit the steering wheel with my fist when I look at my house. Shanelle is sitting on the front steps with Mama.

I shake my head and grab my backpack from the passenger seat.

Mama and Shanelle both look up and kinda shrink into the step. I know I look mad. I try to tone down my anger and take a deep breath. Shanelle really hasn't done anything wrong. This is my mess and I need to deal with it.

"Hey, Mama. Shanelle, how ya doin'? Can we talk a minute?" I wait for her to stand up and put my hand to her elbow and steer her inside. Bad idea. I should have led her directly to her car. As soon as we get in my room, she turns around and tries to straddle me.

"Shanelle, we need to talk." I gently push her leg down.

She bites her lip and comes in for a kiss. I hold my hand up.

"Please. Can we talk? I can't do this. I don't want a relationship with you. Thought I could, but I can't." I look at her and hope she will take it easy.

"What? Are you kidding me? You sure as hell better be kidding, right? Dammit, Isaiah! I mean, don't you be thinkin' you can come back after this. What's wrong with you? Are you into men? Because," she waves her hand along her body, "nobody turns this body down. Nobody." She looks at me with disgust.

"Nope, I'm into women. Just not you." And with that I usher her out of my room and don't stop until we reach the front door.

I slam the door behind her and storm off to my room.

Mama comes in not far behind me. "What did you say to *her*?"

"That I wasn't into her." I pull my books out of my bag and sit down at my desk.

"Well, that isn't a very nice thing to hear," Mama

fusses. "I liked her, she was a nice girl."

"If you'd just heard the mouth on her, you wouldn't be so sure," I tease.

Mama has a thing about girls cussin'.

Her eyes get wide and I can tell she's trying to imagine Shanelle cussing. She can't do it.

"Well, you've gotta give someone a chance, son."

"I did try with her, Mama. I slept with her, all right? Are you happy?"

She clutches her chest and I close my eyes. God, what is wrong with me? I stand up and go over to her. She backs out of the door.

"Don't you be gettin' some girl pregnant, Isaiah. I raised you better than that."

"I was careful, Mama. I won't."

"We've worked too hard for you to make something of yourself for you to just throw it all away on a girl it sounds like you don't even like."

I nod my head and keep my eyes down. "You're right, Mama. I just want to forget Caroline." I press my fingers to my eyes and push down, squeezing them shut. "I can't forget her. I don't know why. I just can't."

Her face softens a little. "I know there is no one like Caroline."

She turns around and I hear her sniff. She still gets sentimental about Caroline.

"I loved her too, you know."

"I know, Mama."

"Have you talked to her dad lately?"

"The last time I tried, it just rang and rang."

"Well, why don't you call him again…see if he knows anything new?"

"Okay…I'm sorry, Mama. I shouldn't have said that the way I did. I don't want to upset you."

"You're a man, I know you've got desires like anybody else. But you've always been smarter than everybody else too. Don't blow it all for a few minutes of fun…get done with school, find somebody you care about, settle down. Someone else will come along that you *do* care about."

If I could count the times my mom has said that last sentence, I'd be a rich man. She really believes it. But she's never had a love like mine with Caroline.

I CALL DAN later that night. It rings and rings and rings. He seemed well the last time I talked to him. I hope he hasn't had a relapse. Since he went back to Tulma, I've talked to him less and less. Maybe I should make a trip there on my next day off.

❀ 33 ❀

FULL CIRCLE

THE HOLIDAYS ARE grueling. Gracie is the only bright spot. Everything reminds me of Davis and I can't get past the injustice that someone like him is gone. I'm fighting to get out of bed every morning. Now that my dad has made himself right at home, I feel the finality of Davis being gone. Dad works on the house, doing the projects Davis would have done and making it more evident that he isn't coming back.

It's strange that all the men in my life have been builders.

I keep putting off going to find Isaiah. My dad has tried the number he had for him and didn't reach him. He's not sure he has the latest number, so I'm not sure what to do next. Dad says he's not sure how he'll get the new number unless he gets home and Isaiah happens to call.

I want to tell him to go home then, but I don't. I do tell him that I won't be going to Tulma with him, so if that's what needs to happen, he better go ahead and then come back for me when he has the number.

He keeps staying though, and before I know it, we're

halfway through the month of January.

"Why don't we just go look for him at the University?" I ask one morning.

I'm not sure why I haven't just taken off to do it myself at this point. I guess I still have some daddy issues. I don't want to look to him for help, but I wish that he would come through sometime.

"We could," my dad says. "But…it would just be more difficult if he didn't have any warning."

Ruby and Papa are busy *looking* busy in the kitchen. I know they're listening to every word. I study my dad's face. He eats his toast and reads his paper. I snatch the paper out of his hands.

"You don't want to leave here, do you? You'd like to stay forever and be pampered just like I pampered you at home. Except Ruby, don't you do it. He's a grown man. He can take care of himself."

I storm out of the kitchen and practically trip over one of our guests.

"Caroline!" my dad calls out behind me. "Hold on."

I turn around and give him an exasperated look.

"You're right, I don't want to leave, but it's not because I want someone to wait on me. I guess I'm not wanting this time with just us to be over. I've been enjoying getting to know the adult you."

"Why?" I lift my shoulders. "It's not like I'm even nice to you."

"True." He laughs. "I must be a sucker for punishment." He puts his hand on my arm. "Caroline, look at me. Even when you're mad at someone, your sweetness comes through. You might mouth off here and there, but I know your heart. I do know who you really are, whether you believe me or not. And I deserve every piece of crap you ever give me. I know that."

I shift on my feet and he drops his arm.

"Now listen, if you really want to go, we'll go as soon as Ruby is fine with the Inn schedule. Do you want to look at that and let me know?"

"Okay, I'll go ask her."

"All right. Let's do this." He winks at me and my heart softens just a touch.

THAT AFTERNOON, RUBY and I look over the schedule and decide that I should go the following week or the next, before the guests start pouring in. The whole month of February is a busy one, so I'll need to be back by the 1st. For the next few days, any time there's a lull, I pack for Gracie and me. She's excited to go on a trip.

We set out on a Monday morning and drive as long as we can before Gracie needs to stretch and go to the bathroom. We're about halfway to Memphis and get a bite to eat while we're stopped.

It's been so long since I've been anywhere besides Bardstown that I had forgotten how people look at a white woman with a black child. In one restaurant stop, at least four people openly view me with disgust.

One guy was smiling at Gracie, thinking she was so cute as she did a little dance while we were waiting to be seated. When she turned and said, "Mama, we eat soon?" and he saw that I answered, he rolled his eyes and looked away, disgusted.

It's a vile thing. I'm reminded of why I've worked so hard to protect Gracie from it. Dad notices and during one particular glare, he puts his hand on my shoulder and tells the men to keep moving. Thankfully, not everyone is that way. We have a nice waitress.

We eat quickly and get out of there. I hope Memphis will be better.

We pull into Memphis late in the afternoon, and Dad checks us into a motel not far from the University. I give Gracie a bath and then she wears herself out bouncing on the bed. When she falls asleep, I get in the tub and think about seeing Isaiah tomorrow.

My dad calls several numbers in the phonebook but doesn't find him. He thinks they keep their number unlisted because of all that went down in Tulma before they left. We'll just have to go to the school and see if we can find him, I guess.

The next morning is warmer than usual for January, but we dress in layers, just in case. I'd like to think that I don't put any extra care into my appearance, but I do. When I come out of the bathroom, Dad whistles. I roll my eyes. He laughs.

With Gracie, though, I put on her cutest outfit and make sure her hair is just so. It's not every day you meet your daddy.

Before we leave to stalk Isaiah, I look up to heaven. "If you're up there, Davis, put in a good word with God. I just want Isaiah to know her. That's all. I don't expect anything else but that."

We park in front of the long brick building. Not so bad, I think...until I see all the other buildings around it. It will be a miracle if we find him.

Dad goes to the left side of the building and I go to the right. We're there about ten minutes before a rush of students pours in from everywhere. Some are walking, some park their cars and others lock their bikes to the rack next to the sidewalk. I scan all the bicycle riders, thinking Isaiah would naturally be riding his bike, but then shake my head, aggravated with myself. He's not a kid anymore.

When the traffic slows down, I walk around to Dad's side.

"See anyone who looked like him?" he asks.

"No. Would I recognize him? Does he look the same?"

"It's been a while since I've seen him, but yes, I'm pretty sure he looks the same, only taller and better looking. Or maybe it was just that he looked better once I got sober."

I smile at his joke and think he's probably right. Because there's no way Isaiah Washington could get any better looking than he already was.

My dad goes to some of the other buildings. He goes to the admissions' office too, but he's already tried calling there and they don't give out information about their students.

Gracie plays with her dolly under different trees and picks a few flowers on the sly. We walk to different parts of the campus, and I think, to her, it's just another day outside.

We give up around five that night.

"What if he takes night classes?" I ask as we get in the car.

"We need to eat, honey. Keep your strength up. You've given Gracie all your snacks today."

We come across a Popeye's and I'm reminded of that day here so long ago. I wonder if he thinks of that every time he passes it…that I abandoned him while he went to get me food. The guilt drowns me. If what Daddy said is true and Isaiah never got my letter and looked for me for a whole year and a half…and is finally moving on…why would I turn his life upside down now?

I look out my window, miserable. For Gracie. I need to swallow my guilt and my pride…and move heaven and hell to make sure they have a relationship.

THE NEXT MORNING, we are about to go out the door when our phone rings. Dad and I both pause, and then I say, "It's probably just the front desk wondering when we're checking out."

"Probably," he says.

I answer it.

"Sugar? That you?"

"Ruby! Yes. Is everything all right?"

"Yes, baby girl. Listen, 'member that cousin I told you 'bout that was friends with Sadie back in the day?"

"Yeah, kinda…"

"Well, you're not 'gon believe it, but she called me this mornin' and she say she saw Isaiah in *Tulma*."

"No! Was she sure?"

"She sho was. She say it is him and lord did she evah go on about his good manners…"

"She talked to him?"

"She sho did. And said he was the sweetest thing. She

also itchin' to introduce him to her granddaughter, but I told her she better leave him alone."

I laugh at her.

"Girl, it is good to hear you laugh. Now you better get on over to Tulma. He ain't in Memphis!"

"Okay, Ruby. I'll tell Dad and see what we need to do."

We hang up and I tell him everything.

"I can't go to Tulma, though. It just...I can't," I tell him.

"I'll drive over there...you stay here, have a day or two at the pool with Gracie. I'll go find him. It will be much easier to find him in Tulma than here."

"Thank you, Dad. I appreciate you doing all this."

"You're welcome, sweetie. It's the least I can do." He goes to his suitcase to take out a cooler shirt and stops halfway to the bathroom. "I don't know why I didn't think of this. Can you call Ruby back and have her call her cousin back...to get Sadie's number?"

I whack my head with my palm. "Yes! I was not cut out for this!"

My dad laughs at me.

I call Ruby right away and within ten minutes, she calls me back.

"Here 'tis. Oh girl, I can't believe you gon' find him!" She sounds so excited.

I hand the number to Dad and he calls Sadie. I bite my nails while he dials. My heart stops when he says, "Hello? This is Dan Carson. Is this Sadie Washington?"

And it plummets all the way back to Bardstown when he says, "It is! Hello, Sadie, I'm so glad we found you!" He gives me a wide-eyed grin and continues talking to her.

"He is? Well, I've been looking for him too. I've been out of town for a while. Mm-hmm, been visiting my daughter." He laughs then and I get choked up.

Sadie. I wonder if she still thinks of me with as much love as I think of her.

"She's doing really well, Sadie. Really well. Yes, ma'am, she is. I know it, makes me so happy too. She's been in Kentucky. Yes. Mm-hmm. We sure did…I guess we didn't go far enough into the country, she was there… so is…yes, I know it. Is Isaiah there, by any chance?"

He looks at me and grins again.

"I can't believe it. Well, are you able to tell him to come on home? Oh, he will? I think we can stick around until then." He laughs. "Yes! We sure are. She's here with me."

He throws his head back and laughs again. I grin in spite of myself.

"I'm not lying, she's here with me."

He holds the phone out and I hear Sadie wailing and thanking the good Lord Jesus and God Almighty…Peter, James and John too.

I put my head in my hands and weep.

My dad puts his hand on my shoulder, and I sit down on the bed.

When he speaks again, his voice trembles. "I sure am grateful too. Yes, ma'am, hang on, I'll get one." He pulls a pad of paper out the motel desk. "Okay, shoot. Mm-hmm. Yes. Oh, is that by the new white brick bank there on the corner? I know right where that is. Okay, yes. Got it…what time would you like us?"

"All right, we'll be there."

He gets off and I stare at him expectantly. "When?

Tomorrow night, the next day?"

"Tonight at five."

There went my stomach dropping again.

I'M READY BY three and pace the motel floor, back and forth, back and forth. Gracie trails me the first twenty minutes, until I even wear her out.

"I need another shower," I mumble and head to the bathroom to at least freshen up with a washcloth, since I don't want to do my hair all over again.

I come back out and start pacing again. It's been three years and four months since I've seen him. A lifetime ago. I've grown up and so has he.

"Relax, Caroline. It's gonna be okay." My dad gets up and puts his hand on my elbow. "Really, it will."

"Weyax, Mama." Gracie chimes in.

"Oh, don't you start piping up." I reach over and tickle her.

She yelps and laughs a belly laugh.

As soon as I stop, she holds her hand up and says it again, "Weyax, Mama." And then dies laughing when I tickle her again.

We do it until she can't breathe from laughing so hard, and I have to help her stand up. I barely hold my hand up now and she starts laughing like I'm tickling her.

"You're such a good mama, Caroline."

"Thanks, Dad." I'm still taken aback when my dad pays me a compliment.

"You were always the grown-up in our little family of

three," he says. "The one who knew how to love the right way."

I sit down and look at him. "There were a few memories of you that held me over during the rough times."

"Really? Like what?" He leans forward, eager to hear what I have to say.

That, in itself, is something I keep thinking is going to pass. He'll surely look over my shoulder, see alcohol in the distance and go hunt it down. So far, this time, knock on wood…it hasn't happened.

"Clovis the Bunny…that was always a special thing, when you'd make up a Clovis story for me."

He smiles, pleased and maybe even a little embarrassed.

"There were some birthdays that you made sure I was taken care of, and like I said, you stood up to Mama for me a few times."

I hold up my "C" necklace and he gets tears in his eyes.

"I can't believe you still wear that," he says, choked up. "I wish I'd done better, Caroline. Every day I wish it. I was selfish and a child…and consumed…I'm sorry."

"You've already said you're sorry. I'm not gonna make you say it forever. Once was enough if you'll stick around this time."

I turn to him when I say that last part and hope that he sees I mean it.

He does. He stands and comes over to me, pulling me into a hug.

"I love you, Caroline. Thank you for this…"

He backs away awkwardly and goes into the bathroom. I hear him blow his nose. When he comes back out, he avoids my eyes and his face is all red.

I smile. Maybe he really has changed.

He looks at the clock. "We should probably get going!"

"Are you sure?" I touch my chest. My heartbeat needs to slow to at least half the rate it's pumping or I'll be passin' out before I even get to him.

"Yeah, it'll take us a little while to get over there. We'll have a little traffic, going that way."

Gracie grabs Dolly and a scraggly blanket she insisted on bringing on this trip. I tried to talk her into a prettier one, but she would have none of it.

✾ 34 ✾

ALIVE

I TRY TO think about everything but what is actually happening as we drive to Isaiah's house. Just those words, *Isaiah's house*, are enough to make me feel chewed up and spit out. *Oh, Lord*, I turn to praying, *don't let me lose my lunch on his shoes*.

We pull in front of Isaiah's house fifteen minutes early, and Gracie is bouncing up and down between Dad and me.

"Oh my goodness," I put my hand up to my mouth, "I haven't…"

"What is it?" Dad looks at me, concerned.

"I haven't told Gracie who we're seeing. I've been so wrapped up with how *he's* gonna take it, I haven't told *her*."

"Baby, it's all gonna work out. Nellie used to say, 'I just know it in my knower'…that's how I feel right now."

I try to gulp a huge breath, but it doesn't really work.

"You've got time to tell her, if you want to…"

"What if he doesn't-?"

"He will," my dad says emphatically.

"We're gonna see your daddy, Gracie," I say it before I can choke back the words.

"*My* daddy?"

"Your daddy."

"I wanna see my daddy!" She tries to crawl over me and get out the car door.

"Okay, hold on, we're going."

I hold onto Gracie and open the door.

We're starting to go up the driveway when the garage door opens and I hear the clank of the lid being put on a garbage can. As the door opens all the way, he turns around and it's *him*.

Isaiah sees us and sets down the can. The look on his face is pure shock. His mouth drops. He puts his fist to his mouth and I see his shoulders raise with his breath. He steps forward, narrowing his eyes to see if it's really me. And then he looks ecstatic. He comes running out.

"Caroline! That can't be you, can it?"

The smile on his face and his sheer joy at seeing me makes me lose it. I start crying through my wobbly smile. And then he comes to a complete stop when he sees Gracie.

"Caroline?" he asks, tentatively.

"It's me," I say shyly. "Did you not know we were coming?"

He looks confused and shakes his head. "No," he laughs, "I just got home from Tulma! I-I'm shocked!"

I walk the rest of the way to him and he studies Gracie. His mouth drops again and his face crumbles when he looks in her eyes.

"This is Gracie," I tell him. "Your little girl."

I look at our girl. "Gracie, this is your daddy."

She holds her arms out to him and he takes her and wraps her in a hug. She squeezes him tight, and his eyes close as he breathes her in. When he opens them and looks at me, I expect to see bitterness, but all I see is relief.

He holds out a hand to touch my face and I remember all the reasons why I never got over him.

"This is really happening?" he asks.

I begin trembling, and I reach out for him so I won't go down. He hugs me to him and my tears get his shirt all wet. He smells like he just got out of the shower.

"You sure feel real," he says.

We hug until Gracie squeaks, "Yook! That moon's got yong yegs yike mine!"

She's pointing up at the moon, and sure enough, the beams look like long legs shining down on us.

Isaiah looks at her in wonder. "Did she really just say that?" He stares at me. "You're so beautiful. Both of you. I've gotta be dreamin' right now…"

I smile at him, my insides pouring out gratefulness that he doesn't hate me. And another feeling that I'd long ago tucked away under an extremely heavy protective coat and put in the freezer for safekeeping.

My dad clears his throat.

"Dan!" Isaiah holds his extra arm out to my dad and they hug. Then they're in some sort of a headlock. "Thank you for bringing her to me."

The sight of my dad and Isaiah obviously having a connection does something for me that I didn't expect. My chest feels like it's going to burst right out of my skin.

"I tried to tell her that you searched the world over for her for a long time. I think she might believe me now." Dad turns around and winks at me.

I go all splotchy.

"Caroline!" Sadie comes out of the door and runs straight for me. "I didn't even get to tell him yet! He snuck in on me!" She hugs me. "As I live and breathe, child, I can't believe it's you. Look at you!" She looks at Isaiah then. "And who is this you've g—"

She puts her hand to her mouth and a sob escapes. "Oh sweet lamb of God, that is your child, Isaiah." She looks at me then with her eyebrows bunched together.

I confirm. "She is. I-I wasn't sure when I was pregnant, but as soon as I saw her, I knew."

Gracie looks at Sadie and waves. "Hi."

Sadie giggles. "Hi. I'm Sadie, your grandma."

"Gwacie," she pats her hand on her chest and nods, "I Gwacie." Then she reaches out her arms for Sadie to take her. "Gwandma, Gwacie, Gwacie, Gwandma." Gracie laughs at the sound of that and it's as if she's tapped a magic wand over us. Her laughter puts us all at ease.

Isaiah holds out a hand to me. "Come inside? Sorry, we've kept you out in this cold for so long. I'm not thinkin' straight. I seriously did just drive in from Tulma." He shakes his head and doesn't take his eyes off me, even when he talks to my dad. "I was worried about you, Dan…since I couldn't get an answer at your place."

We walk inside and Sadie tells us to have a seat. Gracie is already chatting her ear off.

Dad speaks up, "I tried to call you too, back before I ever went to Caroline's, but when I didn't get you I thought it must be meant to be. I didn't know if you were needing to…you know…not think about it all for a while."

Isaiah looks at me and smiles. "I tried that. It didn't work."

I swallow hard and wish for the cold air again to cool me off.

"I always loved how your cheeks turned pink when anyone talked about you," he says so only I can hear.

Sadie clears her throat and says, "Dan, would you like to help me set the table for dinner while these children catch up?"

"I'd be happy to," he answers, and they go in the other room with Gracie.

I look down at my hands and he takes them in his. I'm overwhelmed by all the feelings that are still there. Tears blind my vision and I try to blink them away, but they stream down my cheeks.

"I'm sorry, Isaiah. So sorry."

He sucks in air and blows it out. "Why didn't you tell me we had a baby, Caroline?"

I look at him then. His eyes are so hurt and yet, still full of love. It's blinding. He looks ready to say something, when suddenly, his hand stops rubbing mine. He looks down and his face falls.

I look down and see what he's staring at—my engagement ring.

"You're married?"

There's the voice and look I expected. Hurt, anger, disbelief.

"No, but I almost got married," I tell him honestly.

"Tell me everything," he says. "Start from the day you left me...that killed me, you know."

He gives me a look of anger then, and I know my explanation will never be enough.

But I try...from when I realized that I couldn't keep hurting him and holding him back from being all he could be. The reasons I left him that day. Meeting Brenda and deciding to stay in Bardstown. What I felt when I saw how crazy he was about his girlfriend…

He holds up a hand. "That was *not* my girlfriend… that was my cousin, Nia. And I am crazy about her, you *are* right about that part…but as a cousin."

He scowls at me and I want to take back that day more than anything.

"Well, I really wish I'd cleared that up with you that day…would have saved me the gutting that took place in my heart." I try to say it lightheartedly, but it's not believable.

I have to try or else I won't be able to wipe myself up off the floor. Why? Why didn't I go to him anyway?

Isaiah leans his forehead over on mine. "Can I do this?" he asks.

"Yes," I whisper.

"Dammit, Caroline, I can't hate you. I-God knows I've tried, but I just can't. You're here. I've been lost… okay, then what happened?" He runs a finger along my jaw.

I tell him all about Papa and then Ruby coming right after Gracie was born. "They saved me. I don't know how I would have made it without them…"

"Thank God you had each other," he whispers, his hands running through my hair.

I'd forgotten how just a look from Isaiah would send shivers down my spine. The feel of his hands in my hair makes me shudder.

I tell him about writing him the letter on Gracie's first birthday and then guilt that I didn't have the guts to tell him sooner.

He gets up and puts his hands on his head. Then he bends over, hands on his knees and takes a breath.

"I can't believe I've missed out on her whole life. She's what—two and a half?"

"Two years and eight months," I clarify. And cringe. And wish a hole would swallow me up.

"What the hell, Caroline?" He looks at me with such anguish, I go to him and put my hands on his cheeks. The tears are running down both our faces.

"Isaiah, please…I-it doesn't make sense. I wasn't thinking right. I realized I was wrong and when I found out I was pregnant, I knew that even if the baby wasn't yours, I had to tell you. I wish to God I hadn't left that day without telling you! And then time just went on…I waited too long to write you and I just couldn't seem to go back to Tulma…to this day I can't."

He puts his hands on the wall and doesn't turn around for a long time. His shoulders are taut and the anger is bouncing off of him. I try to say something and can't find the words. I made a huge mistake. I knew better than to think he wouldn't want his baby girl.

"I'm so sorry, Isaiah. I-I should have done everything it took to find you and tell you, whether I thought you wanted to hear it or not." I move closer to him. I reach out to touch his shoulder and lose my nerve.

The ticking of the clock sounds like a bomb, ready to go off. Each second that ticks by feels like I'm losing him all over again. Just when I think I can't take another ounce of silence, Isaiah takes his hands off the wall and sniffles. He doesn't look at me, but takes a deep breath.

"You knew me better than anyone. I don't understand how you could have kept the truth from me. It was hard enough that you left the way you did. I would have done anything for us to be together, Caroline. *Anything.*" He swallows hard. "You disappeared on me...I've never gotten over that."

"I thought I had to," I whisper. "I thought I was doing the right thing for you."

"That you'd think I'd move on so quickly..." He shakes his head. "Surely you have more faith in me than that. I *loved* you."

It feels like a slap across the face. *Loved.*

"I love you now," he whispers.

My heart quickens with those words.

"But I never dreamed of this," he continues. "I can't believe we have a child."

For a moment I think he's going to hit the wall, but he doesn't. He balls his hands into fists and looks angrier than I've ever seen him. He keeps speaking in a monotone voice.

"I would have raised her even if she wasn't mine. You know I would have."

I nod, but he doesn't see me. And then he looks at me and the air in the room feels less stifling all of a sudden.

"By the time you sent a letter, there was no house for it to be mailed to..." He rubs his eyes and wipes his hands on his pants. "We moved so much, I doubt the post office knew what to do with all our mail around then." He looks away but laces his fingers through mine. "I wish you'd told me the minute you found out, Caroline. I wish you'd never left," he admits. "I wish I'd had this time with my baby girl. I've missed so much." He shakes his head. "*But,*" he bites his lip to keep it from shaking, "you're here now. And I have wished every single minute of the last

FORTY MONTHS that you were here." He pinches his arm. "Right? You're here? I can't believe this is happening! I know, I can't stop sayin' it! We have a *lot* of time to make up for…"

When he finally looks my way again, the hurt is still there, but it's tempered with a tentative smile. "It's gonna take me some time to wrap my head around all this, but I'm…well, just tell me the rest," he says.

I tell him about the bed and breakfast and then Davis…

"He was my best friend and then overnight, practically, he was more. I was going to marry him."

"You love him," he states, no question. He looks worried.

"I did love him. No one could ever take the place of you, but I did love Davis in a different way."

He nods. "That's hard for me to hear, but I get it." He looks up at the ceiling and then back at me, his eyes ashamed. "I tried to fill the hole that you left…but couldn't. I just gave up trying a week ago, as a matter of fact."

I don't even want to know. I just want to take what is happening right now and live in that moment. He wants to know, though.

"So why haven't you married him?"

"He died before I could."

"Oh, Caroline. Really? I mean…I'm so selfish to be relieved you didn't marry him, but I'm sorry you lost him."

"Thank you. The truth is, I would have never been with him if you'd been there. We would have all been friends, though, I know that."

"I love you, Caroline." He closes his eyes and when he opens them, they're shiny. "I've always been honest with you and I have to more than ever now, while I have this chance. I'm angry with you right now, but I...I feel like I've been given too much of a miracle in having you back to waste time on that. The day you left me, I wished I could *die*. And at the same time, I understood why you felt you had to do that. I didn't agree, but...I understood."

He's quiet for a moment, just looking at me.

And then he says, "Are you here to be with me now, Caroline?" He puts both hands on my face and looks into my eyes. "Please say that you are."

"Once I knew where you were and that you'd been looking for me for so long, I had to let you know about Gracie."

"I can't believe we have a daughter. I love her, already I do..." He studies my eyes. "But is that it? Are your feelings for me gone?"

I bite my lip and his eyes follow my mouth.

"No," I whisper, "that's not it. I still love you."

He draws a deep breath. "You do?"

"Always."

"Are we gonna do it right this time, Caroline? Are we gonna be together? No matter what?"

"I don't want to be without you another second," I tell him. "No matter what."

He leans down and kisses me, and every nook, chink, crack, fissure, cranny, fracture—*crevice*—that has been broken or dried up or closed off or frozen or *dead*...sparks back up in full, living, breathing color.

I'm awake and I'm never going to let go of this feeling again.

GRACIE AND I decide to stay a couple of days with Isaiah and Sadie. She sets up a little pallet for Gracie in the room next to mine. Gracie wanted to sleep in there because it's pink.

"Is this okay?" he asks before he crawls into bed with me. "I was gonna take some time to process all this, but...I know that I don't want to live another moment without you."

"Is your mama okay with this?"

"Because it's you, yes. She knows I already belong to you. And that I don't want to miss another thing. Not with you, not with Gracie. Never again."

"After all this time and all I've done, you still want me?"

"I'll never stop, Caroline."

I'm complete.

We make love, all night, after not seeing each other in so long. And it feels right. There is nothing tentative or awkward about it, even though we're silent, so nothing can be heard. It's perfect, just like coming home.

Seeing him again, I know I'm willing to endure any persecution that might come. And I can't sacrifice my happiness for his anymore, not in that way. I could if it was giving up that extra pork chop or letting him have the better pillow...but not my love. I can't withhold my love from him for another second. Because that could never be better for him. Our love is like air and we need each other to breathe.

THE NEXT NIGHT Gracie falls asleep in our room while we're talking. Isaiah watches her sleep. He's enchanted with her. When we start to get sleepy, he carries her to her pink bedroom and then has to check on her one more time before getting back in bed with me.

"She is so beautiful. I think she knows I'm her daddy, don't you? She can tell there's something different with us. I feel it," he says.

"Yes, she absolutely does," I assure him.

"Are you sure you're ready for me full-time?" he asks.

He's looked into transferring credits to the University of Louisville and has already gotten the process started. I love him for being willing to do that without ever even setting foot there.

"I'm positive," I tell him. "And Bardstown has been good to us. It will be easier there, I think."

"Just promise you won't leave me again and I'll go anywhere you want to go." He kisses my shoulder and makes his way down my neck, stopping to kiss along my scar.

We let our bodies say the rest of what needs to be said.

SADIE DECIDES TO stay long enough to sell the house, but she doesn't have ties to Memphis without Isaiah, so she agrees to come see what she thinks about Bardstown in a few weeks. I know she'll love it.

I never dreamed I would be bringing him home. I get giddy when I think about Papa and Ruby knowing him. To have my family all together, it's more than I can take.

Papa and Ruby welcome him into their lives, just as they have me. They've heard so much about him, it's like they already knew him, but when he's actually here, he has this way of making everyone know how important they are to him. He thanks Papa and Ruby for taking such good care of us, for loving me and Gracie and embracing him. I look at him with Papa every day and realize that he needed Papa just like I did. We don't take it lightly, we recognize what a gift we've been given.

Dad goes back to Tulma to be with Grandpaw. And I have to admit that I'm sad to see him go. We write letters back and forth and he comes to visit every couple of months. I'm finally trusting my heart to him, and he's not disappointing me.

All my concerns that it might be odd to have Isaiah in the place where I've spent so much time with Davis are put to rest the moment he's here. Because, really, Isaiah was never out of my thoughts. He has already been part of every memory. Even if I was trying to push him out, he has always been a constant.

But in the flesh is so much better. I look at him every morning and inhale him. We've moved out to the carriage house and it feels like a dream. We can hear Gracie's feet pitter patter across the floor as she runs to our room every morning. She dives into bed with us and lands right smack-dab in the middle of us every time.

Isaiah and Gracie are head over heels with each other. I hear her telling him all the time. "I yove you, Daddy.

You stay here with us forever?"

And he'll reassure her that he's not going anywhere.

I know it will take time for us to believe we really get to keep all this happiness.

❀ 3̄5̄) ❀

THE GOOD

IN APRIL, A tornado comes through and wipes out all the gardens and a lot of the grapes. The shell of my house with Davis is also destroyed, and I grieve the loss of him in my life all over again. It hasn't been long, but it feels like an eternity since he died. I thank him every day for healing my heart enough to get through my time without Isaiah. He didn't fix things completely, but his love covered my bruises and got them on their way to healing.

His truck is just fine and what I drive most of the time.

Since there's less to work on right now with the gardens, I spend more time writing. It's something I've neglected for a while. Once I'm done with my responsibilities for the Inn and usually while Gracie is napping, I'll sit down with my notebook and pour it all out. I think the therapy I got from working out in the garden was worth more than I knew. I'm starting with my story, in hopes that, in time, every past wound will at least scab over...I know I'm not there quite yet.

Writing is like taking all your insides out, stomping

on them, and stuffing them back inside hoping they'll fit. *Especially* when you're writing your history.

All that, and yet, I still feel like it's helping.

One night, when the air is not so chilly, Isaiah, Gracie and I take a walk outside.

Isaiah is holding Gracie and his hand is around my waist. He seems to be leading us somewhere and I let him. We walk to my favorite archway. All the wreckage and it remains untouched.

Isaiah pulls me under the structure and we look up at it. It's still beautiful. Weathered, but strong.

"This survived, just like we did," Isaiah says.

"It sure did." I smile at him.

"Listen, I know we've tried to get married a couple of times…"

We haven't been able to get anyone to marry us… we've tried three places. Mixed marriages are apparently against a few religions.

"How about we get married right now and then plan a big party once we get it looking pretty out here again?" Isaiah raises his eyebrows. "What do you think? Will you marry me now?"

"Yes!"

"Just us. Right here, right now." Isaiah smiles.

"Okay. I like it." I smile back.

"I, Isaiah Cornelius Washington, take you, Caroline Josephine Carson, to be my wife. I will cherish you forever, live to make you smile, love you beyond the day I die, and do whatever it takes to make you happy, so long as we both shall live."

I lean up and kiss him.

Gracie giggles.

"I, Caroline Josephine Carson, take you, Isaiah Cornelius Washington, to be my husband. I will spend every second of the rest of my life loving you and only you. I will always be grateful that we were given another chance, and when hard times come, I will know that we've already endured the worst. We can handle anything as long as we're together."

Isaiah nudges Gracie and she says, "Now?"

"Now," he whispers.

"You may kiss the bwide," Gracie says proudly.

Isaiah kisses my lips and Gracie kisses the rest of my face and then moves on to his.

ISAIAH GETS DONE with the school and the very next day we have a huge birthday party for Gracie. She's three years old and very excited about it. Everybody's there—Papa, Ruby, Sadie, Brenda, Charlie, Shelby, and right before it starts, Dad and Grandpaw arrive.

I get to Grandpaw's side of the car before he even gets out good.

"Why, look at you," he says and gives me a big hug. "You're prettier'n a tom-cat's kitten!"

"Grandpaw, it's good to see you."

"It's good to see you. I'm glad to see you so fine. Now, what's this I hear about you giving me a nigger baby?" His stomach starts bouncing up and down while he laughs and shakes his head.

"Grandpaw, if you're gonna talk like that, you can just get right back in your car and go back to Tulma. I'm

334

not having my daughter or my husband hear our family say that. You hear?"

"Oh, Caroline, don't be actin' above your raisin' just because you're out here on all this." He waves his arm out over the plantation. "You are who you are."

Isaiah comes up behind me then and puts his hands on my shoulders.

"Hello! Welcome," he says to Grandpaw.

Grandpaw nods at him but doesn't say anything.

I open my mouth to say something and Isaiah nudges me. I look over my shoulder at him and he gives me a subtle shake of his head. He walks around to Dad and they hug.

Grandpaw behaves the rest of the day. He doesn't say much, but that's just as well. He probably hasn't gone a day in his life without telling one of his racist jokes, so I guess we can't expect to retrain him all in the course of a day.

GRACIE DOESN'T EVEN know what to do with herself —all her favorite people, all in one place.

It's fun to watch Brenda and Charlie. They're really happy together. I think they'll be getting hitched soon, if Brenda has anything to say about it. I look around at all the adults and realize we need to get Gracie around more children…fast…she needs some little friends. Or a sibling. Pretty soon…I might be convinced to work on that before too long. For now, I want Gracie to have her time with her dad. And I want to enjoy Isaiah as much as I can just like this. I smile over at him and he smiles back.

"What?" He comes over and nuzzles my neck.

"Nothin'." I smirk.

"Oh, you're thinkin' somethin'," he says.

"I'll tell you later—when I can actually do something about it."

His eyes light up and he kisses the back of my neck.

Sweet Jesus, I love him.

MY BIRTHDAY COMES a few days later and Isaiah takes me camping to celebrate. He says we're around such splendor all the time at the Inn, we should get out and enjoy the nature around it. So we hug Gracie, who is happy for her own little adventure with Ruby, and we head out in the truck with a tent.

We park not too far from a lake we found a few weeks ago and find a good place to put the tent. I pull out the huge picnic basket and laugh at our version of camping. Ruby has sent food for twelve.

There's no one around. It's our very own secluded hideaway.

We go swimming and talk about that day so long ago when we were swimming in our clothes. The subject comes up because Isaiah has stripped me of my suit.

"If we had just done this back then, it could have all been settled," he teases.

"You think so?" I laugh.

"Mm-hmm."

"I wish I'd known back then that it would all work

out."

"I do too, but you know what? We might not have seen all the good if we hadn't gone through all the bad."

I give him a scowl and he shrugs.

"It's true," he says.

"You've always seen the good."

"You're right. Because I've always seen *you*." He wraps my legs around him and kisses me. "*You* are the good."

I lean my head back in the water, which happens to bring my breasts right up to him in easy access...

"See what I mean? It's your birthday, but here you are, giving *me* presents." He leans down and kisses them one at a time.

I laugh and bring my head back up to meet his lips. "I already have everything I want, so I might as well give you *something*."

This time we have a hard time even getting our lips to meet because we're smiling so wide.

EPILOGUE

BACK TO THE BEGINNING
1977

ISAIAH WILL BE here soon. We're adding onto the carriage house and since I'm paranoid that he could have an accident like Davis did, he has to always work with someone else. After weeks of bad weather and workers canceling, he finally had help this week. We have to get it done soon, if we want it ready before the baby comes. We rode down with Ruby and once she got here, she went to visit her family. She didn't want to leave me; I forced her out the door. She takes care of me enough, as it is. Papa and Sadie will be making the drive with Isaiah.

I promised him I'd be all right. But I should have known better. I've been a wreck being in the house without him or Dad.

I hear a noise and jump a mile. I shake my head and stand up to see where it came from. All the times I spent in this house alone…how did I ever do that? I feel like more of a child now than I did then.

The door opens and Daddy walks in. I rush over to him and hug him. He hangs on tight for a minute and then pulls back.

He wipes the tears off my face. "I'm so sorry—I got held up with the funeral arrangements. You takin' it hard about Grandpaw?"

I shake my head. "I mean, yes, it's sad, but…just havin' a hard time bein' in this house again. Too much."

"I was supposed to be here when you got here, honey. I told Isaiah I would and I tried real hard, but the Gentrys would not let me go!"

"It's okay. You're here now and Isaiah and Papa will be soon, too."

"Gracie outside? I didn't see her when I pulled in."

"She's on the hammock."

"Okay…oh and I've got somebody you'll like to see," he says when we step outside. He lets out a loud whistle.

A dog comes running and when he gets closer, I yell, "Josh!"

He hightails it to me and I sit down so I can pet him and hug him. His whole hind end waves back and forth.

"I can't believe he's still looking so good," I say to my dad.

"Yeah, he's been happy as can be back here with me. He wasn't faring too well after Nellie."

Gracie hears the commotion and hops off the hammock to run toward Granpapa.

"Look at you. You're all stretched out!" he yells.

She laughs and hugs him again.

"Speakin' of stretched out," Dad says, as he turns and pats my stomach, "think that baby will make an appearance while you're here?"

"I hope not. I'd like to get home and settled before that happens!"

Dad sobers a little but gives me a smile.

"Now that Grandpaw is gone, maybe I can get over to Bardstown more often," he says. "Maybe even something permanent. This isn't my home anymore either."

"I'd like that," I say, leaning my head on his shoulder.

ISAIAH AND PAPA get to the house just in time to shower and go to the funeral parlor. The relief is immediate when I see Isaiah's face.

He kisses my eyelids, my nose, my cheeks, and lands on my lips, all the while rubbing my stomach.

He finally holds my face out to study me. "You okay?" he asks.

"I am now."

"I kicked myself the minute you walked out that door," he tells me. "I let you talk me into staying and I shouldn't have."

"Maybe I needed to face all this on my own."

"No, you've done enough of that. You never need to do that again."

I pull him to me and kiss him hard.

"Now, go get ready," I say. "We gotta go."

I pat his behind as he walks away.

WE WALK IN as a fierce unit. Dad, Papa, Ruby, Sadie, Isaiah, Gracie and me. My family. We stand by the casket together, as people come and pay their respects. Rumor got out a long time ago that Isaiah and I were married, but the residents of Tulma still seem a little taken aback that we're all here together. Not even Isaiah knows this, but Daddy has set up guards all around the building, just in case any of Les's or Leroy's family comes to give us any trouble. He also didn't want any of the Klan setting one foot through the door.

Miss Sue smiles so big when she sees me. "Caroline Carson! Uh, I mean, Washington! How are you doin'?" She eyes my enormous belly and tries to give me a hug around it.

"I'm really well. So good to see you, Miss Sue."

I hear her before I see her. Miss Greener comes up in a half-trot, church hat askew. She's wiping tears and beaming at the same time. Miss Greener is one of the few people in Tulma that I wish I'd kept in touch with...

"Look at you," she says. "If I could tell you how many times I have thought of you over the years," she shakes her head, "why, I am fuller than a tick! My heart aboundeth over!"

I get tickled. I'm gonna have to remember that one for later.

We talk for a long time and even later, we get more chances to visit. She's still the same quirky, fun lady. She tells me right away that George died just a year ago.

"He was the best dog..." she says sadly.

The Owens' family sent a beautiful bouquet with a sweet note, saying they wished they could've made it to the funeral. Clara Mae met a nice guy from North Carolina when she went off to college. When she got married, her parents moved out there too. I hear Thomas moved to Dallas and has done really well for himself in real estate.

And then I see her—standing at the back of the

funeral parlor—my mother. She clutches the arm of Mr. Anderson, who is balding and quite round, and makes her way to the front. My mouth drops when the people clear away and I can fully see her.

She's pregnant too.

She averts her eyes when she sees me. When she lifts them back up, I can't read them. She walks up the rest of the way and pays my dad her respects. She stands and looks at Grandpaw for a moment and puts a handkerchief up to her eyes. If feels like the whole room went quiet the minute she walked in.

Then she squares her shoulders and walks up to me.

"Caroline," she says.

"Mama," I say.

She looks down at Gracie, but barely for a second before her eyes reach mine again. She just stands there, studying me from head to toe.

"Like what you see?" I ask.

"Looks like you've certainly grown up," she says. "And out," she adds under her breath.

"I should hope so," I reply. "It's certainly no thanks to you."

I'm holding Isaiah's and Gracie's hands so hard, I have to consciously loosen my grip.

"You never needed me," she says.

"I know, you've said that before. I *did* need you, Mama, but I managed to be all right *in spite of you*." I feel the blood boil in me and step forward, dragging Isaiah and Gracie forward with me. "Why don't you just go ahead and bring that baby to me once you have it, since we all know you're not capable of taking care of anyone but yourself."

Mr. Anderson shifts awkwardly next to her, but he doesn't jump to her defense.

She puts a hand up to her hair and her skin turns a mottled red.

I guess that's one way we're alike.

And that's where the similarities end. I have no desire to know this woman. I take a step back, and Isaiah and Gracie stumble back with me.

My mom takes a step back too, and then turns around and walks out the door. I never see her again. And that's fine by me. I do pray for that baby of hers every day, though.

I HAVE NEVER been so glad to see home and my bed in all my life. We pull in late the night after the funeral and Isaiah leads me straight to the bed. I'm trying so hard not to waddle in front of him, but I am spread out like a church picnic...way bigger than I was with Gracie.

Isaiah takes my shoes off for me and I lean over to kiss him before I lie back.

"We did it," I say. "We faced that town and all those people."

"It wasn't so bad, was it," he says, "well, except..."

"You know," I interrupt, "it was even good to see her. I can know in my knower, as Nellie would say, that she is never gonna want to be my mother. There's some closure in the knowing."

"Well, I'm glad then. Because I wanted nothing more than to carry her right off the premises as soon as I saw her come through that door."

I pat his cheek. "My savior."

"Your love."

I nod. "My love. Always."

———————————— ❀ ————————————

IVAN DAVIS AND Daniel Isaiah are born the very next afternoon. I feel all the same emotions of wanting to murder someone as I did while giving birth to Gracie, only now *two* reasons to feel that way. I guess it's a good thing I have that 'perfect birth canal'…

We all dote on the boys; every minute they're cover-ed by someone's attention. I think they're relieved to get in their beds at night, to have a little peace. Gracie is in heaven, having two babies to mother. They're little spittin' images of their daddy too. I just love looking at them all day long.

When they're about a month old, I set up a time for everyone to meet, get the boys dressed warm, and we all make our way to the barn.

Isaiah and Papa bend down and together they pull up the slabs of wood that open to the secret tunnel. Ruby and Sadie hold hands. My dad is holding Daniel and Brenda is holding Ivan. Gracie takes my hand, and when Isaiah stands back up, she takes his too. We stand there and look down in the cavernous space that set so many people free.

I look at those surrounding me, the ones who might not be my blood, but are every bit my family. There's a variety of shades represented and the thought makes me happy, a new generation of color.

I clear my throat and look each one of them in the eye. "Thanks for coming out here with us today. I wanted to do something special to commemorate this place and dedicate my family to this ground, the meaning behind what happened here…and to each of you. I found this scripture the other day," I laugh and roll my eyes at Papa, "I know, I know, don't be lookin' for me on the pew Sunday—it's just a scripture!" I tease. "Anyway, I found it in Isaiah."

I wink at my Isaiah.

"It says: 'When they cry out to the Lord because of their oppressors, he will send them a savior and defender, and he will rescue them.' In one form or another, each of you have been that to me. To say I am so grateful sounds small, but know that I mean it times a hundred."

Papa grins his sweet crinkly grin and says, "Martin Luther King, Jr said: 'Darkness cannot drive out darkness; only light can do that. Hate cannot drive out hate; only love can do that.' You've brought the light into our little world here, Caroline. Shown me what love and life is really all about…which is no small feat at my age." His shoulders shake as he laughs.

I move over to kiss his cheek. "Thank you, Papa. You're the one who did that for me."

I look at Isaiah then and take his hand. "I'm embarrassed now when I think about how I did the cowardly thing and nearly gave up on something beautiful." I motion to the dark cave. "I'd like to think that in some small way we're a part of this powerful legacy that paved the way for us—a way for Gracie and our boys to know freedom."

"Amen," Ruby says.

Each one echoes after her.

"All right, now let's go have some peach cobbler to celebrate."

And with that we head home, hearts light.

THANK YOU

To my husband, my kids, my family, my friends
My betas, my street team, my support system.

Thank you to all of you who keep me sane,
you know who you are.

Thank you to the authors
who have given me your love and support.

Thank you to every single reader—
I will always be so grateful to you for reading my books.

Thank you to all the bloggers out there who are making a
difference, both for the author and the reader.

FOR INFORMATION ABOUT WILLOW ASTER AND
HER BOOKS VISIT:

www.willowaster.com/

Facebook
https://www.facebook.com/willowasterauthor

Goodreads
www.goodreads.com/author/show/6863360.Willow_Aster

Made in the USA
Lexington, KY
02 February 2017